In paradise, the only limits to passion lie in your imagination . . .

After a life filled with hardship, landing on a lush tropical isle is heaven on earth for mariner Heath Garrison. And it comes complete with two angels who bring out the very devil in him. Identical twins Netta and Aimee are guileless and seductive, living and loving without jealousy. Days of longing, nights of carnal bliss make choosing one over the other seem impossible, but hungering for both sisters is taboo.

Aimee and Netta's devotion to each other helped them survive the vicious pirates who overran their home. Will a virile Englishman come between them now? When their enemies return, determined to vanquish the islanders for good, Heath races to save them along with his countrymen. But survival will bring a choice—between the life Heath has known, and a love that changes all their destinies . . .

Books by Tina Donahue

Dangerous Desires
Loving Lies
Wicked Whispers
Passionate Pursuit

Pirate's Prize
First Comes Desire
Days of Desire
Forbidden Desire

Published by Kensington Publishing Corporation

Forbidden Desire

Pirate's Prize

Forbidden Desire

LYRICAL PRESS
Kensington Publishing Corp.
www.kensingtonbooks.com

Lyrical Press books are published by
Kensington Publishing Corp. 119 West 40th Street New York, NY 10018

All Kensington titles, imprints, and distributed lines are available at special quantity discounts for bulk purchases for sales promotion, premiums, fund-raising, and educational or institutional use.

To the extent that the image or images on the cover of this book depict a person or persons, such person or persons are merely models, and are not intended to portray any character or characters featured in the book.

Special book excerpts or customized printings can also be created to fit specific needs. For details, write or phone the office of the Kensington Special Sales Manager:
Kensington Publishing Corp.
119 West 40th Street
New York, NY 10018
Attn. Special Sales Department. Phone: 1-800-221-2647.

Kensington and the K logo Reg. U.S. Pat. & TM Off.
LYRICAL PRESS Reg. U.S. Pat. & TM Off.
Lyrical Press and the L logo are trademarks of Kensington Publishing Corp.

First Electronic Edition: December 2017
eISBN-13: 978-1-5161-0064-4
eISBN-10: 1-5161-0064-6

First Print Edition: December 2017
ISBN-13: 978-1-5161-0067-5
ISBN-10: 1-5161-0067-0

Printed in the United States of America

To Tina's Romance Rebels, my street team, and to my PA Pamela Leonhardt. Ladies, you are the greatest. I couldn't have done this without you.

Acknowledgments

To all the wonderful authors who've given me immeasurable joy with their works, and have taught me so much about writing.

Author's Foreword

Since I read my first historical romance in high school, I've been fascinated with exotic locales, pirates, and the women they can't seem to tame. I've also been intrigued by ménages and have written quite a few over the years. This, however, is the first time I've paired two women with one man. Lucky guy. In my mind, I picture Heath grinning and thanking me. (You're welcome, sweetie). More than an erotic romance, Forbidden Desire is a love story between characters from different cultures and locales, who surmount nearly impossible odds to form a family that works for them. They celebrate diversity and prove love does conquer all.

Chapter 1

Heath Garrison swept his spyglass northwest past the Mozambique Channel. Thousands of miles in the distance lay England. Home. Odd word for a place where he'd faced unending struggle and barely survived. Still, a man couldn't easily dismiss his birthplace, even when compared to this island paradise.

A balmy breeze grazed his naked chest and tugged his hair. Sun poured down. Lush vegetation, the sea's tang, and flowers perfumed the air.

Or perhaps the sweet fragrance came from elsewhere.

Despite his captors' innumerable warnings, he inched his glass to Netta and Aimee, island women no more than twenty. Born identical twins, a cruel pirate's rule had put an end to their exact resemblance.

To Heath, they couldn't have been more perfect.

He settled the glass on them.

His pulse quickened.

Their backs were to him, their focus on the leaves and flowers they gathered. Wind stirred their dark brown hair that hung straight and long to their waists. Both women wore silk tied low on their lush hips, one's cloth a deep rose shade, the other's bright blue. The fabric fluttered above their bare feet.

They abandoned the bush in favor of another.

He edged to the side, careful not to snap a twig that would disturb them. An insect buzzed near his ear. He brushed it away.

White petals overflowed Aimee's palms. She dropped them into the silk sack Netta held. The difference in their hands gave away their identities.

He edged closer for a better view of Netta's old wound.

A lemur cackled on its perch. Its companions jumped from tree to tree, rustling branches and leaves.

At the sound, Aimee and Netta turned. Their naked breasts quivered. The enticing nipples pebbled, ideal for a man's mouth.

Heath's watered.

Previous warnings rang in his head. He wasn't to approach, talk to, or look at the island women. Didn't matter. Weakened with desire, he couldn't back away or flee even though they spotted him.

Their lips parted.

Their softened gazes and heightened color showed their approval at seeing him. Willing surrender registered in their dark eyes. Rose bloomed in their light brown cheeks, their skin satiny, flawless with youth, and surely scented with musk. An invitation no sane man could resist. If he didn't mind being beaten or possibly set adrift from this isle located a week or more from even the most primitive civilization.

Heath lowered his glass. Face down, he called himself a bloody fool for entertaining the idea of enjoying two women at once, much less sisters. This place certainly wasn't London, but that hardly meant he could behave like a rutting animal.

Dead leaves crackled beneath feet.

He didn't dare acknowledge Netta and Aimee's approach or retreat. Wasn't his business what they did. He pivoted and froze.

Royce Hastings glared. The expression he always reserved for Heath and the other captured mariners. Months before, Heath, his mates, and Benedict Bishop had landed here to take Tristan prisoner. Royce promptly put a bullet in Bishop's head and the fear of God into most of the crew.

"What are you doing here?" Royce stormed closer and put out his hand. "Give me the glass."

Heath gripped the instrument. If need be, he'd fight for it. He'd done nothing wrong, except in his thoughts. "It's mine, as you well know. Tristan allowed me to keep it to watch for intruders."

"That would be ruthless pirates or worthless mariners like you and those bastards you sailed with. Not Aimee and Netta. What did I tell you about bothering the women?"

Too much. Despite Heath's background, he wasn't a schoolboy who needed daily lectures on how a proper gentleman should behave. Good sense told him nothing would come of his attraction. He'd have more chance to woo King George's wife, Sophia, than he would either twin. "I haven't said a word to them or any woman here, not even to thank the ones who give me food and drink in exchange for my work. Most think

I'm addled or mute."

"Keep it that way. Leave the islanders to their own people."

"As you did with Simone?" She was the island's healer and several months pregnant with Royce's child.

He rested his palm on the pistol shoved in his breeches waistband. "You dare mention my wife's name? Do you want to die?"

Heath held up his hands. "I'm not the enemy. I've stated repeatedly, I'm with you and everyone else here. Bishop only told us Tristan needed to hang for his piracy. Not once did the swine mention his intent to claim Diana and the treasure here. He certainly didn't disclose his plan to sell the islanders as slaves. At least not to me. Given what I escaped as a boy, I wouldn't have signed on for that."

"So you say. Why should anyone believe you, considering your attack?"

A strange argument coming from a man who'd posed as a shipwrecked merchant to infiltrate the isle for Bishop and help him bring down Tristan. How convenient Royce had forgotten his misstep. "We both came here for less than honorable purposes. Or have you forgotten your role in Bishop's unending plot to see Tristan dead?"

"I had good reason for what I did."

According to gossip, to save his mother and sisters servitude and worse in the Colonies. "Indeed. And I sailed to this isle solely because a man must work to eat. My employment was on ships. Unfortunately, I wasn't born a noble like you."

"You didn't have a wastrel father either who lost every farthing to drink, whores, and wagering."

"How right you are." Heath smiled pleasantly. "I had no father at all, good or bad. If you find me so distasteful and untrustworthy, allow me to leave when the other islanders come here to trade or we go there."

The only solution. He couldn't be an outcast for life. His early years proved hopeless enough. To witness other men building their lives and families while he remained alone was inconceivable, especially with Netta and Aimee tempting him. He didn't think he'd survive their union with men they'd someday love. There wasn't a thing he could do to change their futures, nor would he approach them in any way. But that didn't make him a blasted saint without human need. "I want to leave during the next visit."

"Impossible." The wind blew Royce's dark hair. He pulled it back. "Tristan can't risk you telling the world about this island."

"As you told Bishop, bringing him, me, and the rest here?"

"Tristan spared your hide, which means you're here for life. You're lucky we feed you."

Heath tightened his fists. "I labor for each morsel, same as everyone else."

"Not today you haven't. We need you in the courtyard to set up tables for the celebration. Come on."

"Wait. Diana's already had the child?" Her and Tristan's first in an unlikely union. Despite being a reverend's daughter, she'd waylaid Tristan to rescue her younger brother from a pirate's life. Tristan captured her instead and made her his.

"She's begun the ordeal. Simone said it shouldn't take long. Follow me."

Some distance past his original spot, Heath lost his resolve not to glance back.

Surprise crossed Netta's and Aimee's faces. The look women wear when caught doing something they shouldn't, or when a man gazes into their hearts and souls to uncover their secrets.

Netta returned to her work first, her movements forced, unsettled. Aimee blinked slowly as one would when drugged.

Rumfustian had never intoxicated Heath as they did.

He lumbered forward and bumped into something.

"Watch where you're going." Royce shoved him.

Heath twisted to regain his balance and reined in irritation. Better to earn Royce's trust than to trounce him and get a bullet in his brain or heart for the affront.

They passed through the forest and an opening in the courtyard walls. A sprawling stone mansion, white as snow, surrounded the vegetation.

Naked island children of varying ages scurried past palms and plants. Their laughter rang in the heated air. Men set up plank benches and tables. Squawking chickens flapped their wings in an effort to avoid too many feet.

Tristan's blond hair stood out like a beacon. So did his heavily scarred back, courtesy of a cruel captain who'd nearly whipped him to death. He paced to and fro, his usual bronze complexion pasty, features haggard, a pistol in his waistband. Diana's silver-and-diamond marriage collar dangled from his fist.

James, his friend and former quartermaster, watched from the side, red locks flapping in the breeze. Also armed, he caressed his two-week-old son to his heavily freckled chest. The infant's complexion was islander brown, like his mother's, not a spot in sight. James spoke to Tristan. "You've nothing to worry about. Simone's taking good care of Diana. Gavra is too when she should be here tending to our Willy. He's hungry."

Willy squirmed and wailed.

James simultaneously bounced his son and followed Tristan. Both wore a path in the dirt.

Heath quelled laughter at the once fierce pirates. If their enemies and those whose ships they'd taken could see them now...

A screech tore from a side room.

Tristan whirled around and reared back before he ran into James. "Bloody hell. That was worse than the last one. I thought having Diana take off the collar would allow her to breathe more easily, not scream like the devil's after her. What in damnation is going on in there?" He pushed past.

James grabbed his arm. "You don't want to go into the birthing room. Trust me. What you'll see is for no man's eyes. It could stop your heart."

"Don't be daft. I have to help her."

"How? Was you who got her into this or have you forgotten?"

Tristan yanked his arm away. "If Diana survives her ordeal, I'll never lie with her again."

James howled. "No bloody chance of that happening. If you don't take her, she'll do that to you, at the point of her rapier if need be. The same as when she captured you at the Quest before I saved your hide."

"Must you keep reminding me of—"

Diana's prolonged moan cut through the other noise.

James gestured Royce over. Heath followed. They surrounded Tristan, keeping him from the room.

He glowered. "I know Gavra will try her best. Simone too. However, that doesn't address all eventualities."

James transferred Willy from his right shoulder to his left. Willy spit up yellow liquid that oozed down James's back. He groaned. "You speak of events that will never be. My mother birthed eight children and survived each ordeal. If not for her advanced age, she would have had ten more."

"That's you—her. A farmer's daughter used to hard labor, sturdy to a fault. Diana's father did nothing except preach and rail at her for everything she did. Her days with him never prepared her for life on this isle."

Royce chuckled. "I would think not."

Tristan shot him a look.

He lost his smile. "I'm only saying with the woman going about as they are—not Diana of course. She's always fully clothed—that is, her gowns are quite nice. They suit her, because she's English, not—I'm not sure what I meant. James is right. Since time began, woman have birthed with few problems. My mother thrives in England with my two sisters."

Diana swore in English then even louder in French, the islander's language Heath understood.

Once his goal had been to better himself, learn all he could, and become more than what he'd been born as. Being a lifelong celibate on this isle hadn't been in his plan. He should plead his case to Tristan and James.

Tristan scowled at Heath. "What have you to say?"

"Nothing." Surely he hadn't spoken his thoughts aloud. "I'm here to work." He backed away.

Tristan gripped his forearm. "What of your mother? How many infants did she have and survive through?"

"I don't know. I never saw her."

"Because she bloody well died giving you life?" Tristan dug his fingers into Heath.

Pain shot up his arm. He suppressed a wince. "No. The workhouse beadle told me I wasn't an orphan like the rest, which annoyed him greatly. My mother left me there because she couldn't feed herself, much less me. After that, I have no idea what happened to her."

James gestured dismissively. "Probably married some willing fellow and had half a dozen more children. Isn't that right?"

For Heath to say otherwise might get him killed. Even pirates hunting a prize weren't as ruthless as a future father worried about his wife and coming child. "I'm certain she had the largest family she could and is with them as we speak."

"There you have it." James smacked Tristan's shoulder. "You can calm down. To make certain you do, I'll have Aimee and Netta check on Diana." He motioned them over.

They approached gracefully, more a glide than walk, their breasts bouncing with each step. Aimee held her silk bag in front. Netta hid her left hand. Both peeked at Heath.

His legs weakened, cock stiffened.

"*Bonjour.*" James smiled. "*Allez-vous verifier sur* Diana? *Voir comment elle va?*" Will you check on Diana? See how she's doing?

Diana wailed.

Tristan covered his eyes.

"Now." James shooed them away.

"*Oui.*" Aimee grabbed Netta's wrist and hurried to the birthing room.

* * * *

Simone met them at the doorway, her rounded belly leading the way, a leather marriage collar adorned with brightly colored beads about her throat. "What took so long?"

Aimee frowned and became as outspoken as Netta. "We returned as quickly as we could. The plants you wanted would confuse anyone. They all look the same. Green and more green."

"Each color is different."

"To you, a healer. Not to Netta and me." She pushed the bag at Simone. "You should mix a potion for Tristan. He's darting back and forth like a frightened chicken and is making everyone dizzy. Is Diana all right?"

Nude, Diana sagged against the whitewashed wall, her once pale skin flushed and slick with sweat. Her long black hair clung to her breasts. Each pant shuddered through her. She gripped Follie's and Gavra's hands and screamed, this outburst more deafening than the rest.

Men's voices stopped.

Tristan's loud oath sounded.

Children quieted.

Simone rifled through the bag. "Tell *Capitaine* his wife is fine. The best potion for a man is ale. Fill him with it so he no longer hears her cries. Where's the bloodstop?" She dug deeper and made a face. "Did you forget it?"

Netta stiffened. "No. Look at the bottom. Aimee picked the bloodstop first. I added extra before we found the other plants you wanted. Do you expect Diana to bleed?"

"All mothers do, but too much will risk her life. Never tell Tristan that."

Netta clucked her tongue. "And have him shoot me if I dared mention such a thing? I have no wish to die."

Simone waddled to her mixing bowl and cups. Her green cloth matched Royce's eyes. She told the women she'd prayed to *mère de l'homme*, the goddess who created this isle, for her unborn child to have Royce's coloring. "Diana's infant should be here before sundown. Tell Tristan his wife is as brave and healthy as any islander."

Aimee doubted he'd hear those words even if James shouted them. Only Diana's silence and Tristan's son's or daughter's thin cries would quiet his worry. She took Netta's hand. "We can tell him together."

"No." Netta pulled away. "You go. I want to wait here."

Only because Heath was with Tristan. Nothing Netta said or did could convince Aimee otherwise. They'd been together in their mother's womb and each second they'd drawn breath. Netta was too ashamed of what a pirate had done to her to let any man close, particularly Heath, whom she desired. She'd rather hide from him forever than risk him spurning her.

Aimee pressed her mouth to Netta's ear. "You saw how Heath looks at us. He wants both, not only one."

"He looks at you, never me, unless he thinks I might be you. Then he wants me until he sees..." She cleared her throat and kept her voice low. "Go to Tristan then stay with Heath. I can help Simone and the others with Diana."

"And leave you without any man to love?"

"Go." She shoved her gently. "I need no one. I never will."

"Not even me?"

Netta's dark eyes filled. She embraced Aimee. Her scent matched the sweet flowers she rubbed on herself. As girls, they played at being young women and perfumed themselves to tempt the boys. Their giggles filled the air, as did their boasts about how they'd each capture the strongest and bravest man's heart.

The pirates came and changed everything.

"Of course I will always need you." Netta hugged her even harder. "But only when you can take time away from the man who makes you mistress of his house and fills you with his children. Heath's young and handsome with kindness in his eyes. If he wins your heart, he may let me care for his sons and daughters while you and he take time for your love."

"No." Aimee gripped her. "Never talk that way. Your loneliness would kill me."

Netta's features grew stony. "You see sadness when there is none. I know what my future brings and what I can never have. I accept my fate."

She cupped Netta's chin. "You have to fight for what you want as you did when we were girls. No matter what the pirates did, you and I are the same. If Heath refuses your love, he can never have mine."

"Foolish talk." She pushed Aimee's hands away. "Never again will I be whole like you."

"None of the islanders or the Englishmen cares about that." She lowered her voice further. "Royce adores Simone despite her scarred leg. Look at Adamo. He can barely see out of one eye. His face is disfigured, his arm limp from the pirates. Zola gladly became his woman because he proved to be a good man. She made him forget Canela's cruel treatment and lies."

"That may be enough for Adamo, but I want no one's pity or disgust." She turned away. "Go. See to Tristan. Speak to Heath. I know you want to."

"Not without you."

Netta joined Simone at the table. "Teach me what to do so I can help."

"With Diana?"

"Other women too and the men. I can heal as you do. When Aimee's time comes, I can keep her safe and present her husband with his new son."

Simone glanced at Aimee, her gaze questioning Netta's sudden desire to heal.

Netta had never shown interest before. Sickness frightened her. She, like the other islanders, had known too much death from pirates.

"What of your infant when you have one?" Simone regarded Netta. "Do you intend to look after yourself during that time rather than have my help?"

"For me, that time will never come. There will be no children or marriage to any man. Aiding others is all I ask. Make me a healer like you."

Aimee's throat constricted. Simone had saved many but she couldn't give Netta back what the pirates had taken from her. Heartsick, Aimee left the birthing room and stilled.

Heath had remained with the other men.

He looked at her.

The world stopped and then spun too swiftly.

Sun blanketed his broad shoulders and turned his bronze skin to gold. Light brown hair fell in soft waves to his shoulders. Stubble shadowed his face, intensifying his masculinity.

She locked her knees. Her tightened nipples stung.

Even next to Tristan and Royce, a capitaine and a man of noble birth, Heath stood out. Hard labor on ships had sculpted his powerful body. Tall and sinewy, he had large hands that could destroy anything or provide great pleasure.

Instinctively, Aimee recognized his gentle nature and longed to see mischief and lust flare in his hazel eyes. For her to experience his protective embrace, heated skin, and breathtaking scent would be heaven.

Netta should be here, seeking what every woman needed, a good man to comfort and cherish her. Wasn't fair or right to deny herself. Nor would Aimee let it stand.

Tonight, she'd change things for her sister, herself, and Heath. Somehow.

Uncertainty and her inherent shyness ate at her. She pushed her unease aside and marched to Tristan to tell him what she'd learned about Diana.

* * * *

Simone pointed. "Tell me what this is."

Netta had no idea other than green leaves, similar to the others on the table. She hadn't listened to Simone's endless droning about plants that cured and flowers that saved lives. To Netta, blossoms made a woman smell good for a man. "Ah…"

Diana shouted vile oaths.

"You should go to her." Netta gestured. "The pain seems worse. Her language certainly is."

"The infant gets closer to its new life. Nothing to worry about. Pay attention. This is the soothing plant." Simone shook it. "After I crush the leaves, I mix their juice with the others I showed you so I can..."

Tristan spoke loudly, the distance muting his exact words. James or Royce laughed. Others joined in. Perhaps Heath.

Netta ached for his voice, the briefest touch. Madness. Wanting him would only frustrate and hurt. He belonged to Aimee, looked at her alone. The few times he'd glanced Netta's way, she hadn't the courage to remain and search his expression. He'd never crave her. Men wanted perfect females, especially if those women weren't white like the English.

Simone shook Netta's arm.

She pulled away. "What?"

"I asked you about this plant."

"Is something wrong with its leaves? Should it have flowers?"

"No. Tell me what it does."

"It stops blood or soothes pain?" Most seemed to do so even though they resembled each other.

Simone dropped her head.

"I can guess again. Does it cure rashes like Henri had before you treated him?"

"Are you certain you want to learn this? You barely listen to what I say."

She'd focused too much on the courtyard, Aimee and Heath possibly leaving together for a private moment. Netta loved her sister more than life but she didn't want to witness Heath embracing or kissing her. Their intimacy would wound too deep. "Forgive me. Can you repeat what you said?"

"Later. The infant is coming."

Its head had crowned.

Unneeded, Netta backed to the doorway.

Children played boisterously, chickens clucked and squawked, feet shuffled, men grunted.

Royce and Adamo hauled a long table across the courtyard. Other men did the same or hoisted plank seats. Near a stand of palms, James and Tristan spoke quietly. Tristan's color had returned.

Aimee must have convinced him all was well, yet she wasn't around.

Heath was.

Unrelenting heat poured through Netta and curled deep within her belly. The folds between her legs dampened.

He carried two seats, one on each shoulder, and barely puffed from the weight. Scars cut across his back.

He'd known the same cruelness Tristan and Diana's brother Peter once endured. The English had much to learn about kindness and decency toward others. Netta longed to stroke the horrible marks and bring Heath joy.

He faced her. His eyes widened in recognition. Perhaps surprise or maybe revulsion.

Shamed, she hid her hand as best she could and ran to the stone house.

Chapter 2

The setting sun streaked distant clouds orange, purple, gold, and rose. A mild breeze ruffled palm leaves and delivered wonderful scents: roasted beef, bacon, rice bread, bananas, pineapple, and other island fare for the celebratory feast.

Aimee prayed tonight would turn out joyous for her and Netta. No one could find a better evening for love. She delivered grapes to a courtyard table.

Netta placed a tray with sizzling fish next to the fruit.

Men lit numerous torches. Musicians played their reeds, lutes, and drums. Younger children bounced in place to the tune. The older ones wove in and out of the adults, getting in everyone's way.

No one scolded. The goddess had created these moments to rejoice over a new life.

Tristan, Diana, and their daughter Merry had yet to leave the birthing room. To Tristan's delight, the infant had Diana's dark hair and lovely violet eyes.

Royce and Simone took seats at an empty table. Gavra sat to their side. James handed Willy over to her and settled close. Laure and Peter joined them. They barely stopped kissing to sit.

Heath wasn't about.

Aimee hoped he hadn't offered to keep watch for pirates or mariners who might approach the isle. If he did, she'd have to drag Netta to the point on the pretense of bringing him food. Hardly the romantic mood to strike.

She stopped her friend Follie before she passed. "Who watches the shores tonight?"

"Adamo. Zola went with him."

Of course. Zola adored her man and Adamo would willingly give up the festivities to prove his loyalty. Nearly a year ago, he'd betrayed his people for Canela who'd said she loved and wanted no one except him. All lies. She persuaded him to watch for pirates and direct them to these shores so the islanders could take back the land from Tristan. She hadn't mentioned that she'd then rule with the pirate capitaine. When Yellow Scarf and his crew had arrived, she'd torn off Adamo's marriage collar and begged the invaders to murder Tristan for choosing Diana over her. Tristan, James, and the islanders had captured the pirates instead. Canela's people banished her, Yellow Scarf, and his men to a distant isle where they would serve those people for life.

Children and adults chose their tables here.

Heath strode from the stone house, Tristan's spirits in hand.

Relief flooded Aimee. Excitement and hard lust filled her too.

Netta padded to the closest table.

Aimee grabbed her hand and pulled her back.

"What are you doing?" Netta twisted her arm. "Let go."

"In a moment." Before they chose a table, they needed to know where Heath would sit. "I want to make certain we brought everything out that we should." She made a show of glancing around.

Netta tapped her foot.

Heath placed the bottles on the table near Royce and sank to the empty bench opposite him.

Given Royce's scowl, Aimee wasn't convinced Heath would stay there long.

Royce eyed the brandy. "Some is missing."

Heath smiled coolly. "Care to smell my breath?"

"Enough." Simone elbowed Royce and frowned at Heath. "You two bicker worse than the youngest children. Try to get along."

Royce wrinkled his nose. "With him? Never."

She jabbed him again. "Have you forgotten how James wanted to shoot you when you brought the white devil here?"

"You mean Bishop." Peter dragged his hair off his shoulders. Sun had bleached his dark locks and turned his skin golden. "Bloody swine. I haven't forgotten what Royce did."

"Nor have I." James leaned across Gavra and Willy to glare at Royce. "You still deserve a good thrashing."

He slumped. "I have apologized repeatedly."

"As I have." Heath drummed the table. "Unlike Royce, I didn't know what Bishop had planned. I was an innocent bystander."

Aimee pulled Netta to the bench. "I believe Heath. He meant no harm." To hide Netta's hand, she shoved her sister to his left.

Netta sprawled on the bench, her cloth falling away from her legs. Heath stared at her thighs. His breathing picked up. "Allow me to help."

She shrank back.

He lowered his hand. "Are you all right?"

Aimee answered, "She is."

"I doubt that." Royce pointed to a faraway table. "There's room over there."

Aimee bristled. "Netta and I have a right to sit here. How dare you ask us to leave."

"Hold on. I haven't. What I said was meant for him." He jabbed his thumb at Heath.

"Everyone stays here." Aimee spoke to her sister. "Go on. Sit. Now." She blocked her from leaving.

Jaw clamped, Netta swung her legs over the bench.

Aimee lifted her cloth and sat to Heath's right. "We should forget the past and look to the future." His clean, musky scent drew her closer. She touched his forearm. Pleasure unlike any she'd known rolled through her. "You must be hungry from carrying so many benches and tables."

Peter sniffed. "Do be serious. We all did that."

"Not you." Netta chuckled. "I saw. I heard." She made smacking sounds to resemble lovers' sloppy kisses.

Peter colored worse than Laure did.

Heath's shoulders shook with suppressed laughter, as did James's and Royce's.

Aimee offered Heath a grape cluster. Juice from the plump fruit splashed his wrist. She resisted an urge to lick the drops. "Netta has a wonderful way of making everyone smile and laugh, no?"

He swallowed his grape and nodded.

"We both like to tease, but she's much better at it that I am."

Netta lowered her face. "I am not."

"You are." Aimee leaned into Heath. Her breast snuggled against his arm. "Go on, ask her if she is."

He stared at Aimee's nipple. His face turned a deeper red than Peter's had, closer to Netta's current shade.

Until he and she got over their shyness with each other, as Aimee forced herself to do, none of them would know passion.

Aimee prodded gently. "Ask."

Netta kept her face down.

Simone, Gavra, and Laure leaned forward, not even breathing as they waited for Heath's first word. Even Willy had quieted. The men rolled their eyes or shook their heads.

Aimee gave them a hard stare.

Heath cleared his throat. "I don't have to ask. I'd say Netta does have a splendid sense of humor, which is greatly appreciated. Well done."

Netta's eyes rounded, but she managed a smile. "*Merci.*"

He made an appreciative noise. "I'd say the thanks go to you. What else can you tell us about poor Peter? Something amusing I hope."

"Always. But I better not."

"Why?"

"We may never get away from the table. It would take me until sunrise and past to finish."

Everyone laughed.

Peter drew in his scrawny shoulders. Although tall like a proper Englishman, he'd yet to put muscle on his lean frame. "Are none of you going to eat? Must you stuff your mouths with foul words rather than food?"

James poured his ale. "Indeed we must. Making sport of you is far more enjoyable, unless someone would care to tell Heath what happened with Royce during our last celebration."

Simone put up her hand. "No one speaks of that again."

"I will." Peter crossed his arms over the table. "He tried to teach us the marionette."

"Minuet." Royce curled his upper lip. "A marionette is a puppet."

"No different from how we looked with your foolish dance."

Netta laughed. "Gavra bounced up and down like a ball. Right, Aimee?"

"She did. Peter and Laure bumped into each other. Like this." She smacked her fist into her palm. "He nearly knocked her down. Zola and Adamo couldn't keep up with the steps. One went this way." She pointed. "The other that way." She swung her finger. "Some went in circles. A few hopped like birds. If the priest had been here, he would have said the white man's devil had possessed everyone."

The women laughed until they couldn't breathe. The men's delighted roars shook the benches. Even Royce and Simone joined in.

A pleasant meal followed. Everyone joked, ate, drank. All good friends and part of the island family now.

James caught the last brandy drops on his tongue. "Do we have more of this or are we to deprive ourselves on this grand night? Heath? You're in charge of spirits. What say you?"

"What else? I'll bring more. Excuse me." He eased his leg past Aimee.

His knee grazed her thigh. Riotous heat filled her. She should have moved but couldn't. Wouldn't.

Netta didn't give him extra room either. She stared at his

muscular arms and back.

Free of the bench, he breathed hard and tramped to the stone house.

"We need more bread and fish." Aimee stood and grabbed Netta's hand. "Help me with the trays."

Royce cleared his throat loudly.

Even if he'd threatened Aimee with his pistol, he wouldn't have stopped her. She tugged Netta inside the house and pulled her toward the liquor supplies rather than the kitchen.

Netta resisted. "What are you doing?"

"Seeing to our future since you refuse to."

"Is this about Heath? It is. No. Release me."

"In time." She patted Netta's hand. "You want him. Never lie about that. I know the truth."

"That I accept my fate? I have and intend to live alone. I will never have a husband. No children either. Or—"

"How wrong you are. Promise not to leave my side no matter what happens." Netta cringed. "What do you plan to do?"

"Give me your word and stay by my side at all times. Do as I do. Please."

"You ask too much."

"I only want your happiness and mine. Quiet."

They'd reached the small storage room lit by a lone oil lamp. The bobbing flame couldn't eat away the shadows. Stuffy air intensified the musty odor.

Netta sneezed.

Heath spun around and stared. His eyes shone golden in the scant light. Moisture gleamed on his throat and brawny chest.

Words failed Aimee. Her need proved too great to deny. She cupped his bristly cheeks and brought his mouth to hers.

He inhaled sharply.

Sagged against him, she drowned in his heat, savored his scent, and parted her lips.

His tongue filled her and explored.

She did the same with him. The tastiest food had never satisfied as he did, his clean taste indescribable and pure man. The same as his whiskered cheeks rasping hers. No weapon could have made her feel safer than he did. He gentled his brute strength and held her carefully.

Her ears buzzed. She came alive as she never had, wreathed her arms around his shoulders, and pressed close.

The prominent bulge between his legs nudged her mound. Her sex responded and grew damp, congested, wanting of him.

The same as Netta's surely did. Aimee knew her sister too well to believe anything else. Reluctant to leave his embrace, Aimee nevertheless pulled away and snatched what breath she could.

Her moisture shone on his lips. Carnal hunger burned in his eyes.

She stepped aside and left him to Netta. The only woman she would ever share him with.

* * * *

Netta had always believed the moment Aimee and Heath embraced, she'd bolt and would banish their intimate moments from her mind.

Her legs barely supported her. Unable to flee, she froze.

Heath pulled her into his arms and claimed her lips, his mouth hard yet tender, his beard-roughened skin more balm than irritation.

She drove her fingers into his thick, silky hair and suckled his tongue. Complete madness. This couldn't last. She should have strangled Aimee for pushing her past temptation until she couldn't control herself.

Netta's tongue played with his then forced it from her mouth so she could fill him.

He made an amused sound and allowed her what she willed.

Her smile touched his.

If Netta could have decided the future, she would have joined him and Aimee in his mud house, worn his marriage collar proudly, and given him the sons all men craved. Daughters too. He only had to want her as she did him.

She'd lied about surrendering to her fate. From his first night on the isle, she'd yearned for a kind word, a loving touch, respect, acceptance, this.

He deepened their kiss. His chest crushed her breasts. He pushed his magnificent sex against her mound. They shared each breath. Their hearts beat as one.

Lightheaded, she tore her mouth free and gulped air.

Aimee joined them.

* * * *

None of Heath's bawdy dreams had matched this.

Aimee kissed his throat, Netta his chest, their lips softer than velvet, tongues wet. Even the sun couldn't match their heat. They smelled of flowers, clean skin, an ocean breeze, a summery day. Life at its best.

Pity if he had to die for these few moments.

Muted laughter and music sounded from the courtyard. No growls or orders from Royce. Yet. Once he happened by this room, the accusations and threats would surely come.

Heath would deal with them when he had no other choice. He pressed his toes into the cool marble to keep still so Aimee and Netta wouldn't come to their senses and leave.

They all should, though together, and remain that way throughout the night and tomorrow, perhaps the following weeks. This confined space wasn't large enough for him to take them fully or repeatedly unless they stood. Only a bedchamber would do. There were certainly enough in the mansion.

Though besotted, he wasn't mad enough to invade Tristan and Diana's home. That left his mud house or the surrounding forest. The trees were closer. He should suggest them.

Netta captured his mouth and slipped her tongue inside, blocking any possible words. He suckled her deeper then took command and filled her mouth instead.

She slumped against him, a prisoner to his will.

Aimee kissed his scarred back and stroked his ass and thighs.

His hair stood on end. Her touch branded him, the same as Netta's mouth. He swayed into one then the other, unwilling to neglect either, unsatisfied because he couldn't get closer.

They bumped into a rack. Glass tinkled. A broken bottle would cut their feet and put an end to enjoyment.

He pulled away to warn them to take care.

Aimee slanted her mouth over his. Netta cupped his balls and stroked his cock.

Delight barreled through him, impossible to contain. He shot to his toes.

They followed. Aimee enjoyed his mouth. Netta unfastened his breeches and stroked his thick curls.

His cock stiffened so much his skin stung. His balls ached. Nothing on God's good earth seemed more fitting than taking them here and now without end.

Feet slapped the hall floor.

Fear slammed into him. Not for himself. Netta and Aimee. No telling what their people would think of one man with two women. Heath being English only made matters worse.

He twisted away from Aimee and grabbed Netta's hand, or rather what remained of it.

She recoiled.

Heath should have let go but couldn't. Up close, the injury was far worse than he'd dreamed. Three fingers and a good portion of her palm were gone leaving only her thumb and forefinger. Whoever mutilated her had used fire to sear the wound, resulting in ragged edges no longer charred but grayish white against her rich brown skin.

He couldn't hide his horror at what she'd endured.

Tears slid down her cheeks. She yanked her hand away and dashed from the room.

"Netta?" Gavra spoke from the hall. "Wait." She called out. "What happened?"

He'd done it this time and had to make things right. Heath buttoned his breeches and eased past Aimee.

She grabbed his arm. "If you follow Netta that will make her run faster. She believes you find her ugly because of her hand."

"What? Never. I'm sickened by what the pirates did to her."

Surprise crossed Aimee's face. "How did you know that?"

"I overheard your people speak of the men who came here and brutalized everyone. It doesn't make sense they'd do so to Netta. She couldn't have been more than twelve or thirteen at the time. Still a child. Why did they choose her to maim?"

Sorrow registered in Aimee's lovely eyes. She glanced past him. "Netta should tell you when she can."

Heath couldn't imagine when that would be. His reaction had crushed her.

"I have to go and comfort her." Aimee brushed her lips over his. "In time, we can all do this again."

Not likely. He needed to leave this isle before his base desires hurt Netta even more. Aimee too. If he could have swum to a populated island, he would've done so tonight.

Once Aimee's footfalls faded, he left the room.

Gavra blocked him in the hall. "What did you do?"

He spoke French as she did. "I sailed here with Bishop when I shouldn't have. Where the hell is Tristan? I need to speak to him immediately."

Even if Tristan decided against the departure, Heath would never look at, speak to, or touch Netta or Aimee again.

God help him if he couldn't get to the other island.

Chapter 3

Faucon Island

Sweat poured down Canela's face and chest. The puny wind did nothing to cool, pushing her hair against her damp neck instead. She clawed it away and grabbed soiled breeches from a pile that reached her calves when she stood. On her knees like a slave, she pounded the cloth against a rock as she wanted to do to her captors who kept her prisoner on this loathsome isle. Their ugly faces evolved into Chadwick Vincent's, the pirate who'd betrayed her and failed to kill Tristan. He became her next target then the Englishwoman Diana.

Canela longed to punish, crush, and kill.

Frenzied with hate, she beat the clothing mercilessly.

Feet shuffled close. Fanette huffed. She couldn't have been more repulsive, her ankles thick, toes fat and hairy. She thought she ruled the world. "Put a hole in those and you go without food until sunset tomorrow."

White-hot loathing roared through Canela. The fare here was barely edible and not enough to keep a child alive. In the past, she'd eaten the finest meats and fruits. Then her hair shone, skin glowed, her beauty surpassing everyone's even the Englishwoman's.

Now though…

Her hands bore calluses from hard labor and her shoulders drooped from lugging baskets too heavy for an Englishman to carry. She labored from dawn to dusk but it was never enough to satisfy these vile beasts.

She longed to have Fanette's head between her hands and battered the breeches accordingly.

"Heed what I say." Fanette smacked Canela with a switch.

A searing sting raced down her arm.

Fists tightened, Canela pushed up, ready to beat the woman senseless.

The switch came down repeatedly, driving her to the ground. She covered her head with her arms and wailed. *"Pardonne moi."* Forgive me.

"For being foolish and lazy? Or for defying me?" Fanette struck again.

Canela cried out. "Everything. Please."

Breathing hard, Fanette stopped. "When will you learn to do what we ask without destroying everything you touch? No wonder your people wanted to get rid of you. Clean those breeches properly then do the same with the others. If you dare leave here. I promise to bring more and more for you to wash. Today you go without food. Tomorrow too if you fail to learn submission to your betters."

Canela would have gladly starved before considering them or anyone superior to her.

"Do you understand? Or do you need more of this?" Fanette brandished the switch.

Canela forgot pride, for the moment, and bowed submissively. Under Fanette's watchful scowl, she cleaned the breeches carefully and hung them on a branch to dry.

"Do the others now as you should. The women's cloths come next. Then whatever else needs washing. That pile had better be much lower when I return. If not, prepare for true punishment." She trudged away.

Surf flowed around the breeches and licked the sand. A small, green lizard skittered past, skirting the water.

Canela scooped up the creature. The thing snapped its jaw, trying to bite. She twisted its slender body. Bones cracked. Smiling, she hurled its limp form into a wave and winced. Her arms ached from washing too many clothes and from welts where the switch had struck. Several stripes bled lightly. Her perfect skin ruined again.

She trembled with outrage but didn't cry. Weeping was for fools and those she'd make pay for the abominations done her.

Torture and death filled her thoughts. Horrific images made the day pass more swiftly.

The moon was high before she finished her tasks. She gobbled wild berries to quiet her growling belly. No one watched or guarded her. There wasn't anywhere to escape. Endless water separated this isle from the next. Wild boars roamed the forest. The sturdiest man wouldn't survive an attack.

If she chose to live outside the settled areas, no islander would complain. They'd have one less mouth to feed. She, alone, would have to find enough food and fresh water to sustain her.

With no other choice, she carried the basket on her back as a beast would.

Despite the short walk, the cleaned breeches and cloths grew unwieldy, forcing her to stop for breath and what strength she could gather.

She plodded into the island community, a series of mud homes. No stone house like Tristan's. No jewels, colorful silks, or looking glasses. The comforts here were horribly primitive, yet still denied her and the other prisoners. The men had a penned off area where they slept beneath the sky no matter the weather. They had to endure the worst rain and storms.

So did she. As the only female slave, her open-air enclosure was far smaller than the one afforded the hogs.

She dropped the basket in front of the cowhide that served as Fanette's door. If good fortune was with Canela, Fanette would trip over the clothes and break her neck.

At this hour, most everyone slept. One man guarded the shore. None the community. The male prisoners had their ankles shackled. They could barely shuffle much less walk, run, or cause trouble.

As a woman, she could move freely. No one worried about her.

If she had a blade they would.

To get to her dirt bed, she had to pass the crude wooden fence surrounding the men. Clouds shrouded the moon and cast the world into deeper shadows. Dark shapes littered the ground. The prisoners, she guessed.

A soft trill sounded. Perhaps from a bird. Perhaps not.

Canela slowed. Wind stirred her cloth and hair.

Another trill, this longer, quieter.

The silvery light dimmed further, then went out. Similar to when one extinguishes a candle or an oil lamp. The moon no longer able to pierce the heavy clouds.

Something rustled and scuffed.

Unafraid, she gave into curiosity and padded closer.

A hand clamped her wrist. "Scream and I'll break your neck."

Chadwick Vincent. Yellow Scarf to her people. A name given because of the bright cloth he wore on his head. In the dark, she couldn't make out the color or his ugly face, but she'd never forget his hideous voice.

She'd offered him Tristan's stone house, the island she'd called home, its riches, and herself, even speaking the English Vincent knew. He'd wanted Diana. Only white skin would do for him.

Canela clutched his balls and squeezed. "Release me or regret it."

His hand fell away from her. He panted, agony in each breath. "I only wanted you to stop and not alert the others."

He'd once threatened to put a bullet in her head and promised to strangle her if she didn't answer his endless questions quickly and truthfully so he could take Diana as his own. When Canela had still offered him her flesh, he'd given her to his foul pirate crew saying they might want a savage. He was better than that.

Not any longer.

She increased the pressure on his sac.

He made an angry sound.

She wasn't afraid. He might be able to break her fingers or arm, though not before she crushed his manhood. Her labor during these endless months had made her quite strong. "Why would you want anything from me, a mere savage? You craved Diana."

"I still do. I dream of her neck between my hands as I squeeze the life from her. Surely, you've thought the same."

"Why would you care?"

"Don't you want to escape?"

She'd thought and dreamt of little else. "Do you?"

"What do you think?"

"That no man could be a greater fool than you are. You wear shackles, sleep in a pen like an animal, and have no pistol to protect yourself, yet you dream of escape." She laughed quietly. "Have you prayed to your white god, hoping he would save you? Why would you ask him to help me?"

"We can band together, or you can stay here and work until you're old and ugly. I'd say a few more years of endless labor should do it. No man will want you then, English or islander. The choice is yours."

She dug her nails into his testicles. His breeches provided some protection, though hardly enough.

He winced.

"Tell me how beautiful I am. Make me believe you."

"You are." He gulped air. "My men wanted you immediately."

She clenched her jaw. "Not them. You." She sank her nails deeper.

He groaned.

Her smile widened. "Tell me how much you want me."

"If you harm me, you'll never have my answer or know what I have planned for us."

"Us?" She gave him a hard squeeze.

He gasped.

She let up slightly. "Tell me your idea. I may listen."

"I can't. Not while you're hurting me. Please stop."

So the invincible pirate was finally on his knees to her where he belonged. "Say or do anything that displeases me and I promise to make you regret it." She eased her grip but didn't release him. "Tell me how we can leave."

He swallowed loudly and sucked in air. "You know French, I don't. Nor do the men. Only Storley did."

The pirate who'd claimed Canela after Vincent had pushed her away, disgusted by her brown skin. Storley had died the second month here, trampled by a horse. An accident, their captors had said. Canela knew better. Storley had wanted to die. "After all this time you need me to tell you what the islanders say?"

"This is the first chance I've had to speak with you. I've tried since the bloody moment we set foot here. You must get the key to these shackles and learn where they keep their pistols."

"So you can shoot them then me. I think not." She let go and backed away.

"Trust me, or you're a slave till death. That may be fifty years or more. Think you can stomach that? Alone, you can never leave. You need help from me, my men, and the other prisoners here."

Canela edged closer. "To do what? Take the sloop the islander's now have? The newest captives said it came from Benedict Bishop, a white merchant."

"I have no idea of its origins. Though a fine vessel, I don't want it. I'll settle for nothing but Tristan's."

She gripped the rail. "You expect to take it when my people come here to trade?"

"What else?"

"To return to my land?"

"I'd enjoy nothing more."

She wasn't certain if he lied. "Why not use Bishop's ship?"

"Have you forgotten Tristan has men watching his shores? If they see a sloop other than his approach the cove, they'll warn the others. We need surprise on our side. With his longboats and some of his men rowing to the beach, those who guard won't suspect anything's wrong until it's too late. By then, we'll have the upper hand and can mount our attack."

"Not until you arrive there. You need to leave here first."

He made an impatient noise. "With your help in getting the key and the weapons, me and the others can overpower Tristan's crew. We'll already have defeated the islanders here. We can then sail to Tristan's island and take it as we should have before."

Her excitement dimmed, replaced by rage. "And Diana too?"

"I want that bloody bitch dead, same as you. Maybe you want it more. What say I let you have the honor of doing her in?"

"Let me? Without my help, what can you do? I no longer need you to agree. Tell me you understand that."

He breathed hard. "I do."

"Remember it well or die here, a slave for the islanders to whip and work to death."

"Yes, yes." He made an impatient sound. "Have these beasts discussed the next time Tristan's sloop will arrive?"

Even though they had, Canela wasn't about to tell Vincent. He'd used her cruelly. She'd make him pay. "When they do, I may tell you."

"Best you make that will, instead of may. Do you know where the pistols are?"

She did. Her time spent here hadn't only involved filthy work. Early on, she'd learned where the men stored the weapons. At first, she'd wanted to use them on herself. Soon, she daydreamed about killing the islanders. Now, she'd indulge in her fantasies about shooting Diana, Tristan, and Vincent. "I can find out. The islanders here outnumber your men. How do you hope to fell so many?"

"Do they have drink? Spirits? Ale or rumfustian?"

"No."

"What about potions and things savages call magic? Something to put them out, hopefully for hours."

They had a healer who mixed potions to make one sleep, the same as Simone did for her and Canela's people. "We shall see."

"You'll need to do more than that or this hellhole is your future."

Not any longer. "We can speak about this again tomorrow when the moon rises. Not before." Confident in her new power, she padded to her enclosure.

* * * *

Vincent sneered at Canela's retreating figure and cupped his aching balls. Wasn't like him to cower to any woman, especially a savage, but he'd play her game to get what he wanted then make her regret everything she'd done tonight. First though, escape.

Another moment here would drive him mad.

Even growing up wretchedly poor in England hadn't prepared him for such deprivation. His stomach growled constantly, begging for any food, even the leaves and grass he forced himself to eat so he could sleep. These island bastards worked him near to death, worse than any captain on a merchant or pirate ship.

Next to them, Tristan had been kindness itself.

Vincent couldn't wait to slit Tristan's bloody throat for causing this misery and starting these problems.

As captain, Tristan had been honor-bound to share Diana. That's what pirates did. After everyone enjoyed her womanly charms, Tristan and the crew could have ransomed her to Bishop, collected the funds, and gone on their merry way.

But no, Tristan had demanded her flesh for himself alone. His notion of a grand romance. The pirate prince and the reverend's daughter.

Vincent spat. Both would regret what they'd done to him. Canela too. He'd save her death for last, the moment he no longer needed her.

* * * *

These last days, Heath's worries had kept him from civilized niceties. His stubble itched. He hadn't combed his hair. Even when he was in the courtyard, as now, he kept to himself as much as he could to avoid seeing Netta and Aimee.

Thankfully, they hadn't crossed his path.

He missed them terribly.

Tristan emerged from the mansion freshly shaved and wearing clean clothes.

Heath left the loom he'd yet to repair.

Gavra grabbed his arm. "Where are you going? Follie needs this to work so she can finish here and help me in the kitchen."

"I'll fix it in a moment. I have to speak to Tristan first."

"No. Before you do that, you see to what we need."

"Forgive me, but no." He shook her off as gently as he could and blocked Tristan from leaving the courtyard.

Tristan backed into a child. The girl tumbled to the ground and wailed loudly. Tristan glared at Heath. "What is the matter with you?" He patted the youngster's head. "Pardonne-moi. *Vous souhaitez un tour?*" Forgive me. Would you like a ride?

Her tears flowed but she lifted her chubby arms.

Tristan swung her above his head.

The other children gathered and bounced, each screaming for him to twirl them around.

He laughed. "*Vous porterez sûrement me out, mais chacun d'entre vous a votre tour.*" You will surely wear me out, but each of you shall have your turn.

Heath wanted to bellow. He'd already waited an interminable time to settle matters and end his torment on the isle.

Tristan couldn't have been more perverse. He gave each child a particularly long ride. They staggered past him like drunken sailors, their giggles and shrieks blending.

Finished, he stepped around Heath.

"Wait a moment." Heath grabbed his arm.

Tristan clenched his jaw. "Take care with what you say to me and do. This is your first and last warning."

"Understood." Heath released him. "I need a word. I've waited days to speak to you."

"Is something wrong with the crops? The cattle? The pigs or horses? James and Royce are here. So are the islanders. Why didn't you speak to them? My God, man, you've been here long enough to know I don't have time to settle every single thing. I have my wife and daughter to tend to now. I deserved a few days without interruption."

"Yes, I know. Congratulations. I wish all of you long lives and good health, but only you can resolve this."

Tristan sighed loudly. "If this is about Royce loathing you, there's nothing I can do to make things better. Quit coming to me like a silly schoolgirl and settle the matter between yourselves."

Heath danced to the side to keep Tristan from leaving. "I don't care if he shoots me. In fact, I welcome it. His hatred isn't what I need to discuss."

"Then what is? Out with it."

"Not here. A private place is best. We could speak in the room where you store the liquor or where you keep your books."

"No. Stay away from my library. Peter's finally doing his lessons. I want nothing to keep him from them. I'll educate him as a gentleman even if it kills him. If I don't, Diana will have my head." Tristan pointed. "Never repeat that."

"I swear I won't. Isn't there anywhere else we can talk without anyone overhearing?"

"Why? The women and children don't understand English. Even if they did, what have you to hide?"

To mention his desire for Aimee and Netta would most likely coax Tristan to a more secluded area. Unfortunately, Heath hadn't the courage to face Tristan's outrage, though he had to say something. "This is about me and the island women."

Tristan's color rose.

Heath guessed it wasn't from embarrassment.

"Come with me." Tristan strode into the birthing room and crowded him. "Talk. Or should I say confess? What have you done?"

"Nothing. Nor shall I. As long as I'm here, I can't be a proper man. Much more of this and I'll surely go mad. I'm no bloody priest."

Tristan's mouth quirked as he struggled not to smile. "Is that all?"

"You can't be serious. I know Royce expects me to endure celibacy for my remaining days, but you do too? I refuse."

Tristan got in Heath's face. "You what?"

"You heard me." He no longer cared if Tristan killed him. Anything would be better than this. "I want to leave. I must."

"How? You expect to take a skiff to civilization? Surely, you don't think we'd let you have the Lady Lark. Or leave for that matter. You are aware there is a price on my head. James's and Peter's too."

"I've done everything I could to win your trust, yet you still believe I'd bring the authorities or pirates here."

"Money does terrible things to men, even honorable ones."

"Should I include you in that assessment?"

Tristan's face darkened. "I don't care about such things."

"Neither do I. I want my freedom. The chance to live a normal life. I'd wager you and the others wouldn't last a minute in my position, yet you expect me to endure and to thank you for the restrictions. Where's the fairness in that?"

"Who said life was fair?"

Heath spoke through his teeth. "A decent man would let me go."

"I hope you know an insult isn't going to sway me."

"I'll beg if I have to. Do you want me on my knees?"

Tristan growled. "Of course not." He rubbed his forehead. "I can't give you an immediate answer. I have to think about this."

Heath threw up his hands. "How long will that take? Please don't tell me years. I won't last that long."

"Has an island woman shown interest in you? If so, I want her name."

"Why? Do you intend to lecture her?"

"No. Until Diana can speak fluent French, I'll have to ask Gavra or Simone to keep the women in line when it comes to Englishmen, including you and your shipmates." Irritation flashed across Tristan's face. "Bloody hell. Have they been having the same problem as you?"

"I have no idea. They work in the fields or with the animals. We don't converse now any more than we did on the ship. I only met them through Bishop."

"Never mention that swine again." Tristan paced the opulent room. Marble abounded along with silk coverings on the bed. "It isn't bad enough I have no end of trouble with the crops, animals, and Peter, now I have your problems to consider." He stopped and looked over. "You've yet to give me a name."

"There is none."

Tristan laughed. "Liar. I see the truth on your face. It's Veronique, isn't it?"

"I have no idea who that is. If she or the other women have shown interest, I wouldn't know. On Royce's orders, I'm not to look at or speak to the females here."

"He's a good man. You should follow his lead."

"By wedding an island woman and getting her with child?"

Tristan planted his hands on his hips. "You bloody well know what I mean. Keep away from the women while I sort this out."

"I want to leave with the islanders who come to trade. They should be here in weeks, surely no more than a few months. They have to travel before the cyclone season begins. To get rid of me even faster, Royce and the men here could take me to Mozambique in the Lady Lark or to the other natives' isle as they did Bishop's crew. Blindfold me. Keep me in the hold so I don't know the route. Bishop never told me. I wasn't his captain or quartermaster. Without the knowledge, I could never repeat it to another soul. Not that I would anyway. I give you my word."

"Which counts for nothing if pirates waylay the ship and beat what information you do know out of you or scuttle the sloop and everyone drowns. At that point, I'd have Simone's and the other women's grief to contend with, plus worrying about a possible attack on these shores. No thank you. Why didn't you consider this before you agreed to stay here?"

Heath could barely contain his outrage. He squeezed his fists to keep from shaking. "What choice did you allow me? It was either give you my allegiance as a free man, or be a slave for life to the other islanders, the same as Canela and the pirate everyone calls Yellow Scarf. No one said I'd never lie with a woman for the rest of my days. If they had, I would have spared you this trouble and shot myself."

Tristan's mouth jerked again.

Heath clenched his jaw. "This isn't funny."

"No one is laughing. Nor do I wish you ill. You have proved repeatedly you can be a good man, but that doesn't give you license to behave as an islander. This is their land, not mine. We must respect their people, in particular, the women. If we don't, they could revolt, then where would we be? There are no habitable islands around here, save this one. I expect you to remember that while I speak with James and Royce to determine the best course. I'm sorry for the suffering you have to endure, but these things can't be rushed. You'll simply have to understand and behave yourself. That above all." He left the room.

Heath sagged against the wall, no further now than he'd been days before.

Tristan could drag this out for months, clear to the storm season when the weather trapped everyone here. After that, he could conveniently forget the problem. By then, Diana would most likely carry a second child. So would Simone and Gavra and countless other women. Peter could be wed. Aimee too. And Netta, despite her hand. They'd have children. They might expect him to care for the babes until he died from loneliness or old age.

He tore into the courtyard.

The women looked up from their looms, the wash, and the potter's wheels.

Heath raced to the wall.

Gavra shouted, "Where are you going?"

Heath had no idea. He dashed into the forest. Bushes and trees rushed past. The cliff came up sharply. He veered before he shot over the side, bolted the way he'd come then back once more. A futile race to nowhere that he couldn't stop until his calves ached, feet hurt, and lungs burned.

He sank to the ground and could have cried. Despite his fatigue and pain, the clean, sweet air reminded him of Netta and Aimee. Their lips on him. Hands searching, arousing, comforting.

Everything he could never have.

Chapter 4

The morning dawned brighter than any other, the sky clear, breeze warm. A good omen Aimee wasn't about to waste. She hurried to the basin in her and Netta's mud house, washed, combed her hair, and rubbed fragrant petals over herself.

Netta tied a yellow cloth around her hips. "If you take all my flowers, what will I use?"

Aimee snatched two silk sacks and tossed the bright red one to Netta. "We can pick more."

"Before we eat?"

Excitement chased away Aimee's hunger. Yesterday, she'd learned where Heath would be this morning. "We can bring food with us and eat as we work. Diana wants berries for her bread. In the loaf, I think. If what Gavra makes tastes good, we can have as much as we want."

"If Diana chooses the right words in French. Many times, she still doesn't. Gavra's berry bread could end up feeding the birds. We best stuff our bellies before we gather anything."

"I can see to what Gavra needs. You should pick leaves and petals for Simone's potions."

Netta sagged. "They look the same no matter what she says. What if I choose poisonous ones rather than those that heal?"

"She always knows which to use. You have to at least try or things will never change." After their kiss with Heath, Netta had refused to leave their house for days unless she absolutely had to assist Gavra in the kitchen or mothers with their children. Once she finished those tasks, she raced back here.

"You do it." Netta held out her bag. "Being a healer is too hard. I like helping others with their work, not their good health."

"Then help me." She padded to the cowhide that served as their door. "And stay close no matter what happens."

Netta drew back. "What do you mean? What do you expect?"

Aimee couldn't tell her the truth. They'd never leave. "I expect lemurs, lizards, even flamingoes. No end of animals that could make you bolt."

"What are you talking about? I like the pink birds and the other creatures never bother me if I do the same with them. You always jump and squeal when an insect buzzes too close."

"Then you best protect me. Come." She gripped Netta's wrist and pulled her from their home.

"Wait. We forgot our food." She ducked back inside and took too long to gather their morning meal.

During their walk to the stone house, Netta ate bread and fruit. Aimee declined her share. Her stomach fluttered too much to eat.

Heath's scent, warmth, and strength lingered in her thoughts.

Netta stopped.

Aimee strode past, unwilling to delay their arrival.

"Where are you going?" Netta stood near the courtyard wall.

Aimee hadn't seen it or anything else except her fantasies: Heath in her and Netta's home, them in his, each sharing laughter, converse, meals, evenings, love.

Sun spilled past trees and drenched the courtyard in a golden glow. Earth gave up its rich morning scent. Dew clung to grass and leaves.

Near the looms and potter's wheels, women hugged each other in greeting and smiled. Children dashed around vegetation or played quietly in the shade. Infants fed at their mother's breasts and waved their tiny fists aimlessly.

Aimee's chest hurt. She yearned for a real home, a large family, a future no one could take away. When the pirates had invaded, she'd lost everyone except Netta. During those dark times, she dreaded having a babe. After what those beasts had done to her, she wasn't certain she could.

Melancholy pressed close. She pushed it away, ready for a new future even if she had to pull Netta into it kicking and screaming.

They greeted their friends and exchanged pleasantries.

Simone shuffled into the birthing room.

Aimee elbowed Netta. "Maybe you should give healing another try. Or at least helping Simone. Go on and ask her what the plants and petals should look like so you can collect what she needs." Troubling over them in the forest would keep Netta busy before they ran into Heath.

"I think not." She shoved the remaining bread in her mouth. "She may try to teach me about her potions again. When she talks, my head hurts. Tell me what berries you need."

"The red ones near the trees."

She followed Aimee past the wall into the forest. "Which trees? Tall? Short? Those with large leaves? Others with small ones?"

Follie had said Heath needed wood to build cribs for the coming infants. A task Royce had set him to do. "The sturdy ones." What other kind could he use to make a bed?

Netta gestured to the trees surrounding them. Sunlight streamed through the heavy canopy and left bright dots on her palm and hair. "These look sound to me."

"They have no berries nearby. We need to search for the bushes that do."

"Where?"

"There." Aimee pointed. Once they roamed that area, they could try another. Eventually, they'd come upon Heath.

She wandered through the woods, neck craned, alert to every sound.

Birds squawked and sang. Lemurs or other animals bounced the branches and shook leaves. Spotted butterflies took wing. Ones bluer than the sky joined them.

"Wait." Netta inclined her head. "The red berries are over there. Enough to fill our sacks."

"Those are the wrong ones."

"How can you tell?"

She asked too many questions. "Because I can. Over here." She avoided leaves and twigs that might mask other sounds.

Netta wasn't as careful. Shuffling and crackling noises announced her steps.

Aimee stopped. "You need to be quiet."

"Why? Will the berries hear us and run away?"

"You may coax out a snake."

Netta chuckled. "Noise frightens the creatures. It never causes them to strike."

"If you stand near one, it might." A yellow snake slithered back into the foliage.

Netta shuddered. "I promise to take care."

"While you follow me, you should look at the ground to make certain we avoid anything that might hurt us. I can search for the berries."

They prowled through the vegetation. The air grew warmer, the breeze died down, and animals quieted, already sluggish from the increasing heat.

Perspiration clung to Aimee's throat, intensifying her flowery scent. She ached to smell Heath's. Fevered and wanting, she rushed through the vegetation.

Netta trotted to keep up. "Why are you running?"

Aimee halted.

Netta bumped into her and sucked in a breath.

Before Netta could flee, Aimee grabbed her arm.

Heath stood within a stand, his back to them. A large blade hung from a loop in his waistband. He ran his palms over a slender trunk and shook it.

Birds squawked. One left a nest and dove at him, its wings flapping furiously.

He covered his head and ducked. The thing persisted, trying to peck.

Netta pulled away from Aimee. "Take care!"

Heath twisted to her. The bird followed him. He staggered back.

Aimee waved her arms to frighten the thing. "Shoo. Go away."

Netta threw a rock.

The bird shot back to its nest.

Netta reached him first. "Are you hurt? Did it peck you?"

"I don't think so." He ran his hands over his face and naked chest. "Is there any blood?"

"No." Aimee cradled his freshly shaved cheek, her thumb on his bottom lip. Never had she felt anything as silky and warm.

Netta touched his chest. "The mama was only trying to protect her brood." Tiny chirps sounded. "You need to be careful."

"I shall. I didn't know they were there. I...ah...I..."

Aimee leaned in. "You what?"

He made a frustrated sound and pulled them into his embrace. He kissed Netta hard and long then Aimee.

She accepted his tongue willingly.

He tore from her too soon and returned to Netta. Back and forth he went, his passion deepening, their lips and mouths molding. They fought to get closer. Netta moaned. Aimee couldn't find enough air to produce a sound.

Heath pulled away and backed into a trunk. Longing blazed in his eyes. Fear too. "Go to the courtyard. Now."

Netta took Aimee's hand. Together, they approached him, both of them brave.

Aimee spoke first. "Why do we have to go?" No one was around. If they had been, she would have chased them away. "We want more of your kiss."

Netta squeezed her fingers. "Far more. Everything you have to give."

Sadness replaced his previous emotions. He spoke to Netta. "I want to apologize for the other night in the storage room. I didn't mean to hurt you because of your..."

She turned from him.

He slumped. "Please don't do that. You have no reason to hide from anyone. You and Aimee are the loveliest women I've ever seen. You're both perfect. Exquisite beyond compare. You need men who'll protect and love you."

Netta stiffened. "Other men. Not you."

"Never me."

"Because of my hand."

"I didn't say that."

"I know what's in your heart. I can see it in your eyes. Refuse me, if you must, but take Aimee. Make her yours. Love her."

"No." Aimee wrapped her arm around Netta's waist. "Love us both."

"I can't." His face reddened, neck muscles corded. "Netta, hear me out. What I'm saying has nothing to do with your hand. You're beautiful. Always will be. Even if the pirates hadn't done any harm, I can't let either of you near me."

Aimee's hope sank. "Because our skin is brown not white?"

"Damnation. None of that bloody matters. The most enchanting Englishwomen can't compare with the two of you. You're too good for me. I'm nothing. I don't deserve you. You need good men. Not—"

"No." Netta stamped her foot. "Never say those words again. No man is finer than you."

"I'm leaving the isle as soon as the other natives come here to trade or your people sail there to do so. Surely no more than a few months, hopefully in a week or two. Before long, I'll be gone and won't return. Ever."

Netta covered her mouth.

Bile rose to Aimee's throat. The world kept spinning and she couldn't make it stop. "You want to leave because being with us makes you unhappy?"

Heath growled. "Don't you understand? I want you both too damn badly. It's all I think about and dream of. I can't—I won't take either of you, alone or together. Matters are already settled. If you refuse to leave here, I will." He sprinted into the forest.

* * * *

Canela hadn't kept her word to speak to Vincent. She liked toying with him as he'd done with her. Let him think she'd forgotten what they'd discussed. Let him worry that she'd told their captors about his plan.

More than once, he'd tried to catch her eye by whistling, waving his hand, or bouncing in place like a foolish child. She pretended not to notice.

His scowl faded to concern then panic. The same as hers after his betrayal.

Today he tended the hogs. His bony frame was no match for their bulk. Their snouts poked him. Their grunts and squeals demanded food. Snarling at them, he dumped the swill. Greasy hair clung to his head and neck. His yellow scarf had faded beneath the sun. Holes decorated it. Its worn state and his ugly scowl didn't improve his homely features.

Deliberately, Canela strolled close to the pen, her hands filled with tubers for the cook's stew.

Vincent stared then glanced over both shoulders.

No one watched them. She'd made certain before edging near.

He made a noise to get her attention. She raised her eyebrows to acknowledge him but didn't stop. He'd have to wait until she decided to hear him again. In a few days, perhaps. Maybe a week. Her people weren't expected until next month, if they came. She'd learned that shortly after she and Vincent had spoken.

At the community fire, Canela offered the vegetables to Ismay, the cook. She was half Fanette's size. Ismay's food was terrible but she was young and easy to fool. She'd agreed readily to Canela helping her, not guessing why she'd offered this time but never before. "Are these all right? If you want, I can dig for others."

"Those are plump enough but you need to clean and cut them so they soften in water." She handed Canela the blade.

Its long, sharp edge would easily slice through human flesh and make the victim squeal. Canela smiled sweetly. "Merci. Do you need anything else? Rice perhaps? Or herbs? I can fetch them."

"The spices are already here. Yoland keeps the herbs." She was the community's healer.

Ismay named what she wanted, explained how each looked, and where Canela could find them.

"If I forget, will Yoland help me?"

"She's with her mama today. No one expects the poor woman to live. The priest is there to help her journey past life."

He'd done nothing to save Canela's people when the pirates invaded. Like a meek woman, he'd hidden in the forest. Here, he barely looked her way, unconcerned with her suffering. Him, she'd truly enjoy killing. "Should I disturb them to get what you need?"

"Both are at her sister's. You can go to Yoland's home."

"What if she finds out I was in there instead of you?"

"How would she? I have no plan to tell her."

Despite the assurance, Canela bit her lip, feigning caution.

"Fanette will never know either. She's also with the sick mama. Now go." Ismay flapped her hand.

"Merci." Putting on a show, Canela kissed Ismay's fingers and darted to the mud house.

It stank of dried earth and filth, identical to everything else on this isle. Herbs filled bottles and cups. In the past days, she'd learned which Yoland used for the sleeping potion. However, now two cups held similar brownish-green contents that resembled dried moss. Canela wasn't sure which was for food, the other for rest, or if they were the same.

She took both, along with what Ismay had requested, and delivered them with a tentative smile. "Are these the ones you need? As stupid and foolish as I am, I can never be sure."

"These will do." She took everything except the second bowl with the brownish-green substance. "Bring this back and never use it."

"Why? Is it poison?"

"It has powerful magic to make one sleep."

Her pulse leapt. "By putting it on their eyes?"

Ismay laughed. "In their food. Too much and they may never wake."

Excitement warmed Canela more than a man pleasuring her. "I promise not to even look at it lest I grow tired from its power." Fighting her smile, she raced back to the mud house.

* * * *

Netta wrung her hands. "We have to fix this." Heath couldn't leave. He'd given her the greatest gift, desiring her and accepting who she was despite her deformity. "You have to fix this."

"Me?" Aimee paced their home the same as Netta. "How? We searched the forest, shore, and beach for him."

"We should have gone to his house. I can do that now."

"Wait." She caught Netta at the doorway. "How can we make things better when he speaks nonsense? He wants us so much he has to leave? What man ever said anything that foolish? An islander would have made us his on the forest floor and moved in here or asked us to join him in his home."

"Heath is English."

"Do their men behave as he does?"

Tristan couldn't keep away from Diana. James was the same with Gavra. Simone and Royce were always within each other's arms. Peter was the worst. He thought of nothing except taking Laure. "Do you think he has an illness only some Englishmen get?"

"We have to find out."

"How?"

"By asking someone who's English. Come."

Netta dug her toes in the dirt and refused to budge. "Not Tristan. He wanted to keep Royce away from Simone. They suffered greatly because of him. What if Tristan does that to us and Heath?"

Aimee cradled Netta's face. "We can ask Diana to help us. She knows about English men."

"What does it matter if she does? Although her French is improved, it's still too poor for her to converse easily. Everyone has to talk slowly and point to things to make her understand. With her help, we might send Heath away even faster."

"We can have someone turn our French into her English and back again so everyone understands each other perfectly and quickly. What Tristan calls translate."

Aimee wasn't making sense. If they asked Tristan to help, he'd know everything then. As a woman, Diana might keep their conversation secret. No man would, unless… "I know who can help us. Come with me."

* * * *

Diana rested her head against the bedchamber chair, Merry on her lap. A more perfect child didn't exist. A noisier one either. Hour upon hour, she cried. Diana nursed and changed her repeatedly. She rocked her and walked so much, she'd nearly worn a path in the marble floor. The screams didn't abate. She showed Merry the splendid English gown Tristan frequently asked Diana to wear before their bed play. The rose silk and scandalous cut always set him on fire.

Unimpressed, Merry bawled endlessly only to stop without warning. Like now. She even slept. Blessed peace at last.

A fist hit the bedchamber door hard enough to shake the wood.

Diana flinched. Merry wailed.

Peter, Netta, and Aimee piled into the room. Peter screwed up his mouth. "Can we come in?"

"You already have. You woke Merry."

Netta and Aimee exchanged a glance. Peter translated.

Netta gestured imploringly. "*Nous pardonner. Nous voulions dire aucun mal.*"

Sounded like an apology, but Diana couldn't be certain. Fatigue had muddled her brain. English was hard enough at this point, French impossible.

"Please tell them everything is all right and to sit."

Peter rattled off the words effortlessly, his accent as fine as Tristan's. There was hope her baby brother would eventually be the gentleman Diana wanted.

Aimee and Netta perched on the mattress. Peter paced like a caged animal and kicked the door.

So much for civilizing him. "Stop that." Diana bounced Merry to calm her. "Why are you here?"

"They forced me. I had no choice. Everyone threatens me with Laure."

Diana stroked Merry's back. "What did you do with that poor girl now?"

"I took a moment, one single moment from my studies to speak to her. Aimee and Netta saw me and threatened to tell Tristan unless I brought them in here. They want to ask you something."

"What? Why me?"

"I have no idea. I'll ask."

French flew furiously between him and the young women, the words so quick they slurred, confusing Diana completely.

Peter laughed.

Netta stood, hands on her hips, jaw clenched.

He sobered. "They want to know about Englishmen, in particular Heath. Why he's behaving as he is."

Good heavens, more problems. First Peter with Laure, then Royce with Simone, now this. "What has Heath done to Aimee? Or did he do something to Netta?"

"Before I tell you, you must promise not to scream or swoon. I'm not good with women who carry on so."

Diana's irritation doubled. "Poor Peter. We do try your patience, don't we? Tell you what, I'll try to keep my head as I did when Vincent threatened to shoot you and me in the longboat. Will that do?" Peter had nearly wept then. She'd been eager to tear Vincent apart and would have if given the chance.

Peter's face colored. "I suppose. Heath said Netta and Aimee are both lovely, perfect in every way. He can think of nothing else. He wants them for his own but must never touch them. He plans to leave the isle and live amongst the natives we trade with or work his way back to England. Aimee and Netta don't understand."

Diana didn't either. "Are you saying he wants two women at once?"

"Since they look alike, it's probably like having one to him."

"Have you lost all good sense? What he's proposing is unheard of. In England, he'd probably face arrest. Perhaps hanging."

"We're not in England any longer."

He kept reminding her as did other things: bare-breasted women, naked children, and Diana making love with Tristan behind vegetation during previous festivities. The celebrants hadn't been far away. If that didn't convince her they were no longer in England, she'd fought off pirates, had her nipples rouged, and had worn a diamond in her navel on her wedding night. Clearly, they were no longer in the civilized world. Even so, one man and two women was unthinkable. "Does their culture allow such a thing?" Tristan didn't need the island men killing Heath over his randy ways. Perhaps Heath planned to leave to spare everyone the trouble he'd cause. "Does anyone here do that?"

"I'll ask." Peter snickered while doing so.

During her answer, Netta waved frantically, unmindful of her mutilated hand. A first. Aimee spoke rapidly too. They interrupted and talked over each other.

Peter gestured for silence.

They calmed and looked at Diana expectantly.

She did the same with Peter. "I believe I heard love is love. After that, I couldn't keep up. What else did they say?"

"That love is sent to us by mère de l'homme, the greatest goddess of all. She's the one the islanders believe in. For them not to accept what she offers is a terrible insult. She might not call them home to her loving arms when they die. The priest said the goddess is wrong and what they think she said is actually wicked, made up by depraved men who'll be damned to hell's eternal fires for their vile lust. Aimee explained the priest meant well, but they believe the goddess. Nothing you say will change their minds. Netta made a point of that."

Diana suspected her father would have run screaming from the isle. He'd taken morality seriously and lived a life of prayer, deprivation, and unending gloom. She preferred the island ways no matter how unconventional. "We certainly can't tell them to rebuke their goddess. What did they want to know from me? If I approve? I'm afraid I'm too English to give them my blessing. They must do what they think is right for their situation."

"I'll tell them."

More discussion followed and grew heated, the words flying too fast to catch or translate. Netta kept pointing at Peter then Diana and the door.

Thankfully, Merry's newest crying spell had worn her out and she slept peacefully.

Peter sighed loudly. "Are you ready for this?"

"Quit being dramatic and tell me."

"Very well. They want to know if all Englishmen act as Heath does.

Kissing and loving one moment then running away the next and threatening to leave. They wonder if he's sick in the head. I believe he is. If two women wanted me, I certainly wouldn't—"

"Have you forgotten Laure already?"

Peter's cheeks turned pink. They were as smooth as Diana's. Whiskers had only begun to sprout at the corners of his upper lip.

He shifted his weight. "I was boasting. Please don't say anything to Laure. What should I tell Netta and Aimee?"

"I can't read Heath's mind, but I can guess since he's English he feels what he wants is wrong. He was raised to believe differently than them. Not that either of their upbringings matter. You said he's departing when he can. Is Tristan all right with that? Do we have anything to worry about from pirates or authorities finding us here?"

"Tristan wouldn't let him leave if there's a problem. Perhaps Heath's going to forsake England forever and live out his life with the other islanders."

She'd have to ask. "If he does go, he'd abandon Netta and Aimee. They could be with child by then. That wouldn't be right. Please tell them to think carefully about what they intend to do. I don't want them hurt. Go on."

"I hope this is the end of it."

"Present your case well and it will be."

He spoke longer than Diana expected.

Aimee and Netta listened without comment, their lovely faces not giving away their thoughts.

"There. Finished." He strode to the door.

Aimee stood. "*Votre soeur doit dis àpersonne ce que nous dit. Même pas son homme. Nous voulons sa promesse.*"

Diana couldn't wait until she knew French fluently, especially the islander dialect. Aimee had spoken so quickly, the words blurred into each other, all incomprehensible. "What did she say?"

"She doesn't want you telling anyone what they said."

"I don't like keeping secrets from Tristan, but I won't betray their trust. Nor will you. Promise me you'll say nothing to him or the other men."

"If you insist."

"I do. Go back on your word and risk my wrath. Do tell them their secret is safe with us."

He rattled off his comment.

Aimee nodded.

Netta shot to her feet. *"Demandez votre soeur combien il est facile de changer d'avis de l'anglais."*

Diana rubbed her forehead. "What now?"

"She wants to know how easy it is to change an Englishman's mind."

Chapter 5

Heath cut more trees than he needed and didn't stop despite his aching arms and his cramping back. The pain and physical activity should have calmed his thoughts and killed his coarse needs. If anything, his feelings magnified. He tasted Aimee and Netta on his lips. Their scent followed him everywhere no matter how far he traveled from where they'd been. Their dewy flesh, tightened nipples, and ripe breasts beckoned.

Cursing his desire, he lugged the wood through the forest. His initial destination had been his house where he could work in peace. He hadn't the strength to go that far and brought the logs to a far corner in the courtyard, away from the women and children. His search for tools to saw, plane, and fasten the wooden pieces enticed the most curious boys to his side. Once he had everything he needed, except solitude, a few girls had joined the crowd.

The little ones shifted in place and fidgeted. They also stared at him in wonder. As one would a king or a god.

Despite his inner turmoil, their youth and openness touched Heath as few things had. He'd never considered having a family. That was for men who had proper occupations and money, not a roving mariner who had to work constantly to feed himself, his meager wages spent on food and clothing. He should have ordered them to leave or asked their mothers to keep them away from him, but couldn't stomach their disappointment.

Aimee and Netta's were still too fresh in his mind.

He laid his tools in the order he'd need them.

A taller boy toed the hammer.

Heath wagged a finger. "*Personne ne touche à rien. Vous devez garder la bonne distance.*" No one touches anything. You must keep a proper distance.

The girls stepped back readily and held their hands behind themselves.

The boys nodded but didn't move.

Heath ordered them to join the others. "Heed what I say or I won't let you watch."

The one who'd touched the hammer was the last to obey. A born leader or rascal. Heath had been no different, shoving his way through life when he'd had no one to care whether he lived or died or to show him how the world should work.

The boy eyed him and the materials. "What are you going to make?"

"Cribs for the infants."

"How do you do that?"

"Watch and I'll show you. What's your name?"

"Ourson."

Little bear in French. It fit him well. He had a fearless manner and sharp mind. "I'm Heath. Nice to meet you. Care to shake hands?"

"Why would we do that?"

"That's how proper Englishmen greet each other and others around the world. Take my hand and make certain you move yours up and down like I do." Heath shook firmly.

Ourson couldn't have been more solemn. He even put muscle into his grip.

"Well done."

He smiled, showing his missing baby teeth, the adult ones not yet grown in.

The other children clamored to do the greeting. Most giggled so much Heath could scarcely understand their names. "Who'd like to help me with my work?"

"Me." Ourson elbowed those closest to him. "Quiet. I go first."

Heath intervened before they fought. "Everyone will have a turn. Ourson, hand me my blade."

He held it as one would priceless jewels. "Did you make this too?"

"No. A swordsmith most likely did."

"A what?"

"Swordsmith. A man who forges metal into various shapes like the blade you hold. A blacksmith created this hammer." Heath touched the head. "These nails too." He picked them up and showed Ourson.

He stared. "How do you make them?"

"You melt metal and shape it while it's hot."

"Do it now. I want to see."

The other children bounced in place, voices raised, asking for a show.

Heath laughed. "I haven't the materials or tools to do so. I'm certain Tristan took—ah, he found these when he sailed on ships."

"That he did." Peter strolled by. "Along with many other things. What a time that was."

His wistful tone matched an elderly man recounting his wayward youth. Peter had much to learn about the world. When Heath had been his age, he'd already survived on his own for years with no parental guidance as Tristan and Diana tried to show Peter.

Heath hadn't the benefit of books either, as Peter did. Certainly nothing close to the luxury found here. He doubted Peter ever had a moment's hunger in this wild, lovely place. Someone should knock some sense into him. Tell him how lucky he was.

Ourson sat cross-legged on the dirt. Several boys imitated him. The girls drifted away to watch the women who made pottery or wove cloth.

Hands on his knees, Ourson rocked. "Capitaine always brought gifts when he returned from his voyages. Silk for our mothers, tools for our fathers, and toys for us. When Diana came here, he stopped sailing. Will you go and bring us something?"

Once Heath left these shores, he'd never return. Despair filled him, restricting his breath. His chest and belly hurt.

Tristan strode from the mansion, glanced at the gathering around Heath but didn't comment or stop.

He'd either forgotten Heath's plea or planned to ignore it. "Tristan, wait." Never seeing Aimee and Netta again would kill Heath. Remaining here deprived of their loving touch would destroy him.

Tristan slowed but didn't look over.

"Please, I need an answer on what we discussed. Have you decided—"

"No. I'll let you know when I have. No need to ask again. Make certain what you do doesn't hurt the children." He caught up with James and left.

Ourson tapped Heath's hand. "What must Capitaine decide?"

Heath had forgotten to speak English so the children and women wouldn't understand. With each day, he grew more attuned to this isle. He behaved as a native but would never belong. "Matters I spoke to him about."

"What are those?"

His freedom or captivity. If Tristan refused to let Heath go, he'd have to steal an islander's skiff and leave. The man on watch might shoot him. Should he withstand that problem, survival in such a small boat, by himself, wasn't likely but couldn't be worse than the slow death he'd endure in this place. Perhaps he could implement his escape shortly after the other natives who traded here left. He might be able to catch up with their vessel, or stow away on it where they'd anchored. If they took Bishop's. If not, their boats might not be large enough to hide him.

Ourson tapped harder. "What are those matters?"

"Ah, whether we should make our own tools and materials. These surely won't last forever."

"How do we make them? Is it hard?"

"No. All one has to do is pull metal from heated rocks, melt it further then fashion the material into whatever's needed. A blade, saw, pot. I'm certain Tristan has books on the subject."

"When you make those things, I can help."

Several boys shouted they wanted to do the same.

At the noise, the women looked over. Thankfully, Netta and Aimee weren't among them. Heath had learned they helped where needed. At the looms, potter's wheels, the mansion kitchen, or with mothers who were too busy tending newborns to care for their older children.

Wherever Aimee and Netta worked today, he prayed they understood how terrible he would be for them. That they deserved far more. He'd prefer they cursed and hated him rather than hungered for another touch as he did with them.

Weariness washed over him, yet his pulse wouldn't slow. He swung from agitated to tired without pause.

Ourson's endless questions distracted him briefly. If Heath had been lucky enough to have a son, he would have chosen him. Painstakingly, he explained the process of turning a log into furniture. His words didn't register with Ourson, but Heath's actions did. As the pieces took shape beneath his hands, Ourson no longer scratched, bounced, or rocked. He watched transfixed. A future carpenter if ever there was one.

"No one ever showed you this before?"

He shook his head. "The men work at their houses or in the fields and pastures."

"What does your father do?"

"He tends the horses. I want to do that and this."

"A fine goal." Heath ruffled his hair. "You're a bright boy but I'm afraid I'm through for now." The sun shone directly overhead. He'd only made it to midday, his exhaustion complete. If he didn't nap, he'd collapse.

"Ourson." A young woman in a dark blue cloth smiled gently. "Come along. We must go home."

He pushed to his feet but didn't leave. "I want to stay with Heath."

"Another time. I need your help with our meal. Papa expects us."

"Go." Heath pushed him gently. "Never keep your mother waiting. You're lucky you have one."

"Everyone does."

"Not me."

"Why?"

"That tale's for another day. Go or your mama may not let you help me next time."

Ourson raced to her.

Heath had difficulty moving. Everything ached but it wasn't nearly as bad as the pain in his heart. He stored his materials in a safe place the children couldn't access and plodded to his house. He couldn't call it home. This isle would never be that for him. His future lay elsewhere.

Once he escaped, got shot trying, or drowned, Royce would surely rejoice. Ourson might miss him for a day or two. Netta and Aimee would move on. They'd have no choice.

Yards from the mud structure, Heath's feet no longer wanted to move. If not for the sun burning his shoulders and insects bombarding him, he would have dropped to the ground and slept there.

His grass-stuffed mattress urged him forward. He drew back the cowhide over the entrance.

An oil lamp barely lit the interior, its flame turned low. The lamp didn't belong to him. His eyes adjusted to the gloom. Flowers stuffed in bottles or piled in bowls decorated his Spartan surroundings. The fragrant petals competed with the enticing meal on his rough-hewn table: roasted beef, fresh rice bread, boiled eggs, and other fare.

Netta and Aimee stepped out of the shadows.

Aimee undid her purple cloth, Netta her deep rose one.

The silk grazed their sleek thighs and fluttered to their feet. The delicate curls between their legs matched their dark hair.

He clutched the cowhide to remain standing. This couldn't be real.

Netta joined him, her scent musky and sweet, nipples taut, lips moist. Heath wanted to devour her. He didn't dare move.

She pressed closer. Their toes touched.

Heat shot through him. "What are you doing?"

"What we have to. No matter your English ways, our desire will never be wrong. The goddess wants her children to be happy. Diana said to do whatever we want."

He reeled. "You spoke to Diana about coming here, being with me, taking off your cloths?"

Aimee approached, her breasts bobbing with each step. She smelled better than heaven ever could. "Diana promises never to tell anyone, not even Tristan. Everything will be all right no matter what the priest said."

Heath went hot then cold. "You talked to a priest too?"

"Not today." Netta unfastened Heath's breeches. She grazed his skin.

He trembled.

She glanced up. "The islanders we trade with needed the priest so he's with them now. The love we share is not his concern."

Aimee helped Netta lower Heath's breeches.

His cock sprang out, thick and stiff, balls tight to his body. "Stop."

"Why?" Aimee cradled his rod and searched his face. "You want us, no?"

With her caressing him, he couldn't think much less speak. She rubbed her thumb over his crown.

Netta cupped his sac.

Heath's legs went watery. "We shouldn't—mustn't…"

They directed him to his bed. He fell backward onto it. The frame creaked and the sheet puffed up.

On their knees, they pulled off his breeches and tossed them aside. Netta tongued his shaft, Aimee lapped his balls, their mouths wet, hot, loving.

Pleasure exploded in too many places. He writhed and gasped. If possible, he would have jumped out of his skin. "Bloody hell, you're killing me."

They stopped instantly.

"This hurts you?" Aimee stroked his inner thigh.

Even his teeth tingled. "Of course not. It's bloody wonderful. I—it's too much. We shouldn't. We can't."

"Only the priest tells us this is wrong." Netta made a dismissive sound. "We listen to the goddess, not him." She took Heath's cock into her mouth clear to its root, her nose pressed to his hairy groin.

Even the most wanton doxy hadn't relished his sex as Netta did. Feelings he didn't know existed rammed into him with cyclone force and threatened to tear him apart from longing he couldn't resist.

Fool that he was, he clamped her head to keep her at the shameless task.

Aimee tongued his left testicle, eased it past her silken lips, and suckled gently.

He twisted the sheet, needing it as an anchor. New emotions emerged. Excitement, euphoria, tenderness, raw lust, boundless need. He'd never get enough of these two.

They worked as a team, trapping him each time he squirmed, arousing his sex with their mouths as their cunts would.

Their tongues were unbelievably hot and supple, skin softer than a baby chick.

Relief sped close. He shoved it back, not wanting this to end. When it did, he'd have to face reality. Escaping. Leaving. Possibly dying.

If Royce guessed what happened in here, he'd tell Tristan. Nothing good could come of that. Even if the goddess and Diana turned a blind eye, Heath could hardly live openly with two women. When they became pregnant, matters would only grow worse.

The only reasonable alternative was to stop this and leave.

Aimee stroked the furrow between his cheeks.

Netta licked the area behind his crown, his most sensitive spot.

He surrendered, helpless against their charms, trapped by need, affection, and an end to loneliness. What all men coveted and any sane god should want for His children.

Heath soared, unmoored from the earth, adrift in delight. Either the world spun or he did. Impossible to tell which.

His seed spurted into Netta's mouth. Proof he was a bloody beast. He strained to move back to spare her.

She pressed against his thigh. Aimee did too. They each lapped and swallowed his offering and licked him clean.

Panting, he sprawled on his bed and hoped for death. What a glorious last moment this would be, after which his actions would send him straight to Hell. If such a place existed. Never a pious man, he'd always reasoned no eternal torment could be worse than the daily struggle to survive.

Aimee crawled on his right side, Netta his left. Both beamed.

Nothing could match the joy their happiness gave him, the comfort and serenity they provided. He fought a yawn and strained to keep his eyes open. "Proud of yourselves, are you?"

"Oui." Aimee lifted her chin coquettishly. "We pleased you greatly and made you smile."

Heath touched his mouth. He was grinning. He dropped his hand. The bloody thing proved too heavy to keep up.

Netta kissed his knuckles and rested his palm on her nipple. The tip and halo tightened instantly. "Do you need to rest now?"

Not if it meant missing a moment with them. Her plush breasts invigorated him more than prolonged sleep and a hearty meal. Aimee's tender kisses on his cheek and neck stirred the animal within. "No."

He pushed up.

Both grabbed his arms.

Heath shook loose, left the bed, and faced them. "Spread your legs."

Relief filled their eyes, replaced by naked sin. Precisely how women should be with a man who wanted them.

Indulging in this could cost him everything, possibly them too. Caution warned him to dress and leave. Intolerable need wouldn't allow retreat until he had no other choice. Their skin glowed with good health, the color richer and far lovelier than a pale English lass. He'd never seen warmer eyes or shinier hair. They had no rivals.

The soft folds between their legs glistened with moisture and plumped with need. The deep pink shade matched their rosy cheeks.

Heath wished there were two of him so he could enjoy Aimee and Netta simultaneously. He nearly laughed at the notion but didn't, not wanting either to think he made light of this moment or them. However, he couldn't make a wrong move that would lead them to believe he preferred one over the other.

Aimee propped herself on her elbows. "Why are you waiting?"

"And doing nothing?" Netta lifted her eyebrows.

"I'm not sure what…that is… Who wants to go first?"

Aimee fell back and giggled. Netta did too.

He didn't blame them. His question sounded foolish.

Netta's color deepened. "Choose Aimee."

"Not me, you. Choose Netta."

"What say I pick both?" A way had just come to him, his solution quite brilliant.

He settled between Netta's legs, his mouth on her cunt.

She gasped and pushed into him, offering herself.

No man could ask for better. He reveled in her taste, a faint salty flavor and clean skin. Ambrosia to a lonely mariner.

Not wanting to overlook Aimee, he stroked her nub.

She moaned and scooted closer.

Netta wiggled, demanding his attention.

Heath gave it willingly.

* * * *

Enveloped in Heath's passion and regard, Netta forgot her imperfection. She was whole again, pretty, desired, cherished.

His breaths warmed her. His unrestrained sounds spoke of his delight. He suckled her sensitive flesh.

Delight rolled through her in waves, each stronger than the last. She yielded fully. He'd never harm her.

An odd ache settled between her legs. Not painful. Maddening. It edged close, teased, and urged her to rub herself there.

She reached down.

Heath pushed her hand away gently and held her wrist.

Trapped, she had no choice except to submit and endure. She wanted nothing else. For him, she'd be a slave to his passion. He worshipped her flesh even though it wasn't white, and understood her feelings like no other Englishman had.

She hurt as he did, bled the same, needed comfort, acceptance, respect. He stroked her thumb.

The small intimacy opened her heart even more to him and stoked her craving. Her sex became glutted, heavy with desire, needy of an end to this. She hadn't any idea what the finish might be. After the pirates, no man had touched her. Not even an islander.

She hadn't wanted anyone until she'd seen Heath.

He released her hand, explored the separation between her cheeks, and touched her tightest opening.

Her breath caught. Unruly heat and feelings she'd never experienced swirled within, crashed into each other, and pulled her with them.

The pleasure proved greater than she could endure yet not enough. She longed for it to never end.

Another surge hit, too strong for her to battle against. Deep within her sheath, something beat strong and steady, and sapped her remaining strength. Her legs drooped outward. Lifting her lids proved impossible. Heat flowed from her belly to her breasts, legs to her toes, covering her like a warm fog.

Heath kissed her thigh.

Aimee thrashed and moaned.

He tended her, but also stroked Netta's sex, their pleasure not done. She melted into his touch.

* * * *

Heath's hand on Aimee was one thing. But his mouth…

No wonder Netta had shouted loud enough to scare away the insects and birds.

Aimee wasn't certain she could be any quieter. The warmth he generated with one lick and suckle outdid the largest fire or brightest sun. Dazzled, she grew greedy and possessive, wanting him between her legs without end.

Netta made a pleased sound.

Heath flicked his tongue on Aimee's nub. Her excitement intensified. Proof he could take care of her and Netta at the same time.

A more magnificent man had never lived. He couldn't leave. Today bound him and them to each other for all time.

Even if Aimee couldn't give him children, Netta would. She and Aimee would pour their love into him and the babes. Their family would be strong, impossible for any invaders to defeat. He only had to give love a chance.

She clutched his hair lest he try to get away too soon.

He pressed closer and eased his finger into her channel. His size, touch, and passion trapped her.

Aimee surrendered to his dominance that safeguarded and treasured.

Joy bubbled up. The tension between her legs sharpened, burst, and billowed free.

She trembled like a newborn. There wasn't enough air to satisfy her lungs. She gripped the sheet, Netta's hand, Heath's shoulder. None proved able to keep her or his house from dipping and swaying.

Heath leaned up. "You all right?"

She could scarcely speak. "The heat. The spinning. Already they go away." That wasn't right. "I want them back. I want more."

Netta sat up. "So do I."

She and Aimee pulled Heath onto the bed.

He toppled between them. The mattress shook.

Netta spoke to Aimee. "You first."

"No, you."

"Merci." Netta straddled him and grabbed his shaft.

He twisted and swore.

Netta tried to ride him. "Keep still."

"I will not. Stop that."

She froze. "Why?"

He lifted her from him and scrambled off the bed. "Never do that again, do you understand?"

Aimee couldn't hide her surprise. "You never want us to love you as a woman does a man? Do the English do so differently? Will you show us? We can learn."

His face turned red. He grabbed his breeches.

Aimee rolled off the mattress and yanked the clothing from him.

"Damnation. Give those to me."

She pressed them to her, stepped back, and hit the table. The bowls and plates rattled. "Why do you want them?"

"To get dressed. There won't be any lovemaking."

Netta pulled her legs to her chest. "With me. I can leave and you—"

"With neither of you." He pointed at Netta. "Before you say anything else, this has nothing to do with your hand. I want you for who you are now. Aimee too. However, I can't risk either of you having a child with me. I won't be here. Who'll take care of the babe, see to its welfare? A child growing up without a father's guidance and protection wouldn't be right."

But him leaving was? She and Netta had shared their laughter, love, and hope with Heath and he still wanted to flee. When they'd asked Diana how to change his mind, she had no answer. Already, Diana knew the situation was hopeless.

Aimee fought tears. "Netta would have to worry about having your babes, not me. After what the pirates did, I may never have infants."

She threw his breeches at him and grabbed her cloth.

Chapter 6

Heath had never felt as helpless, stupid, or cruel. He didn't want to consider what Aimee meant about the pirates. If he'd had the power, he would have torn those beasts apart.

Not that he had any reason to consider himself honorable. He could have let her and Netta down gently. Instead, he'd presented his argument as he would to another man. Hard sense. No emotion involved.

Aimee's narrow shoulders trembled. Netta swiped her cloth and embraced her sister, both clinging to the other. He didn't doubt they'd done so repeatedly during the awful times they'd faced.

They padded to the doorway.

"Hold on there." He spoke as mildly as he could but did block the entrance so they couldn't leave. Not like this. Every time he and they met, he left them bereft or in tears. "Please. Won't you have some water or the lovely food you brought?"

They kept their faces turned away.

He had no idea how to reason with one woman, much less two. "Sit on the mattress. I'll bring you whatever you want."

"Why?" Netta held Aimee tightly. "You wanted us out of your home and your life, but now you ask us to stay. You make no sense."

"I won't argue with you. I've been awful. I've upset you and Aimee. I didn't mean to or to bring back the frightful events you'd endured."

Offense flashed in Netta's dark eyes. "You want us to stay because you pity us."

"No. Never. I hate the men who hurt you both. I've never known braver women. You survived their savagery. A man might have turned murderous after being used so cruelly and struck out at those around him even though they had nothing to do with his mistreatment. You and Aimee are gentle and kind. No man could ever be as worthy as you."

Aimee lifted her face. Tears streaked her cheeks.

Heath cursed himself for the unkind words he'd said. If he'd had any sense, he would have bitten off his tongue before making a sound. "Forgive me for adding to your distress." He enfolded her in his arms. Netta too.

They didn't fight him. Perhaps they should have. He didn't know any longer but couldn't cause them more pain. "You should sit and have some water. I'll bring it to you."

He settled them on the mattress and filled the one cup he owned. His hands shook so much water sloshed over the container. He crouched near their legs and offered the drink.

Netta gave it to Aimee. She took a small sip and let Netta have the rest.

If they hadn't been this devoted to each other, neither might have survived the pirates.

Too much emotion simmered within him. Sorrow battled with outrage. Sadness for them and the islanders fought hatred for his kind. "Whatever the pirates did to you, I want you to know shame isn't yours to bear. It belongs to the animals who dared come to your land and harmed your people. They had no bloody right."

Aimee fingered away tears. "They changed everything."

"I know."

Netta bristled. "How? It happened to us not you. They treated our people worse than animals." She hugged Aimee. "To them, we had no feelings. No right to be afraid, to scream or fight when they hurt us."

"I'm sorry."

"That changes nothing."

Aimee touched Netta's arm. "Heath means no harm. He wants our pain to go away."

"I won't say anything." He lifted his hands. "Speak if you want, I'll hear every word. If you'd rather be quiet, I'll accept that."

"You have to know." Aimee lowered her face. "I want you to know."

"Then I'll listen."

"Do you mind?" She pressed Netta's ravaged hand to her cheek.

Netta shook her head.

Aimee drew in a ragged breath. "One night we went to sleep in the world we knew and loved. The next morning, pirates swarmed the isle, no different than bugs that destroy crops and leave nothing. Our parents died first then our grandparents, aunts, and uncles."

Tears dripped from her chin. "They killed anyone who was too old to work or brave enough to fight. No islander's blade could win against the pirates' pistols. They rounded us up as everyone's fathers had the animals. They even built pens. Girls in one. Boys in the other. The pirate capitaine had a white woman. She made certain no girls escaped. The boys went to work at once, carrying water, gathering food. No matter how small they were, they had to toil like men, hour after hour from the moment the sun rose in the sky until it sank back into the water. With the girls…" She turned into Netta and hid her face.

Netta stroked Aimee's hair. "Do you want me to tell him the rest?"

Aimee nodded.

Color drained from Netta's cheeks. "The pirates moved into the houses that belonged to our chief and the men who ruled with him. They were dead by then, their bodies outside the entrances, throats cut, bellies slit open and exposed to the birds. So many creatures fed on them. The sounds were awful." She shivered.

Heath didn't know what to say or how to comfort. To hear more would sicken him, a grown man. She and Aimee had been girls when the pirates forced them to brave atrocity upon atrocity. He hadn't the right to turn away or beg them to spare him.

No one had shown them mercy.

Netta wiped her nose. "The pirates took the oldest girls into the houses first. Their screams and pleas seemed to go on for hours. Men laughed. Then horrible silence. We thought the girls had died like our parents and the others."

Aimee grabbed Netta's hand. "When they finally came out we were glad until we saw them. Bruises covered their arms and legs. Some had eyes that turned black. They stared at nothing. They looked like one who's seen the dead or a bad spirit, something too evil to imagine. They curled on the ground away from us. The capitaine's woman told them to get used to what happened. They had no choice. The men came back for new girls. They returned as the others had, bruised and haunted. At last, the pirates took us."

Netta held Aimee's hand to her heart. "The capitaine and his crew fought over who would take us first. We were the only ones on the isle who looked so much alike and had shared a mother's belly. One man argued for this turn. Capitaine shot him. He fell dead at our feet. The others held up their hands and spoke the English. The words meant nothing to us. Capitaine knew our language. He said he would have us first then we would go to his men. That made no sense. Have us how? Go to his men why? Were we to cook and clean for him and them? Gather food? Collect water?"

Aimee covered her mouth to quiet her weeping.

Netta's gaze turned inward, terror in her eyes. "Capitaine pushed me on the mattress and undid his breeches. One of his men hit Aimee to stop her screams. I fought to get to her. Capitaine held me down. I bit him wherever I could and even tore off his earlobe. He slapped me until I was too dazed to fight. His breath stank of spirits. The same that Tristan gives the men at celebrations.

"Capitaine said I would pay for what I did to him. He pulled me to the table and sliced off my little finger to my wrist." She looked at her wound. "No matter how hard I try to recall the pain, it never returns. Blood spilled over the wood and settled into cracks. That I remember and Aimee screaming for them to take her, to hurt her, not me. He cut off my second finger as deeply as he had the first."

Netta breathed hard. "He took my middle finger as he had the others and said he should let me bleed to death but wanted me to live disfigured. The other islanders would know what would happen to them if they dared defy him. His men held me down. One pressed a torch to my hand. The fire sizzled. That was the last thing I heard. When I woke, a pirate was on top of me. Another on Aimee. She was too quiet, not screaming or crying any longer. The pain in my hand was worse than the hurt between my legs. The pirates kept us longer than they did the other girls. They made me watch them taking Aimee with whatever they could find, hurting her worse than me. Capitaine said it was my fault for trying to save her."

Tears stung Heath's eyes.

Netta kissed Aimee's cheek. "In time, I carried a babe the same as the other girls. Aimee never did. After what the pirates did to her…" She shook her head.

Heath cradled their faces. "What happened to your child, Netta?"

"I ate plants Simone said would keep me from birthing. The infant left me. It would have died anyway. The pirates took the newly born babes and left them in the forest. The men hated their brown skin. Those children suffered more than mine did. Now you know why Aimee will never have a child. But you can still love and protect her."

He gathered them to him, holding both equally, kissing their cheeks, tasting their tears. "I'm so sorry for what happened."

Netta stiffened. "We want nothing of your pity."

"You're not getting it. I have only respect for you." He brought her maimed hand to his mouth.

She twisted her arm.

"Please don't fight me. I mean you no harm. I want to honor you." He kissed the ragged scar and protruding bones.

She wept.

He held her and Aimee as hard as he dared and didn't want to let go. He'd crossed a threshold with them and couldn't turn back or run ahead into the future. It remained as murky as the past. They only had the present. Once they quieted, he dried their tears with Aimee's cloth and gave them the cup. "Drink. Then I want both of you to eat. Your stomachs are growling."

Netta finished her sip. "Yours is doing that. Not ours."

"Then we can share the food, if you'll allow it. Please say you will."

Aimee smiled. New tears spilled from her eyes. Netta's too.

Heath hoped they were happy ones.

Aimee scooted to the mattress edge. "Netta and I can serve you."

"No. I won't hear it. Stay where you are. I'll fill a plate that you can share on the bed."

Netta grabbed his wrist. "Will you sit at the table so far from us?"

"I'll be at your feet. My proper place with such lovely sisters. You put every other woman to shame."

Her laughter tinkled, the sound lovelier than songbirds. "Never let Tristan hear you say that. He believes Diana's beauty is greater than the goddess's."

"He's an Englishman. Ignore him."

"But not you?"

"I've seen heaven in your faces and eyes. No man has ever been as lucky as I am to know you. Now heed my words and stay where you are. Let me serve you as I should."

He heaped beef, bread, eggs, grapes, two bananas, and honey on his lone plate and delivered it to Netta. Aimee's protector. He suspected Netta was first born. Whether hours or minutes separated them, she was in charge. He handed Aimee his only fork and knife. "Go on. Enjoy. I'll be back with my food in a moment."

He used the sack they'd brought and settled the silk on his crossed legs.

Aimee peeled an egg and gave it to Netta.

She took a small bite. "Will you stay on the isle now?"

Beef stuck in his throat. Heath forced it down. He shouldn't stay, couldn't if Tristan granted him freedom. Netta and Aimee's frightening history hadn't changed their odd arrangement with him or what would happen if Netta conceived. He doubted Aimee would ever be jealous, but she'd hurt deeply if she couldn't have a child. As to what the islanders would think of him with two women, he didn't want to guess.

Aimee fingered the grapes. "You have a woman in your England? Sons? Maybe daughters? You want to return because you miss them?"

"No. Not at all."

Netta nibbled her beef. "You left them because they failed to please you?"

"No. I've never wed nor do I have children. If I did have a wife or little ones, I'd never leave them. Wouldn't be right."

Aimee lowered her face but couldn't hide her smile from him.

Netta ate the meat, her demeanor far more circumspect. "Do you miss your mother and father? Brothers? Sisters? Is that why you want to go back?"

"I have no one in England. Not even a grandparent, aunt, or uncle."

"How can that be?"

"I was a foundling. That's a child with no one."

"How is that possible?" Aimee exchanged a glance with Netta who looked equally confused. "Everyone has a mother and father or they would never be born."

After the terror they'd been through, they'd managed to maintain their innocence. That endeared them to him even more. They faced life without guile or resentment. Pity everyone couldn't do the same. "I never found out who my father was. Most likely, he left my mother before she birthed me. The beadle at the workhouse where I grew up told me she was too poor to feed a babe so she left me to them for care."

Netta chewed her bread. "What is this beadle?"

"An officer who runs things, much like Tristan does here."

Aimee brightened. "The beadle raised you as his son?"

"I'm afraid not. There were dozens of boys like me who didn't have families."

Understanding flashed in Netta's eyes. "The pirates killed their parents as they did ours."

"No. Some lost their mothers to childbirth, their fathers to illness, war, or endless work that eventually killed them. Since so-called civilized people can't allow a child to starve to death in the street, and still call themselves good Christians, they housed unwanted boys and girls in the workhouse. Before you ask what that is, it's exactly as it sounds, a place where people work. Once a child reaches four or five, they have to do as many tasks as they can to earn food and a place to sleep."

Aimee made a face. "When do they play?"

"Some never go outside or run like the children here. Boys as young as six become chimney sweeps. In England, homes have hearths where fires burn to keep the rooms warm during cold weather. Soot clogs the areas above the flames, like ashes left after a fire. Little boys and sometimes girls have to climb into those narrow spaces to clean them for hours on end. Many get hurt."

Netta touched his wrist. "Did you do that? Did it hurt you?"

"No. I worked with the animals and carried things. I grew too fast to toil in a chimney. The master sweep would have wasted his money buying me from the workhouse since he wouldn't be able to use me for long. When I learned the beadle had indentured me to the Colonies, I ran away and lived on the street with other orphaned children."

Aimee stroked his cheek. "How old were you?"

"Eight. I won't lie, it wasn't pleasant. There was little to eat, nowhere to sleep, but it was better than being a slave in another country with no escape. The other boys and I did tasks for the gentlemen and ladies and earned enough to stay alive. When I was eleven, I went to sea. The work was hard but at least there was sufficient food."

"Beatings too." Aimee fingered a scar on his biceps.

Every hurtful thing done to him faded with her tenderness. "I only had one cruel captain. As boys go, I was lucky. I learned French from the quartermaster who took a shine to me. I'd hoped one day to become a captain."

Netta sucked her lip.

Aimee pressed close to her. "You want to leave so you can command a ship as Tristan did?"

"One needs connections and power to do that. I have none." Being in charge had been a boyish dream. However, this isle wasn't any better if there wasn't a way for him to be with them and not upset everyone. "What you, Netta, and I want and have found in each other isn't easily understood or accepted by the rest."

Netta shrugged. "Why should they worry about what Aimee and I do?"

"They're your people and care greatly for both of you."

"As we do with them, but we must still live our lives."

"I understand that, but I promised my loyalty to Tristan in order to stay here." He stroked her bottom lip. "We can't carry on like Simone and Royce, James and Gavra, or even Peter and Laure. Especially them."

"We can once we wed and you slip the marriage collar around our throats. That will tell everyone we belong to you and you to us."

Aimee nodded.

Such a simple and ludicrous solution. Heath wasn't certain whether to smile or sigh. "I doubt the priest would agree with what we want to do. It's unlikely any holy man would."

"Then Simone can say the words over us." Netta kissed his fingertips. "As our people's healer, she has great power."

There was no arguing with her or Aimee. "We must take care that no one knows of our feelings for each other. Not even your women friends."

"What of our love?" Aimee clasped his other hand. "You taking us as a man should with a woman. Do you intend to deny us your touch?" She kissed his palm.

Netta his wrist.

Their breath tickled and warmed. Their scents aroused. His best answer would be to refuse any carnal thought, touch, or deed. "I don't know."

Netta's eyes sparkled. "There are ways a man can enjoy a woman without creating an infant. Aimee and I can show you."

* * * *

With the midday meal over, Tristan herded James and Royce into the library, far from the females. Gavra, Laure, and others worked in the kitchen. Diana was in her and his bedchamber with Merry.

Unfortunately, the women never stayed put. They roamed at will and heard too much.

The library door flung open. Peter hurried inside without being threatened.

Tristan doubted the boy had developed a love for books as strong as his attraction to Laure. "Leave. Now." Tristan cleared volumes from a chair and sank into it. "Take a ride. Come back in an hour or so."

"Why can't I stay?"

"To do your lessons?"

Peter's challenging look turned sour. "To offer my opinion on what you're discussing."

"The swamp. We're deciding who does what to clear it for arable soil. You can be at the top of our list. How does hauling water and shoveling muck sound?"

"Should I close the door on my way out?"

"It's well advised. You should also keep going. Eavesdrop at your peril. And don't slam the door."

He sighed loudly but closed it with care.

James yawned. "If Peter still served on a ship, the captain would have shot him by now for his cocky attitude."

"Diana wants that honor and has it. I'm a helpless bystander in family matters."

"I face the same." James crossed his freckled arms over the table and rested his head on them. "Gavra rails at Laure whenever she wants. If I dare look at the girl with anything but pure sweetness, I never hear the end of it."

"Did Gavra bend your ear last night?"

"Willy screamed and cried without pause. I scarcely got an hour's rest."

Tristan would have killed for that much. Merry seemed determined to do him in with her endless wails. He gestured to Royce. "What about you with Simone?"

"The closer our child comes, the quieter she is. However, I don't dare challenge her on even the simplest matter. She may look gentle, but I could end up dead."

They laughed.

Tristan stretched out his legs. "It's good to have a family."

"I'm not complaining." James rubbed his eyes. "Did you call us in here to gossip about domestic matters as women do?"

"Hardly. Heath came to me. He wants to leave the island. Even offered to get down on his knees and beg to get my consent."

Royce arched one eyebrow. "It seems he gave you the full treatment. With me, he demanded his release."

James lifted his face. "You don't rule here. Tristan does. Makes perfect sense he'd cower to him."

"I'm hardly king." Tristan folded his arms behind his head. "I merely keep matters from escalating. Everyone here has the same rights. None better than any other."

"Mind your words." James rapped the table. "That means Heath can do whatever he wants."

"He and the other prisoners aren't full citizens until we can trust them. So his privileges aren't the same as ours, all right?" Tristan spoke to Royce. "When did he come to you? Why haven't I heard this until now?"

"He approached me the day Diana birthed Merry. You wouldn't have noticed a gun in your face much less anything I had to say. Since then, I forgot the matter."

"Recall it now and tell me why he wants to leave."

"He said if I found him distasteful and untrustworthy, I should allow him to go with the other islanders when they come to trade or leave with us when we go there."

Odd. Heath didn't strike Tristan as a man who cared what Royce or anyone else thought of him. "He spouted that without provocation or did you say something to bring on his rant?"

Royce rested one arm on the table, fist clenched. "I came upon him in the forest near the point. Rather than watching our shores with his spyglass as he claimed, he had the blasted thing trained on Netta and Aimee."

Tristan hadn't expected that. "Which one specifically?"

"Both in equal amounts."

"I'm not surprised." James wiggled his eyebrows. "At the celebration that night, they flirted with him. Netta was reluctant at first, until Aimee practically shoved her in Heath's lap. After that, they got cozy. When he left the table to get more brandy, they followed."

Tristan brought down his arms. "He told me he was tired of being celibate and would die unless he could be a man again. Did he take both in the storage room?"

"If he did, he couldn't have pleasured them much. After a short absence, he returned with a bottle and a deep scowl worse than any we saw on our captain's face before I shot him. As to Aimee and Netta, they never came back to the table."

This was worse than Tristan had imagined. "The man's mad if he thinks he can have two women at once."

"Like you and I have done in the past?"

Royce laughed. "You've engaged in a ménage, Tristan?"

"Well before I met Diana and only with doxies. One hardly meets virtuous women in ports and foreign lands."

"Except for Diana when she captured you." James spoke to Royce. "What a surprise she turned out to be. Beautiful, courageous, and pure. Sadly, the other women Tristan and I came upon were less demur. One night, two doxies wrestled quite shamelessly and pulled each other's hair out over Tristan."

His face burned. "Each wanted the gold I could give them."

"They loved your manly form. I heard them shrieking that at each other."

Royce howled. His face reddened from laughter.

Tristan kicked his foot. "As a noble—"

"Former noble. I'm content to let my mother and sisters keep up family appearances. Trust me. Peers are no different from pirates. They simply talk a better game. If you mean to ask if I've had a liaison with two women at once my answer is yes. That and far more."

"Is that so?" Though intrigued, Tristan had other pressing matters. "We'll have to hear about your misadventures another time. I called you both in here to determine what to do with Heath. Do we let him go?"

"No."

Royce and James answered at the same time.

"Your reasoning?"

James propped his head in his hand. "Admittedly, he's a good man. Has endless patience with the children and does whatever Gavra demands without pause. However, if he fell into the wrong crowd, he knows too much about this isle to keep everything secret. Especially if he faced a blade or pistol."

Royce spoke to Tristan. "We can't risk it."

He agreed. "That means he stays. What do we do about him and women? As far as I'm concerned, he can be with anyone he wants unless it starts a commotion."

"I feel the same." James pushed back in his chair. "It's really up to the islanders whether they accept this or not. He is English after all. They may resent one of ours taking two of theirs or they could think he's using Netta and Aimee. Many of the women have taken to the priest's teachings about sin, lust, and any joy being a terrible thing."

Tristan rubbed his temple. "I wouldn't want to anger them. When it comes to romance and love, women have short tempers and long memories."

James stretched. "So what do we do?"

"The only thing we can. He remains on the isle and must keep to himself. There's simply no other way to keep everyone safe."

Chapter 7

Fanette raged around the community fire. "Stupid. Foolish. Lazy." She shook her fist.

Canela seethed, but bowed her head and played the meek, frightened slave.

"I should beat you more senseless than you already are. I will." Fanette stormed to her.

Ismay hurried between them. "She helps me now, not you. Find someone else to wash the clothes and clean your house. Or do the work yourself. Keep busy with your own life and stay out of ours and the others."

Fanette glared. "You dare tell me what to do."

"That and more. You have no power over me, only the chief does. From this day forward, Canela helps me and Yoland. Do you want our people to grow ill and die because you denied Yoland help?"

"From her, that...thing?" Fanette spat. "She ruined the men's breeches and our cloths. When she cleaned, she broke my cup and plate. Simple tasks even a child could do."

"Then you should have no trouble without her and will be far happier as you can clean them the way you like. I find nothing wrong with Canela. She brings me the most delicious tubers and plants for my cooking. She picks spices for me and herbs for Yoland. Without her, I have to cook constantly to make enough for everyone to eat, especially you. Yoland should mix a potion to improve your bad temper. Go." She waved Fanette away. "You bother us when we have work to do. See to your own tasks. Threaten Canela again and the chief will hear about it from me and will deal with you."

Fanette stepped around Ismay and hurried to Canela.

She covered her head with her arms.

"This is not the end." Fanette pressed so close, Canela smelled her foul breath. "You will pay dearly for the trouble you caused me."

Fanette would die before then, the first of the islanders.

Ismay joined them. "One more word and I call the chief."

Foul oaths poured from Fanette. She stomped to her house.

Canela fell to her knees and kissed Ismay's fingers. "I promise to serve you and Yoland well. I tried with Fanette but I was too clumsy for the tasks she gave me. She has reason to be angry. Perhaps I should try again."

"No." Ismay stroked Canela's hair. "Gather what I told you I need and the herbs Yoland wants. If you find the choicest for both, you get more to eat tonight."

"Merci." She kissed Ismay's dirty feet, proving what a good slave she was, playing the game that would put her in control. In time, everyone here would pay for what they'd done to her.

"Enough." Ismay stepped back. "Take your sacks and fill both before you return."

"I will never fail you." Canela tore past houses toward the vegetable gardens and forest. Within the trees, she'd find spices and herbs. She'd collect some for Ismay and Yoland to fool them further. Another she'd keep for herself.

Days ago, Canela had found ample sleeping herbs. She'd wrapped them in a discarded silk cloth. While the others slept, she'd clawed dirt and buried the sack where she was supposed to rest. To make certain no one saw what she'd done, she covered the newly turned earth with rocks, twigs, and leaves. The herb waited for her use once Yoland gave up her healing secrets.

The woman delighted in praise. Curiosity about her potions and poultices loosened her tongue even more. Canela had feigned interest and begged to treat wounds, especially the vilest, to spare Yoland the blood or pus. Endlessly, Yoland taught what worked best and didn't. It would be easy to trick her into telling how much sleeping herb to use, and what spices would mask its flavor in food and drink. Already, she trusted Canela far too much.

Canela bypassed the garden and hurried toward the forest mindful of anyone watching.

No one was. If they had been, she would have explained leaves and flowers were lighter to carry than tubers. Those she would collect last.

An easy lie to place her close to Vincent.

He scrounged the forest for fallen limbs and rotted logs to burn. Shackled, he could merely toddle, no different than a young child or the old who neared death. Metal had rubbed raw spots on his ankles. Some bled slightly. Others oozed a yellowish liquid. His filthy breeches hung on him, the cloth little more than rags. Insects buzzed close, drawn to his stink.

Revulsion and hate mingled with Canela's pleasure at his state in comparison to hers. The breeze stirred her freshly washed hair. Flowers perfumed her clean skin. Ismay had no problem letting a slave bathe. That kindness might spare Ismay's life, if Canela felt generous during her coming attack.

Vincent grunted beneath his load and faced her. Shock lit his face.

She needed to see lust, craving, desire so she could torment him further and crush him beneath her heel.

He glanced around frantically. They were alone, hidden within shadows. He shuffled closer. "You'd better have news I want to hear. I've tried to speak to you for days. Did you suddenly lose your sight and hearing? Didn't you see or hear me?"

She smiled and turned away.

He swore. "Wait."

She would not. He no longer gave orders or spoke to her as he would an animal. She'd do that to him.

"Please."

Canela stopped but refused to face him.

Leaves crunched. A twig snapped. He winced and cursed, his approach painfully slow.

She yawned.

Breathless, he reached her. "Have you learned anything new? Are Tristan's men on their way here?"

"You smell. Step away." She flicked her hand. "You make me sick being so close."

His jaw tightened. Rage smoldered in his eyes. If he'd been free, he would have killed her. Fettered and helpless, he edged back.

Canela lifted her chin. "The bird flew away. When it returns, I may know something."

He scrunched his nose, the narrowed tip reddened and peeling from the sun. Sweat glistened on his bristly cheeks. "What are you talking about? Have you lost your bloody mind?"

"Insult me again and you may never know." She pivoted.

"Wait. Forgive me. Please don't leave." He cradled the branches and glanced toward the community. No one approached. "What does our escape have to do with a bloody bird?"

"The creature is a special kind. What the English call a pigeon. The men are using it to send messages to Tristan and he does the same with them. The priest can read and write. He tells Tristan what the islanders need and when to bring it. The men sent the bird away this morning. When it returns, the news it carries will be from Tristan." She shrugged. "I may share it with you."

"Oh, you may? If you don't, prepare to stay here for the rest of your days. You're cunning and murderous, I'll grant you that. But you're also a damn woman. Do you think you have the strength to fight off Tristan's crew or force them to do your bidding? Only a man's power can do that. You need me and the other captives for this revolt and a return to your isle. So quit being sly and let's plan this as we should. Did you find something to put the islanders to sleep?"

Her loathing for him urged her to leave. His usefulness made her stay. "I know what herbs to use for sleep but the healer has yet to tell me how to mask their flavor."

"Put more damn spices than you need into the food."

"I have yet to convince Ismay to let me try my hand at cooking. If I push her too far, too fast, she might suspect something. Is that what you want? Your liberation denied because of your impatience? No wonder Tristan defeated you. A child has more sense. When the time comes, your men will come with me and you can stay here to rot."

"That would be a bloody mistake on your part. They fear me."

"They crave freedom. Nothing you say or do to them will change that. I can give them what they want. Without my help, you offer them nothing."

"Go on then, leave me here. But you'll lose your chance to destroy Diana and make her last moments on earth as horrible as possible. The same for Tristan. I thought you hated them. Was I wrong? Imagine how you and I can play with those two. I often dream of their tortured shouts and pleas."

As she did. When Vincent had trapped Diana in the bedchamber, her alarm and hopelessness provided a wonderful moment. "If I allow you to join me, I decide what to do."

"What about my say in the matter?"

"You never had any. I found the herbs. I made the plan. You do what I want or your men will finish off Diana and Tristan. Their pain will be over. Yours will go on. That is my only offer."

Vincent's anger drained away, replaced by a devil's smile. "Guess I'll take it. When do we meet next?"

"When you smell better. A hog stinks less than you and is more appealing. Tristan is always clean, his hair and clothes washed."

"He wants to please Diana. An Englishwoman. He never truly desired a savage. Like most men, he made do with what he had until someone better came along."

Canela dug her nails into her palms to keep from killing him. "You mock me because of your white skin, but Diana still ran from you as she would the vilest creature. You repulsed her."

"Aye, I did. I'll do so again with your sweet help." He stared hard. "Our revenge for her and Tristan goes beyond the distaste you and I feel for each other. We must work together to succeed. If you're as smart as I think you are, you'll accept my help. I'll wait each night for you to come and tell me what you've learned and what you've decided. Do so at your own pace, if you must, but do it. What we think of each other doesn't matter. What happens does."

He shuffled away.

* * * *

"No, no, no." Ourson pushed Heath's hand from the tools near their feet and shoved the plane to him. "You need this, not the hammer."

"How right you are."

The morning was still new and already Heath had made too many mistakes. He couldn't pay attention to his work, drifting instead to the evening he'd shared with Netta and Aimee. Their playful coaxing for him to take them in a way that wouldn't result in a child.

He'd resisted, though hardly on moral grounds. As most mariners had, he'd indulged in women in every possible way.

His self-control would never survive him mounting Aimee and Netta in their tightest openings. He'd want to be inside their damp, heated sheaths next. Nowhere else would do. Not even their mouths.

Ourson stroked the plane. "Will you?"

"Will I what?"

"Show me how to smooth the wood?"

Heath wasn't certain he should. If he didn't concentrate on his tasks, he'd injure himself or Ourson. "Perhaps you should help your mother. She's having difficulty with the wash. You're a strong boy and can assist her."

His lower lip jutted. "Did I do something wrong? Do you want the other boys to take my place?"

First, Heath would have to corral them to his side. Once he'd become a fixture here, rather than an exotic attraction, they'd searched for other amusements and left Ourson as the sole spectator. If only Heath, Netta, and Aimee could be as invisible to the adults as he was to the children. "Of course not. Tell you what. I'm naming myself captain of the wood and choosing you as my quartermaster. That's a man who helps his captain greatly. A fearless and strong fellow. Do you think you can do the job?"

"I can."

"It's yours...as long as your mother and father allow you to take on the responsibilities."

"They do." He bounced in place. "Can I smooth the wood?"

"'Tisn't easy. Show me your muscle first."

"How?"

Heath made a fist to display his biceps, large and bulging from rough labor. Ourson's eyes nearly popped out. He poked Heath's arm. "Hard."

"A man must be fit to do his daily tasks, as your father does his. Come now. Show me what you have."

He made a fist and grunted but produced little change.

Heath prodded the tiny mound. "Well done. I wager you'll be stronger than me before long. Now lift the plane."

Ourson did.

"Is it heavy?"

"No."

He struggled to keep it up.

"I think you're ready to use it." Heath placed it on the wood. "Grip it tightly." Once the boy had, Heath rested his hand on top. "Push forward at a slow pace. No need to rush. You want it to skim the surface not dig in. Go on." Heath tempered his strength and barely pushed the tool.

Ourson squealed. "I did that."

"Indeed you did. Shall we have another go?"

"Oui."

"Heath." Tristan gestured him over.

"Give me a moment." He spoke to Ourson. "You're not to touch anything while I'm gone. If you do and hurt yourself, your parents will never let you help me again. Do I have your word as my quartermaster not to do anything you shouldn't?"

"You do."

"Will you keep the other children away from these things?"

"If they try to touch anything, I promise to hit them."

"No, you won't. Good men don't use violence, they use words, like your father does. Am I right?"

He nodded.

"I'll return shortly." He joined Tristan. "I assure you, Ourson's in no danger. If he were, his mother would have kept him far from me by now."

"Follow me."

They entered the birthing room. Tristan closed the door and shutter, casting the space in deeper shadows. "After much deliberation, I've decided you cannot leave this isle."

"What? After everything I told you, you still expect me to stay?"

"That's what I'm saying."

Heath wanted to bellow. Leaving this isle was his only recourse and the best decision for Aimee and Netta even if it devastated him. At least, they'd fall in love with island men and would have the homes they deserved. "You said before that I proved myself enough for you to trust me."

"I also said even the most honorable man will talk when faced with a severe beating or death, which could happen if you take to the seas again. We can't risk it. I have a family to think of, as does James, Royce, and many islanders. No one has a right to put the women and children at risk. As to your desire for a woman…"

Heath ached to escape. "I don't want to hear it."

"You don't have a choice." Tristan glared. "If the situation were up to me, I wouldn't stand in your way. God knows I never lasted long without a female's sweet touch. The islanders could feel differently. You have to please them, not me. Until things change, you'll have to endure."

"Wait." He rushed past Tristan and blocked the door. "That's all you have to say?"

"It's my final decision and not up for discussion."

This was madness. "You expect me to continue as I have until things change. In what bloody way?"

"The islanders accepting you as one of them, not an intruder on their land. If a man from another culture came here and wanted your daughter, would you gladly hand her over? I think not. The man would have to convince you of his good intentions."

"By asking for the woman's hand or permission to see her? No adult here has parents any longer. Pirates killed them. Who am I to impress?"

"The islanders who are still here and grown now. Before the slaughter, their parents had forged a strong community. Since then, the survivors are even more protective of each other. I can't blame them. Dismiss their feelings at your own risk. We've never hanged anyone on this isle. You could be the first should you test their patience. I'm only one man. I couldn't stand against eighty or more armed with pistols, clubs, and blades. Again, I'm sorry but this is the best I can do."

He pushed past Heath and left.

* * * *

Netta waited for Aimee and Heath outside his house. He hadn't returned for the midday meal when they'd arrived after helping Gavra. Nor was he here when they'd finished tending the children for their mamas. The sun dipped below the trees. Soon, darkness would blanket the isle.

Worried, Aimee had run off to search for him at the stone house, the fields, pastures, or wherever he might be.

Netta chided herself for allowing Aimee to go. If anything happened to her, she'd never forgive herself. If Heath had left the isle and them...

Impossible. He had no ship. None had sailed from the island or had arrived. The men would have signaled if pirates had attacked. Heath would have been here to protect her and Aimee.

Moist wind whipped Netta's hair and cloth but did little to cool her fevered state. She'd never loved a man before. The turmoil wasn't easy to bear, her fear that she'd lose him always too great, but she couldn't turn back now. She'd fight for Heath to be at her side and Aimee's.

An indeterminate shape bobbed in the shadows.

Netta stood on tiptoe and craned her neck.

Aimee darted into the torchlight, cheeks reddened, chest heaving. "Did he come back?"

"No." Netta gripped her shoulders. "Did you search the courtyard and stone house?"

"Everywhere I could. I asked Diana about him. She told Peter to look. He took his horse and returned without Heath. What should we do?"

Netta lit another torch and handed the first to Aimee. "Take this and go to the point. I can search the glade."

"What if we never find him?"

"We will. Go." Netta ran in the opposite direction.

Heath emerged from the darkness. Netta jumped back, hand to her throat, heart pounding wildly. "Are you all right? Are you hurt? Aimee! Over here. He came back." Netta touched his chest and arms. "Are you bleeding? Did something hit your head? Did you just wake up?"

"No, of course not. I haven't been asleep or hurt. I'm fine."

His nonchalance surprised Netta, turning her worry to quick irritation. "Fine? You keep Aimee and me waiting all day, you tell us nothing, you hide until dark while we worried you had hurt yourself, died, or left, and you say everything is fine?" She turned her back to him.

Aimee rushed to them. "Heath. Nothing happened to you." She threw out her arms.

Netta stood in her way. "He has no bump on his head, no cuts either, nor is he bleeding anywhere. He says everything is fine."

"We should praise the goddess for her kindness."

"Or ask Heath why he kept us waiting during the midday meal and after our work for the new mamas without one word to calm our worry."

"Sorry." He ducked into his house.

Aimee followed. Netta preferred to nurse her anger but joined them.

Heath stared at his favorite foods they'd set out for his midday meal. The bread was hard, meat cold, pineapple dried out. "You shouldn't have done this."

"What?" Aimee padded to him. "Feed you?"

"Go to so much trouble."

"You have to eat."

"I…" He backed away from her, bumped into the bed, and twisted to keep from falling. Not once did he look at them.

Netta felt sick. "A ship is coming. You plan to sail with the islanders. You want to leave."

"No." He ground his hand into his forehead. "I didn't want to have to tell you this. I tried to find a way to avoid it, but there is none. Tristan spoke to me earlier today. He said I can never leave the isle."

Netta's spirits couldn't soar. Heath's face held too much sadness. "Aimee and I can make you happy here. We can help you forget your land. This will become your home for all—"

"Tristan said I couldn't be with any woman here. I'm not an islander like you. I came to your shore with Bishop to hurt everyone. No matter what I do or how I behave, many of your people still don't trust me. Tristan mentioned hanging."

Aimee gaped.

Netta shivered. "He threatened to kill you because of Aimee and me?"

"He said he doesn't care what I do, but the islanders might turn violent if they found out about us. I don't care for myself, but I don't want either of you to suffer."

"How could we?" Netta put aside the torch. "Our people have never been cruel."

"In the past, before the pirates came here. White men like me. My kind taught your people anger, brutality, and vengeance."

"No." She pressed her fingers to his lips. "The boys the pirates hurt are now grown, all kind like their fathers and grandfathers. Yellow Scarf and the others nearly beat Adamo to death and disfigured him for life. He's still the gentlest man I know save you. Even if anyone here wanted to bring you harm, Aimee and I would never allow it."

Aimee hugged his arm. "Netta and I would protect you."

"What if everyone treats you like outcasts because of me?" Heath lowered his face. "Could you bear to lose your friends and standing in the community?"

Netta stroked his whiskered cheek. "How could they be our friends if they refused to understand our happiness?"

"Easily, I would say. Happens all the time where I come from."

"Not here. Gavra tried to keep Simone from Royce. She told Simone he was no good for her and he should leave the isle. I think she may have said he should drown."

"She did." Aimee kissed Heath's shoulder. "Royce brought the white devil here. A terrible time."

Netta leaned into him. "Simone and Gavra argued so much everyone tried to keep them apart. Then they stopped speaking. Simone did what she wanted and now carries Royce's son or daughter. Gavra forgot what happened before. She and Simone love each other again."

Heath sank to the bed, pulling them with him. "How did Royce get everyone to trust him after what he'd done, other than apologizing repeatedly as he's said?"

"He offered his life to protect the islanders. Simone cried but he went to meet Bishop alone on the beach even though Bishop had a hundred mariners with him who carried swords, pistols, and clubs."

Heath arched an eyebrow. "That's not the way I recall it. I was there."

Aimee cupped his hand. "Whatever happened, the English died that night but no islanders did. Simone said it was because of Royce's bravery."

He kissed her knuckles. "I have no white devils to fight to convince your people to trust me and allow us to make a home here."

Netta fingered his breeches. "Ourson's mother said he likes you nearly as much as his papa."

"He's a wonderful child."

"So are the others, boys and girls, women and men. All you have to do is show them how kind you are, as you do with Ourson and us."

He rested his forehead against hers. "That's nearly two hundred people, not counting the infants. Thankfully, those sweet souls have no opinion of me. If they did, it would take months, perhaps years to gain everyone's respect and trust."

"A gentle word, a helping hand, and understanding how someone feels works quickly."

"I've done that without end."

"You have to do more. No one thought they could forgive Adamo but they did."

"The man with the limp arm and crooked face?"

"Oui." Aimee eased Heath's hair behind his ear. "He accepted everyone's anger and told them he was wrong in what he did for Canela. The women forgave him first and then the men. They knew in their hearts he was good."

"The same as you." Netta pressed her cheek to his chest. His warmth and musk thrilled. "Aimee and I can tell the women how wonderful you are as Simone did for Royce. You can speak to the men. Then we can share your bed as we should, no?"

"There are still two of you and one of me."

"Oui. The perfect number."

He laughed.

Netta covered his mouth and stole the sound. She kissed him deeply, for as long as she could before giving him to Aimee.

Tonight had to be the last one they kept themselves from love.

Chapter 8

Heath greeted the new day with dread. Winning over a community once abused by white men wouldn't be easy or perhaps even possible for him. He had no political skills, wasn't a smooth liar, and lacked effortless charm to reach his own ends. If things had been up to him, he would have gathered the group, stated his case, promised his loyalty to Netta, Aimee, and their people, and hoped for everyone's blessing.

In England, the crowd would have laughed at or hung such a fool.

"Eat, please." Aimee offered him the choicest bananas, grapes, and pineapple.

Netta laid out fresh bread and bacon she'd brought from her and Aimee's house. He had no stores here, had never cooked for himself, preferring to trade his work for the islanders' fare.

Despite the appetizing smells, he stuffed himself for Netta and Aimee's benefit. The food went down hard and didn't want to stay in his stomach.

They watched him carefully. He forced a smile. "I'm quite all right. No need to fret." No one had ever worried over him. He wasn't certain how to react.

Netta combed his hair. Aimee gathered his razor and soap.

"You plan to shave me?"

"After you eat. My hand is steadier than yours."

He fisted his fingers. They trembled from reckless desire lashing through him. Cool morning air had tightened Netta's and Aimee's nipples and rosed their cheeks. They'd bathed, washed their hair, and used something to give them a sweet scent. Both must have woken well before dawn to cook and tidy themselves.

Next to them, he was an uncivilized animal. "I should wash."

Aimee peeled another banana. "We can bathe you."

If each morning began like this, he'd find their ardent care impossible to resist. He ate more hurriedly than he'd planned, eager to have them tend him.

Netta poured water into his basin, dampened a linen cloth, and ran it over his neck, chest, and beneath his arms.

Heat surged in places she stroked. He filled himself with her scent.

Aimee guided his head back to expose his throat, her touch lighter than an angel's would be. She spread bubbles over his whiskers. "Take care not to move. The blade is sharp."

Not nearly as much as his senses. Her and Netta's hair glided over his arms and tickled him in the most provocative way. Their fresh breath sweetened the air.

His lids slipped down, weighted by too much need churning inside him. He had to brace himself to keep still.

Aimee proved more than competent with the razor, the sharp edge scarcely touching his face.

Netta tended him lovingly, her cleansing strokes particularly pleasant on his nipples and groin.

Both behaved as women born to the task. Perhaps all islanders shared the same morning ritual with their mates. If so, that strengthened Heath's hope that desire wasn't as forbidden here as in the civilized world. There, government and religious doctrine turned everything natural into something wicked. "Where did you two learn to care for a man this way?"

They stilled.

Not the reaction he'd expected. He forced his eyes open.

Color had drained from Netta's beautiful face. Aimee's cheeks burned.

He'd reminded them of the past. What the pirates had most likely taught and made them do with numerous men. "Doesn't matter. You've pleased me greatly. No fellow is as lucky as I am. However, I am curious about something else."

Aimee stared at the razor, Netta her dampened cloth, both cautious.

He wanted them to smile. "How is it that neither of you find me vile. I'm far too hairy, uncouth, and have abominable manners."

Netta tilted her head. "What do you mean by abominable?"

"Dreadful. A child behaves more properly at the table than I do." He showed them his fingers coated with bacon grease, and gestured to his torso and thighs. Breadcrumbs dotted them.

Aimee leaned against him, her nipple close to his mouth. "You eat as a man should, filling your belly, enjoying yourself."

"We have ways to clean you." Netta sucked his fingers.

Aimee sank to her knees and licked food particles from his thigh.

His toes curled, cock hardened.

They tended him with their delicate touch and heated mouths. Netta suckled his neck. Aimee licked his crown. Unbearable need jolted through him. He couldn't bear another second, much less a lifetime, separated from them.

Restraint evaporated. He grabbed their wrists and led them to his mattress. Their cloths drifted away.

Animal hunger radiated from Netta. "Fill me."

"And me." On the bed, Aimee went to her hands and knees, head lowered, arse raised, her tightest opening displayed for his use.

Netta did the same.

Moisture shimmered on their dark curls and turgid folds. He stroked their clefts. Hot. Damp. Ready for him.

Aimee moaned throatily. Netta breathed hard.

The scent of sex filled the small room.

He couldn't focus on anything else. Not honor. Caution. Good sense. A future that might never be.

No moment was more precious than this or another woman as giving as them. They made him a man more than power or riches ever could.

He dipped his fingers in their musky dew and used it to lubricate their tight, pink rings. "I won't hurt you." He'd die first.

Netta wiggled her rump quite saucily. "I want you."

"And I." Aimee pressed into his touch.

Their softness and heat seized his breath. He didn't know who to mount first. Wouldn't ask. They'd bow to each other's needs as they always did.

He stroked Aimee's tiny nub, swollen now and hard.

She shivered.

Heath guided his crown to Netta's opening and entered her as easily as he could, lest he do harm.

Her passage relaxed around his sex. She rocked into him with more grace than he owned and coaxed his rod inside.

He trembled at her intense heat, the tight fit. Collecting his thoughts proved impossible. He barely remembered to arouse Aimee. With all his will, he rubbed her fast and slowly. Hard. Soft.

Wanton noises poured from her.

Netta was far too quiet for his taste. He claimed her precious kernel. She bucked.

He slid into and out of her with care, each pump meant to please and excite no matter his own need. His balls throbbed, wanting relief. His rod pained him in a bad yet good way. He gritted his teeth and endured.

Their pleasure came first.

Aimee cried out joyously and shuddered. Her newest moisture warmed his fingers.

Netta whimpered and beat his mattress with her maimed hand.

"Am I going too fast?" He slowed.

"This can never end. I have to fight against it so it goes on and on."

He would have laughed proudly if he could have drawn enough breath. Sweat streamed down his face and chest. His shoulders burned. Chest hurt. However, his cock and sac knew real agony. He couldn't find release within Netta then expect to take Aimee immediately. She'd have to wait while he recovered and gained strength. He'd disappoint and perhaps wound her with his selfishness.

That wouldn't do.

He thrust faster and stroked Netta quickly.

Her loud moan tore through the room, signaling her release.

Heath could barely maintain control. He eased from Netta, mounted Aimee, and nearly died. She proved far tighter than Netta unless his delayed passion had thickened his rod even more.

Perspiration stung his eyes and clouded his vision. He clenched his jaw so hard his neck ached.

Her passage couldn't have been warmer or smoother. Pure torture for a man as far gone as him.

Netta gulped air and touched his thigh. "Are you all right?"

Any second he'd explode or would go mad. His ears rang. Skin burned. He'd never hurt in as many places at once. "I'm fine."

"Your face is red. Your shoulders are bulging."

"I'm showing off. Forgive me, I must..."

He lost control and spilled his seed inside.

* * * *

Sated, shaved, and clean, Heath trudged toward the mansion already exhausted before his day began. Too easily, he'd crossed a line with Netta and Aimee that he swore he never would. No telling what tonight with them would bring. Certainly not celibacy. He wavered between delight and fear, unable to calm down.

His mood sparked Aimee's protectiveness and Netta's resolve. They'd insisted on accompanying him rather than arriving separately.

He questioned their wisdom. "What if the others see us together?"

"They should." Netta stopped and plucked a wildflower.

He halted. "Why is that?"

She tucked the blossom behind Aimee's ear. "They need to get used to us being with each other. Once we wear the marriage collar, they have no choice."

She already had them wed.

Aimee smiled dreamily.

Their happiness wouldn't last once the priest was here to lecture them on their sinful ways. They'd surely get an earful with none of it the vows they longed to hear.

Heath would have done anything to make their hopes, and his, a reality. First, though, he had to win over the masses, dodge death, and guard Aimee and Netta against banishment. "Who will you help today?"

Aimee walked backward. Or rather, she skipped, her breasts and hair jouncing. "Gavra. While I make bread, I can tell her what a wonderful man you are."

Netta turned in circles, arms flung out. "I plan to do the same with Simone."

Aimee wagged a finger. "Not if you never listen to what her potions do."

"I have but it's hopeless. I told her I would gladly collect the plants and herbs she wants, but I never want to heal anyone."

"What did she say? Will she take her anger out on Heath?"

"Please, not that." He halted well away from the courtyard walls and kept his voice low. "I'm finishing up a crib today and starting another. Best neither of you say anything to me or do anything either."

Netta stopped spinning and struggled to maintain her balance. "What would we do to you?"

Kiss and touch him. Tear off his clothes. Precisely what he longed to do with them. "Nothing, I'm sure. Forgive me for jumping to the wrong conclusion."

"What does that mean?"

"Nothing." With no one around, he swooped down and captured her mouth then enjoyed Aimee's. His kisses were far too swift but would have to do. "I must go."

They held on to his hands with surprising strength. Netta spoke first. "Will you return to your house for the midday meal?"

"Will you and Aimee be there?"

They nodded gravely as a man does when taking a sacred oath.

"I'll join you then." He broke free, raced to the wall, and slipped inside the courtyard.

With the sun scarcely above the horizon, there was less activity than usual. His tools lay where he'd left them yesterday. Nothing disturbed as

Ourson had promised.

Poor child probably wondered what had happened when Heath hadn't returned. He'd been damn thoughtless and would have to make it up to Ourson. A tasty banana or juicy grape cluster might do as a peace offering. He hurried toward the storage room where Gavra kept the foodstuff that she prepared for Tristan, Diana, and the others who lived in the house. Surely, Gavra wouldn't mind if he took something for Ourson.

Aimee's voice sounded in the adjoining kitchen.

In the storage area, Royce crouched near a large pen filled with pigeons. Some pecked seeds. Others enjoyed water or strutted.

Heath stopped and stepped back quietly.

Royce looked over.

"Sorry, didn't mean to disturb." Heath affected an innocent air and braced for whatever crime Royce would accuse him of. "I wanted to fetch a banana for Ourson."

"Do you often use the children as an excuse to steal?"

Heath wouldn't allow this to come to blows. Royce's goodwill toward him was as important as everyone else's. If Heath couldn't win him over, he'd have little chance with the islanders. Royce would make certain to poison their minds against him. "Tristan told me I had to stay here for life. I'm trying to settle in and do my best. I hope you won't make matters difficult for me, but if you do, I understand. You don't know me. In your situation, I'd feel the same."

Royce opened his mouth and closed it.

Long ago, Heath had learned how impossible it was to argue with someone who agreed with you. "I don't mean to pry, but I am curious. Are you raising those birds to eat?"

There were several younger ones mixed in with the others, each sturdy, though they wouldn't provide much meat.

"Do you always ask such preposterous questions?"

"Didn't know I had. If they're not for food are you keeping them as pets?" Seemed cruel to keep a bird from flying.

Royce blew out a breath. "You are daft. We use them to communicate with the islanders who trade with us."

"How?"

"How else? With messages." He stood and brushed dirt from his knees.

"I didn't realize those islanders knew how to read and write. The ones here don't."

"Not yet. I'm holding lessons for those who want the skill. Only Simone and Gavra have attended with any frequency. As to the islanders we trade with, they have no one to teach them except the priest, if he's so inclined. He's with them now and offered his assistance in telling them what the messages say. Not a simple task given their French and his Portuguese. He knows only enough of their language to pound his teachings into them, request food, drink, and a soft bed. With any luck, someday things may be easier. We just started doing this."

"You found the birds on this isle?" He stepped nearer to the cage, though not too close to alarm Royce. Heath simply wanted distance from the entrance so those in the kitchen couldn't overhear him. "They look like English pigeons to me."

"They are. I brought them here to communicate with Bishop. Unfortunately, that landed you on our shores."

Heath had wondered how Bishop knew the exact coordinates for this isle, how many resided here, and when to attack. "Quite brilliant. But surely Tristan questioned why you had them with you when you washed up on shore or pretended to."

"Why do you want to know? Are you planning on using the birds to bring other mariners here?"

"That would lead to Aimee and Netta getting hurt. The islanders too. So my answer is no. I'd never do anything to harm them. I'm certain you felt the same about Simone before everyone accepted you."

"I proved myself."

"Indeed you did. Aimee told me how you fought off a hundred mariners by yourself, each armed with blades, pistols, and clubs. Some breathed fire."

Royce laughed.

A rather pleasant sound. Certainly better than harsh words, a threat, or growl. "I told her and Netta you were magnificent even if I witnessed the real truth in your brave deeds."

"You have little to boast of. You surrendered immediately."

"I've no wish to die. I thought what I did showed good sense. Would you have done otherwise?"

He regarded the birds.

His silence proved he agreed with Heath. "You strike me as a man who would do anything to protect the woman you love."

Royce tightened his jaw. "Take care with what you say."

"I mean no harm. You would do for Simone what I would for Aimee and Netta." Heath lowered his voice even more. "I realize our feelings for each other are unconventional, but—"

"Immoral is closer to the truth."

Heath conceded with a small bow. "Blame the commoner in me. As a noble, you wouldn't debase yourself in such a way."

Red stained Royce's forehead and cheeks.

Just as Heath thought. Royce wasn't the saint he pretended to be. Few nobles were. "I take full blame for my feelings. As a man, though, I'd like you to counsel me on how you'd love this woman but not that woman, especially sisters so close they practically breathe as one. Do I turn away from Netta and let her believe her hand repulses me? Or do I ignore Aimee because she can't, or at least believes she can't, bear children? Would her hurt be any less than Netta's? Give me an answer to my problem and I'll fix it. Tell me how to stop loving and wanting them so badly I'd rather die than spend my days deprived of their presence. How would you do that with Simone? Your answer would help me."

"It's not the same."

"Because of your noble birth?"

"You're challenging convention."

"As you did by wedding Simone."

Royce threw up his hands. "What makes you think I'd have an answer for your problem?"

"Then tell me what you'd do in my place. The truth. Not a heroic tale like you battling hundreds with your bare hands and steely determination."

Royce lowered his face but couldn't quell his laughter. It soon turned into a frustrated moan. "Very well. What you face would kill me if I couldn't resolve it."

"What would you do in my place? Heed others or do what you had with Simone?"

"You already have the answer."

Indeed, he did. Heath put out his hand. "Thank you. I hope we can become friends. You're not a bad sort."

Royce laughed and shook, his grip firm. "Neither are you. But you are treading in dangerous waters and best take care."

When love was involved that wasn't possible.

* * * *

Aimee kneaded the dough so forcefully her arms ached, yet she couldn't keep still. She feared speaking to Gavra about Heath but had no choice. The other women respected Gavra. If she approved of something or someone, most usually agreed. When she'd accepted Royce, he gained status and became an islander despite being an Englishman.

Gavra had to do the same for Heath. If only Aimee's words would come.

Nose wrinkled, Gavra was cleaning a large fish.

Veronique wiped flour from her hands. "I have to go. I promised to work the potter's wheel."

"I need to tend my son." Follie scooped the crying infant from his cradle and padded to the door. "As soon as he finishes his meal, I can help again."

Gavra nodded. She'd just nursed Willy. He was sleeping in his cradle. With the others gone, only Aimee, Gavra, and her younger sister Laure remained.

"What are you doing?" Gavra pointed her bloodstained knife at Aimee. "If you keep beating the dough, the bread will come out too hard to chew."

She stopped. "Forgive me. I have other matters on my mind."

Laure bent over the table, chin cupped in her hands. She was as lovely as Gavra, eyes large and dark, skin light brown, hair long and silky. "What worries you? Not Netta, I hope."

"No." Aimee had scant time for conversation before Follie returned. She steeled herself to say what she must. "If I tell you something will you promise to keep it in your heart and never repeat it to anyone else until I say you can?"

Laure rocked. "I do. Tell us your secret."

"Gavra? Will you keep your tongue too? Please?"

"I never gossip. What you tell me stays with me." She gutted the fish. "What is this about?"

"Heath. I love him."

Laure smiled.

Her approval gave Aimee hope. "Netta does too."

Laure shook her head. "Does too what?"

"Loves him. We both do."

Gavra sank to the bench. "What?"

"We want him to put the marriage collar around our throats. Please say you agree."

Laure made a face. "Peter has yet to put one on me. Can all of you keep from saying the vows until I do so no one pities me for having to wait endlessly?"

Gavra shot her a frown and gave it to Aimee. "You and Netta want to wed the same man?"

"We share everything. If you approve, you can convince everyone how wonderful our union will be. The islanders listen to you."

"Not with this. No." She stood. "What you want to do is madness. The priest would—"

"Forget him. Our goddess wants us to be happy. When we worshipped her, there were no rules, only love and kindness. White men changed everything. First the French then the English. They made our lives harder and filled us with guilt for not being like them."

Laure nodded.

Gavra slapped her arm. "As free women, you and Netta can do what you want, but many have taken the priest's words to heart. Especially the women. They may never understand what you told us. Some will turn away from you."

"Do you hate me and Netta now?"

"What? I could never do that." Gavra embraced Aimee. "I want both of you to live wonderful lives. With separate men."

* * * *

Herbs scented the healing room. Candles flickered. Netta paced, breathless from her confession to Simone.

She rocked in her chair and cradled her protruding belly. "Does Heath make you happy?"

"Oh yes." She sank to Simone's feet. "I no longer hide my hand from him. He kisses the ragged edge and tells me how pretty I am. The island men always glance away from my deformity, disgust in their eyes."

"They mean no harm, but I will tell you something." She leaned forward. "Until I met Royce, I refused to look at my leg. My scars have never bothered him."

"Then you know how I feel. Aimee too. She may be whole on the outside, but if she wed an islander and failed to birth his children, he might turn away and want another woman who could give him a family. Heath is different. He accepts us as we are and calls us perfect. When he holds me, I feel safe. What islander or Englishman has the right to say our love is wrong or take it from us? No one better try to hurt Heath." She shook her fist.

Simone cradled it in her hands. "You need to give our people time to accept one man loving two sisters."

"How long? If we wed, no one would have a choice except to honor our marriage collars. You could say the words over us."

"Me? You need a priest for holy matters."

"The English and French taught us that. What of our customs before the white men came here?"

Simone lifted her shoulders. "No one speaks of that time or remembers. We do what the priest demands."

"Not any longer." Not her, Aimee, or Heath. They would have their happiness.

Chapter 9

Heath returned to the courtyard, encouraged by his progress with Royce who'd been his most outspoken critic. Next came the islanders.

Ourson arrived with his mother. Upon seeing Heath, delight registered in his eyes but he held back.

Heath couldn't blame him. A wise man always treated a child and a woman's trust seriously. He shouldn't have broken his promise to return or forgotten the treat he'd planned to use as a peace offering. Now, he had nothing more than a smile and gestured him over.

Ourson approached slower than usual, his manner shy.

"Bonjour. Please sit." He patted the ground.

Ourson shifted from foot to foot.

Heath deserved no better treatment. "I'm sorry I failed to return yesterday. I had an important matter to attend. You did a splendid job protecting my tools. You're a fine quartermaster."

He dragged his big toe over the dirt, immune to praise, eager for honesty.

Heath liked him even more for his principle. It would serve him well as a man. "Do you forgive me?"

"I waited and waited. What matter kept you away?"

"Ah…I walked the isle." He had.

"Why would you do that?"

Heath had no choice except to lie. "I worried about using too many nails for the crib. What if I ran out before I finished the other beds? I searched for the special rocks I told you about. The ones metal comes from for tools and such."

"Did you get any?" Ourson sat cross-legged. "Show them to me."

"I failed to find even one. However, I intend to keep looking." Having their own metal source would help the community greatly. Surely, Tristan had books on the subject as he did everything else. Heath wasn't as knowledgeable as him but he could read and would teach the islanders what he'd learned. That would prove he cared about their survival and wanted them to thrive, thus building their faith in him. "If you want, you can come with me next time I search. If your mother and father allow it. I must speak with them first and have their consent."

"Ask them now."

"After I finish with the crib. We wouldn't want to keep Bella waiting for her bed. Are you ready to smooth the wood?"

"I am."

Heath positioned the plane. Another idea struck. "Who among the islanders knows how to carve a name or images to decorate the crib and make it special for Bella?"

"Adamo. He made a box for Zola. She shows it to everyone whether they want to see it or not."

Heath chucked Ourson's chin. "You must always show interest in what pleases a woman. Makes them happy. That's what men were born to do. Where can I find Adamo?"

"By the wash tub."

Using his good arm, Adamo dragged the metal container to where the women wanted it and hefted several buckets of water into the thing with one hand.

His muscles bunched. His strain obvious. He didn't ask for assistance.

Heath waited until Adamo had finished and called him over. "Bonjour." He stood and offered his hand.

Adamo wiped his fingers on his breeches and shook. His fierce strength contradicted his infirmities. One corner of his mouth sagged to his chin. His right lid hung halfway down his eye, its color no longer dark as the other, but milky. A permanent symbol of his betrayal fueled by hopeless love.

Canela certainly deserved her servitude on the other isle for bringing the poor man to this.

"Ourson tells me you're a skilled carver. I wonder if you'd like to decorate the crib I'm making. Flowers would be nice for Bella, unless her mother prefers something also suitable for a future son. Perhaps you can decide what images or symbols would be best. To pay you, I can help with your tasks. Tell me what to do and I'll do it."

"I need no one to help."

Everyone did. "Then I can teach you how to make nails and tools. Would you like that?"

"How do you make them?"

"I have no idea." Heath smiled sheepishly. "I need to read Tristan's books to learn. Once I have the skill, I can show you as payment for your carving."

"I do that to make the islanders happy. But I look forward to learning what you know when you know it. Merci."

Heath grinned. "*De rien.*" You're welcome.

Children squealed behind them.

The girls covered their heads and dashed away from the storage room entrance. Boys formed a circled to trap something within.

Surely not a falcon or eagle. The bird would have fought viciously.

A pigeon strutted past an opening in the children's legs. They tightened their circle to keep it from escape.

"Excuse me." Heath left Adamo and Ourson and rushed to the boys. "Step aside, please. Don't hurt the bird." Fastened to its leg was a small cylinder.

Heath scooped the creature to his chest.

Ourson ran to him. "Will you keep it?"

"No. It belongs to Royce. As soon as I get it back to him, I'll return to you. Guard the tools well."

"Oui."

Royce wasn't in the storage room. After removing the cylinder, Heath put the pigeon in the cage and joined Adamo who studied the cut wood. "Do you know where Royce is?"

"No."

Ourson bounced. "Are you leaving again?"

"Sorry, I must for the moment. I need to find Royce to tell him about his bird, otherwise he may worry."

Heath roamed the stone mansion. Its dining room loomed large and airy, the finely crafted table long enough to serve thirty.

Empty now.

Women's voices sounded in the kitchen, Aimee still among them. Everyone spoke quietly and quickly.

Not wanting to get involved in whatever they discussed, Heath backed away and wandered the halls.

Tristan's laughter spilled from the library. "I told you. We should have wagered on this. I love to win."

"Indeed." Diana made a dismissive sound. "However, you haven't. It's still too early to tell if Merry's eyes will remain as they are or turn brown, gray, or green. All babes have blue eyes when they're first—" She glanced at Heath in the doorway.

James and Royce looked up.

Tristan held Merry on his lap. Bubbles poured from her mouth. Spittle ran down her chin. Quite adorable and a beauty with her mother's pale skin, dark hair, and violet eyes, for the moment.

"Forgive me for intruding but the pigeon came back. Royce." Heath tossed him the cylinder.

James slung his arm over his chair. "Did you read the message?"

"The seal hasn't been broken, I can assure you." He spoke to Royce. "I put the bird with the others and made certain to latch the cage so they couldn't escape."

"Good man."

At the friendly exchange, Tristan and James traded a surprised glance.

Royce dropped the message on the table. "The natives want us to sail to their isle rather than them coming here. They've had problems with the crops and can't spare the men for a crew. They'd like our best seeds for the next planting. In exchange, they'll send the priest back here for christenings and give us more herbs and spices. If we agree, we leave next month."

Diana clutched Tristan's arm. "Please, not you. I know you like to sail, but I don't want you in danger from mariners, pirates, or the authorities for herbs and spices. We have plenty here. We only trade because the other islanders need what we have, not the other way around."

"They have the priest, love. The new mothers here and those expecting infants clamor for his blessings."

"Someone who doesn't have a price on his head for piracy can bring him back. Merry and I need you to protect us. So do the islanders. Whether you like it or not, you are the ruler here."

"I rule no one. We're all free." He shrugged. "I simply suggest solutions."

"And implement them to everyone's benefit. Do so now. Say you'll stay to protect this isle and everyone here."

"Always." He kissed her cheek. "But not because the trip is difficult or dangerous, since it's not. I've far too much to do here to travel elsewhere, especially for such a minor matter."

"Looks like it's settled." James yawned. "Lovely when a couple agrees so readily without screaming and throwing things."

Gavra brushed past Heath, Willy on her shoulder. "What did you say?"

James had spoken English. He shook his head. "*Rien.*" Nothing.

"Tell me."

"We were simply discussing sailing to the islanders who trade with us. Diana feared Tristan going. He won't. He has to protect her, Merry, and the islanders, plus do endless tasks."

"You too." Gavra gave Willy to James. "Before you slipped the marriage collar on my throat, you made me wait too many nights for you to return.

Do you want me to suffer again? Are you trying to make me cry?"

Tristan smiled gently and spoke French. "No need to worry. James knows he has to stay here to keep you and Willy safe."

Diana tapped Tristan's hand. "I wasn't able to translate all of that. What happened?"

He told her.

"Peter remains here too." She crossed her arms. Her red silk gown shone faintly. Diamonds twinkled about her throat. "He also has a price on his head and I'll not have him in unnecessary danger. I can tell Gavra that. Even though my French is far from perfect, it is improving."

"Go on then."

Diana relayed her comments about Peter.

Gavra flicked her wrist. "I can have a word with Laure and she can do the same with him. Peter knows better than to disobey her." She padded away.

Tristan kissed Diana's cheek. "Did you get all that?"

"Most of it. It wouldn't hurt if you told me everything, just to be sure."

"Gavra's setting Laure on Peter like a hungry dog on a bone. The matter is settled."

"Not entirely." Royce fingered the note. "Looks like this task falls to me."

"With Simone even closer to delivering next month?" Diana gave him a scolding look. "Or have you forgotten? What if you're delayed for some reason that keeps you past your expected return? I'd wager she wouldn't want to birth the child without her husband here."

Heath stepped into the room and closed the door lest Gavra returned or Aimee wandered by and heard something she'd want translated. "I can go." The trip would be his chance to finally command a ship and show these people he could behave like a true islander.

Diana turned her disapproval on him. "What about Netta and Aimee? Do you intend to abandon them already?"

"Wait a moment." Tristan leaned forward. Merry fussed. "Sorry, love." He settled her on his shoulder and patted her bottom. "How did you know about Aimee and Netta?"

Diana's surprise matched his. "How did you?" She spoke to Heath. "I swear, I did not betray their trust. When I give my word, I keep it."

"Clearly." Tristan turned her face so she'd look at him. "You kept this from me."

"You hardly shared what you knew."

"Because you're a woman. A mother now. The thought of one man with… I didn't know if you could handle it."

"I sailed the ocean with crude mariners to capture you. I fought pirates to remain at your side. I birthed our daughter with little pain and no screams. At this point, I doubt much would send me into a swoon."

"Your wails during Merry's birth nearly made my ears bleed. Before you retort, I can never thank you enough for the agony you went through to give us such a splendid daughter." He pecked Diana's lips. "You never cease to dazzle me. That said, you keep no more secrets. I'll not have it."

"Nor will I."

Heath cleared his throat to gain their attention. "This island is my home, same as yours. I don't intend to sail to the other isle and work my way back to civilization as I once said. I'd simply like to help when I can. I've no price on my head nor do I have a coming infant to worry about during the voyage."

Tristan pointed. "See that you never do."

"Never?" Diana curled her hand around his. "Heath's a man not a child. We must leave him to his own future."

Her words shocked. Few women would have been as tolerant. Tristan had a true prize in her. "Thank you for not minding about Netta and Aimee."

"I didn't say that." She sighed. "However, it's your life not mine, and this isn't England. As long as the islanders have no argument with what you three want to do, we have no say in the matter."

"Aimee, Netta, and I will take care. I adore them."

"Good God, man, control yourself." James shivered as one would when tasting something foul. "Soon you'll be spouting poetry. I don't have the stomach for that."

Diana leaned across the table and smacked his arm. "You were as bad with Gavra and her with you. I can't count the times she failed to get tea in my cup because you two were making eyes at each other."

James's freckles disappeared beneath his vivid blush.

Tristan and Royce laughed.

"If I may interrupt." Heath stepped closer. "I don't know most of the men so I have no idea who to choose for a crew. However, I would like Adamo to join me. He's a fine fellow."

"No."

Tristan and James had spoken as one.

Couldn't be they didn't trust him. Everyone knew Adamo would gladly die to protect these shores. "Because of his arm?"

"Canela." Loathing erupted in Tristan's eyes. "Wouldn't be fair or kind to expose him to that she-devil again."

"Understood. I didn't consider her banishment to that island."

James exchanged a glance with Tristan. "I doubt she thinks of anything else."

* * * *

Sun poured down relentlessly. The cooking fire raged. Sweat beaded on Ismay's brow.

"Next time use less wood." She smiled weakly at Canela. "I have never been as hot."

"I can do better. I can learn." She pressed linen against Ismay's forehead. "Would you like me to stir the food while you rest beneath the palms? Their shade will cool you."

"I should stay here." She stared at the trees longingly. "My duty is to cook."

"All day, every day? No one helps you, save me. What if you need to sleep longer than you usually do or you fall ill? The others would starve. If you teach me how to measure and mix, I could ease your burden. Together, we could make twice as much and no one, not even Fanette, could complain."

Ismay laughed. "Her above all. Has she threatened you?"

Only her eyes, not the switch she loved to wield. Canela planned to use far worse on her. "I keep away. She frightens me."

"I promise to protect you." She handed Canela the large wooden spoon. "Let the mixture bubble then stir it several times. It will quiet down. Once new bubbles rise, stir again to keep the food from burning. I only need a few minutes' sleep."

"Rest well. If I need your help, I can come for you."

"Merci." She squeezed Canela's wrist and slogged to the trees.

At the forest edge, Vincent and another captive dug a grave for Yoland's mother. She'd passed as Ismay had predicted and would rest next to her husband. His crucifix was on the last mound in a long line.

Vincent stopped digging and stared at Canela.

An islander cursed Vincent's laziness and brought a large switch down on his shoulders. He shrieked and fell to his knees.

Canela longed for the native to strike Vincent again.

He did.

Wind swept the yard. The fire licked the ground and came too close to Canela's cloth. She scooted as far as she could from the intense heat and stirred, amused this slop, more than Vincent's useless male power, would be her way off the isle.

As soon as the pigeon returned and she knew when Tristan's crew would arrive.

* * * *

For Heath's work on the crib, Bella's mother gave him fresh bread, cooked fish, bacon, and boiled eggs. Laden with the bounty and a few items he'd gathered, he hurried to his house to prepare for the midday meal. Today, he'd serve Netta and Aimee.

He tidied up his meager surroundings, collected wildflowers, scattered them throughout the room, and pulled back the cowhide to let in sun and air.

The harder he worked, the more energy he had. Hope fueled his vigor as nothing else could. He fairly burst to tell Aimee and Netta what had happened. How their fortunes were changing.

Everything was ready.

Except for him. Wood shavings, dirt, and pigeon droppings had soiled his breeches. Before he washed them in his basin, he cleaned his face and beneath his arms.

The sweetly scented flowers drew him. He sniffed each kind, settled on one that didn't smell too womanly, and rubbed it on his chest.

If Royce, James, or Tristan saw him now, they'd laugh.

To hell with them. Heath intended to please his women.

Lovely term.

He laundered his breeches and hung them on his chair to dry.

Shadows fell across the entrance.

Netta and Aimee.

He pointed. "You're late. I won't have that." He relieved them of the food they'd brought and danced them around the room. Wasn't easy in the small space. Neither followed his steps. Knees and feet bumped.

He'd have to teach them the few dances he knew. Nothing as fine as Royce's minuet, but fun nonetheless.

Netta laughed heartily. Aimee giggled.

"I trust you're not making light of me."

Aimee rested her head on his shoulder. Her breath skimmed his chest. "What does that mean?"

"Trust?"

Netta wiggled against him. "Making light."

"Teasing me at my expense. Treating me as if I was a bloody fool."

"You smell good." Aimee suckled his nipple.

Netta tongued his ear.

His restraint crumbled. He didn't need words or food, only them. However, he had scant time for their repast before work beckoned. When Heath took them as a man should, he didn't want to rush or leave the bed for hours.

He eased away and grabbed their hands. Unthinkingly, he'd taken Netta's maimed one.

She wrapped her remaining finger and thumb around his. "Is our play over?"

"Never." Aimee pressed her breast against his arm.

They were going to kill him with their innocent lust. "I'm afraid our desire will have to wait until this evening. After we eat, I must go to the courtyard. I have another crib to build. Ourson's helping me. When I told him yesterday I'd be back, I never returned. If I do that again, he may hate me and rightfully so."

Aimee pulled Heath to the table. "Sit. Eat. Then go back. You must be kind to Ourson and all the children so their parents will like you too."

"I have news about that."

She exchanged a glance with Netta. Their lighthearted mood turned guarded.

He added, "Good news."

Their moods didn't improve.

"Do you two have something to tell me first?" Couldn't be pleasant given their long faces. "Out with it."

Aimee bowed her head. "Gavra wants Netta and me to be happy with two men not one."

"Two each? Four men total?"

"No." She frowned.

He smiled. "Forgive me, I couldn't help but tease." He spoke to Netta. "What happened with you?"

"Simone says the priest must say the words over us."

"Is that all? We'll find another way. Do you know why? Diana and Tristan have no say in what we do. Her very words. Tristan didn't argue. My guess is, he wants to stay in her good graces." Heath gave Netta and Aimee bread, bacon, eggs, and fish divided equally on two plates. He'd taken one from the storage room, along with an extra fork and knife, and left a note that he'd pay for it with labor. Tomorrow, he'd start building two more chairs so they and he could sit at the table like a proper family. "Royce and I also spoke."

Aimee pulled bacon from her mouth without biting into it. "Did he frown? He likes to do that to you."

"At first, but we eventually shook hands. We're on our way to becoming friends. He even called me a good man. Adamo and I have also talked. He's going to help me and I'll help him. That reminds me, I must ask Tristan for his book on the subject."

Netta put down her bread. "Subject?"

"About metal. Adamo and the other men can use what I learn to make tools for everyone. Like this." He touched her fork. "Don't know why Tristan hadn't considered it before now. Could be he thought he'd get whatever he'd need from piracy." Heath laughed. "I can't imagine Diana going along with that. She changed his mind on sailing to the other isle for spices and herbs. Told him he was needed here to protect her and Merry. Gavra told James she'd cry if he left. I'm certain Laure lectures Peter as we speak."

Aimee looked at Netta. "Do you understand what he's saying?"

"No."

"Sorry. I'm so excited, I'm not explaining myself adequately. The pigeon came back with a message from the islanders we trade with. They want us to sail to their shores this time. Royce was the only one who offered to go, until Diana reminded him of his and Simone's coming child. Since I have no infant to worry about I said I'd go."

He chomped on bacon from Aimee's plate, his hunger returned and voracious. "I wanted to take Adamo with me, to strengthen our friendship, but exposing him to Canela again would be cruel. I can't believe a woman would do that to any man, even the vilest. She must be quite mad or pure evil." He gobbled Netta's bread and fish, and spoke around the food. "I told Tristan and the others they should pick the crew as I have no idea how well any islander will perform. We sail next month. This voyage is everything I wanted and more than I dreamed." He laughed. "I'm ready to dance again."

Aimee stepped back. Netta joined her. Neither smiled.

Little wonder. He'd devoured a good portion of their meals. "I'm a swine. Don't let me take another bite." He delivered a new helping of bread, bacon, and fish. "Please eat. It's delicious." He sucked his fingers.

Netta put her plate on the table. Aimee's chin quivered the way a woman's does before weeping.

"What have I done?" This couldn't be about food. "Tell me."

Netta wrapped her arm around Aimee's shoulders. "How long will you be away?"

"I don't know. Didn't think to ask. Longer than a week, I would guess. Otherwise there'd be no need to take the Lady Lark. We could use a skiff or the longboats from Bishop's attack."

Aimee ran her toes over the dirt floor.

She reminded Heath of Ourson when he'd been disappointed. "I've troubled you and I don't know why. Please tell me what I've done wrong.

Never keep anything from me." He touched her cheek.

She pulled away. "You want to go. Will you come back?"

"Are you asking if I want to return? Of course." He cradled her face and Netta's. "If it were my choice I wouldn't leave you."

"Then why are you?" Netta brushed his hand away. "Why does leaving us make you happy enough to do your foolish dance?"

He'd never expected such a comment from her. When Diana and Gavra had given their men a hard time, Heath congratulated himself on having not one, but two understanding women who'd never demand, threaten, or rage against him. Apparently, females came one way, sweet one moment, unbelievably cross the next. "No need to fret."

Aimee shoved her plate at him. "You think I'm being foolish?"

"No. I'm just trying to make you understand I'm not going for me. I'm doing this for you and Netta."

"Stop lying to us." Netta poked his chest. "We never told you to go. We begged you to stay. You said you would. Now you want a chance to leave and because you have it, you hop around like a bird. You dream of nothing else except the other isle."

He curbed his frustration. "Let me reword what I said."

"Will it mean that you stay here?"

"No. I have no bloody choice except to do this. Tristan and James have prices on their heads. For them to leave for any reason would be madness. Besides, they have to stay here to see to matters and keep everyone safe. Peter's also wanted for piracy and is far too young and obstinate to be of any use. Royce and Simone are expecting their first child. She requires him more than anyone does. That obviously leaves me. By sparing the others the task, and putting myself at risk, I—"

"What risk?" Aimee grabbed his arm.

Netta grasped his hand. "Pirates? Men like the white devil? A storm?"

Possibly all three. It wasn't cyclone season but squalls did happen without warning. Anything was possible. Simply being alive exposed one to death. "I've no desire to die. I'll—"

"Die?" Netta covered her face.

Tears brimmed in Aimee's eyes.

He couldn't fathom how his promising news had turned dreadful. "The trip's short. Waters calm. Few mariners travel this area. It's not on the usual routes ships take for trade or piracy."

Netta smacked her maimed hand into her palm. "The French came here. Then the English. Both to destroy us. What if they return with you away?"

"They won't. They found this isle and the other by accident. It's unlikely that will happen again. I wanted to make you and Aimee happy. Convince your people I'll do my part to make everyone safe so they accept me being with you and we can bloody well wed."

Aimee backed up. "I would rather you never wed us than have you leave."

"I feel the same." Netta swiped away tears. "You must stay on this isle to protect us."

"Tristan's here to do that. So are James, Royce, Peter, and eighty or more armed men."

"Do they love us? No. Stay."

"Sorry. I can't."

"Another lie."

"Very well. I won't. You'll have to understand."

Netta ran from his house.

Aimee looked at him pleadingly.

Heath held out his hands to her. "You do understand, don't you?"

She covered her mouth and bolted after Netta.

Chapter 10

Heath had never seen so many blasted books in his life, dozens in languages he'd didn't know, and none in an order he could discern. Medical texts mingled with those on agriculture and furniture design. That one he could have used rather than struggling to build the cribs on his own. Hating Tristan's library, Heath shoved another volume back into place. "Where the bloody hell are they?"

Chair legs scraped. Peter stood. "What?"

Royce tugged him back to his seat and tapped the papers on the table. "Do your lessons."

"With Heath muttering and making a racket? It's impossible for me to think." Peter leaned toward the bookcases. "What are you ranting about?"

"Tristan said they'd be to the left. To the left of what?" Heath ran his finger over spines. Some had titles. Others numerals. None useful. He crouched to check the lower books. Hopeless. The gold lettering had worn off most covers. "Do either of you know where I might find information on rocks and metal?"

Royce glanced up from his message to the other islanders. Today, he'd send the pigeon back. "You mean geology and metallurgy?"

"How would I know? I'm a barely educated mariner. I'm sure you studied at Oxford University. The workhouse was hardly that. I fled the wretched place as quickly as I could and had to make do with what I could learn on my own."

"You've done far better than most in your situation. Be grateful for that."

Easy for a former noble to say. Royce had survived a few years as a lowly commoner before landing in this splendor. Heath had never had a proper meal until he'd come here. Once he'd filled his belly, everything else turned dark. No one trusting him. Happiness out of reach. Netta and

Aimee treating him with little consideration and no understanding when he'd done everything he could to have them.

He clenched his jaw to keep from shouting. If the library had been his, he would have thrown volumes everywhere. "Where are the damn books on how to extract metal from rocks?"

Peter pushed his chair to its two back legs and balanced there. "Why?"

"So the islanders can make tools like blades, knifes, and such."

"We already have enough. If we need more, we can gather a crew and sail to secure them and other things. Jewels. Silks. Whatever we come upon."

"You make piracy sound as easy as purchasing the items from a merchant."

"Absolutely not. It's far harder." Peter grinned. "But more fun."

Royce grabbed Peter's arm and tugged him forward. Chair legs smacked the marble floor. "Keep talking like that and Diana will have your head. Once she's done with you, Tristan would finish you off then Laure would have a go. No one on this isle will ever engage in piracy again. Particularly you. How many times must we tell you that?"

"Things change. One day we may need to survive that way."

"Not if the women have anything to say about it. Trust me. They'd see us men dead first."

Or the women would stop speaking and make themselves so scarce they'd be more memory than reality.

Days had passed since Netta had stormed from Heath's house. Aimee's initial hesitation gave him hope she'd return so he could reason with her and she'd do the same with Netta. He couldn't have been more wrong. Wherever they kept themselves, it was well away from him.

Another lonely night and he'd go mad.

He pulled out a volume on the top shelf. Those on either side came with it and tumbled on him. "Damnation."

"I can't think. I need a break." Peter jumped from his chair and backed away from Royce. "I've been at this all day."

"Scarcely two hours." He pointed his quill at a gold clock in the corner, one of Tristan's prizes from his pirate days. "You may go but only to walk around the courtyard or down the halls to shed your pent-up energy. I expect you back here shortly. Don't make me come looking for you or your next lesson will take four hours. Understood?"

"All too well. One day you and everyone else here will have no choice except to treat me as the man I am."

"We look forward to it far more than you ever will."

Peter made a face and slammed the door on his way out.

"Lucky for him I'm not one to draw my pistol hastily. That goes for you too." Royce crossed his arms. "Getting Peter to sit much less study is a constant battle. Your interruption hasn't made it easier."

"That wasn't my intent. I thought I'd find the text by now and be gone."

"The section you're in has Arabic works. I trust you can't read that language. Try all the way to the left."

"I have. The only thing remaining in that direction is the wall."

"And volumes on the earth." He joined Heath and pulled out a large book with a brown leather cover then a slender one in red. The geology and metallurgy texts.

"Why didn't you tell me where they were from the outset?"

"I didn't know what you were looking for and I was trying to pen my message." He returned to the table. "If you're having second thoughts about the journey, speak up. No need to behave like a petulant child. Or even worse, like Peter."

Heath's frustration drained away. He chuckled. "The boy does try one's sanity. I haven't changed my mind, no matter what they think."

"They? Ah…" Understanding flashed across Royce's face. "You mean Aimee and Netta."

"I thought this would make them happy. I'm doing it so the islanders accept me, us, our situation. How is that wrong? I barely got the words out and Netta went quite hysterical, as Diana did with Tristan and Gavra with James when neither man had even considered leaving this isle for the other. Aimee wasn't any better. I haven't seen them since. I have no idea how to make things better, except to forgo the journey, which I can't. I won't. I gave my word and I intend to keep it no matter what."

Royce gestured helplessly. "If I knew how to make things better for you, I'd say so, but I don't. When women get something in their heads, there's no changing how they think. I do wish you luck."

That meant a lot. "Think I'll need it?"

Royce laughed. "Oh yes."

* * * *

Heath read the volumes well into the evening. The oil lamp drew colorful moths inside. He'd hope to entice Aimee and Netta. Had even pulled back the cowhide so they'd see the light if they happened to stroll past.

A furry animal no larger than his hand scurried inside. After a tense moment for the creature, it dashed back into the darkness.

This was pure idiocy. Within weeks, he'd leave. Netta and Aimee wasted precious time they could all spend together, living, laughing, loving. He understood how they felt, or he tried, but some things a man simply had to do. If they had full say in his actions, he'd never leave his cramped room or face anything more dangerous than breathing. It was one thing to civilize him. He surely needed that. Hobbling was quite another.

They'd have to see things his way this time.

After finishing the portions he needed in the geology text, he tackled the metallurgy book. Thankfully, Royce had encouraged him to take along a dictionary to understand unfamiliar words.

The scientific terms proved elusive. As with his other endeavors, Heath pieced things together on his own.

Peter should have this difficulty. Might make him understand how fortunate he was to have such dedicated teachers in Royce, Tristan, and Diana.

One day, Heath had hoped to teach Aimee and Netta English, both written and spoken so they could converse or argue more easily with him.

He left further study until morning.

At dawn, he finished reading, packed the volumes along with his meager stores for a midday meal, and tromped to the mansion, by way of Netta and Aimee's house. Their cowhide was down, no oil lamp or candle lit inside, no activity either.

Uncertain what to do, he carried on to his work.

Ourson met him at the courtyard wall and jumped with youthful enthusiasm. "The cribs are done. Are we going to look for rocks today and make things with them?"

"We are. At least, we'll look for the rocks we can use." Heath ruffled his hair. "If your parents agree."

"They will. Even papa is here so you can talk to him. Come." Ourson pulled him to the couple. Gentleness and acceptance radiated from them.

In his earlier years, Heath would have been envious another child had such wonderful parents. As a man, he wouldn't have wanted anything less for Ourson.

"Mama, Papa, I need to help Heath find rocks. Please say I can go. Please."

"Bonjour." Heath bowed slightly to mama Esme and offered his hand to papa Michel. "The rocks have metal in them the islanders can use to make knives, arrowheads, blades, and other things. I planned to collect them today. If you don't mind, I could teach Ourson what to look for. I assure you, he'll come to no harm."

"Please, please." He tugged their hands. "I must go. Heath made me his quartermaster."

Michel smiled. "What is that?"

"My helpmate." Heath squeezed Ourson's shoulder. "I've yet to find another who follows what I say so quickly and well. You have a wonderful son."

Esme blushed and looked at Michel. He cupped Ourson's chin. "You may go, but you must also behave. Listen to everything Heath tells you."

"I will. Tell them that, Heath."

"He always does. I'll have him back before the sun dips below the shortest trees."

"Wait." Esme held up her finger. "Give me a moment to return." She ran to the mansion.

"I must tend the horses." Michel embraced his son. "Be good."

"Oui, Papa."

Esme emerged with three sacks. Two hemp. One green silk. She gave it to Heath. "Bacon, bread, and fruit for you and Ourson's midday meal. The sturdier sacks are for your rocks." She kissed Ourson's cheek and waved them on their way.

Outside the courtyard walls, Ourson copied Heath's stride.

To have Netta and Aimee give him boys like this...

His longing returned with such speed and power, he could scarcely stand much less walk.

Ourson shielded his eyes from the rising sun. "Where are these rocks?"

"Some are in water. Others in swamps. Some near large hills and within them like the one over there." He pointed to a greenish peak in the distance. "That's a volcano."

"No. It's *Fue de la Montagne*." Mountain Fire.

"That's the name you call it. Like everyone knows you as Ourson, but you're also a boy. A volcano is a mountain that spews liquid fire, steam, and ash. It's all in here." He patted the geology book. "The material we're looking for today...I forget what it's called...is actually everywhere on this isle. It's a deep red color. I read that in the book this morning."

Ourson regarded the path they took through the bushes. "The dirt is red."

"Quite right. However, what we need are concentrated metals in rocks we then heat. A simple fire might not work to pull out the materials. We'll probably have to build a smelting furnace."

"Today?"

Heath wrapped his arm around Ourson's shoulders and shook him. "In the future. It will take many men to do so. Right now, you and I are gathering raw materials to begin the process. The book has drawings and descriptions on what we should look for."

"We already know. The rocks have to be red. Like those." He swung his finger to the right.

Within a clearing stood several boulders stacked next to and on top of each other. Possibly marking an ancient burial or religious site. Nature hadn't placed them like that.

"Those are a bit large for us to…"

Heath forgot what he intended to say. Colors flashed within the adjoining forest. One blue. The other green.

He stopped and wished he'd brought his spyglass.

Ourson tugged Heath's fingers. "What are you doing?"

Yearning. Across the expanse, Netta and Aimee faced him. Their hair floated on the fragrant breeze, cloths billowed then smoothed. Flowers and plants peeked from their silk sacks.

Netta turned away and disappeared into the forest. Aimee lingered.

Heath advanced.

She left and slipped past trees.

* * * *

"Wait." Aimee grabbed Netta's arm.

She pulled free. "If you want to go back then go. Talk to him. Be with him."

"By myself when you want Heath too?"

Netta spun around. "Has he come to us and tried to make things better? No."

"You want him to stay. I do too, but he's going. Are we supposed to let him sail without showing him our love? Is that what you want?"

She covered her eyes. "I fear for him. If he gets hurt or dies…" She shuddered.

Aimee didn't want to imagine sorrow. She'd had too much. "He will return."

"What if he likes the other isle? What if he misses his England home and wants to go there?"

Aimee would never be the same, part of her heart and soul lost. Despite the heat, a chill ran through her. She wrapped her arms around herself. "He loves us. He said so."

"Now. Will it last? His people have different ways than ours. Not gentle and kind. Peter told Laure fathers scream at their children and beat them when they misbehave. Men rage against women and treat them worse than animals. White men have power and riches but they have no idea how to love."

"Some. Not Heath. He knows how to be different. Look how he treats Ourson. The same as the islanders with their sons."

"What choice does he have? If he dared hurt any child, the men and women would beg Tristan to hang him."

"You believe that threat alone keeps Heath from hurting anyone? He disagreed with us and now you consider him as bad as other Englishmen?"

"No!" Netta sagged against a tree, her forehead to it. "I love him so much I ache. I can barely draw a breath."

"Then tell him. I will too. We can catch up and say what we hold in our hearts." Aimee offered her hand.

Netta cowered against the trunk. "I want to speak to him if he comes back from his journey."

"When he does."

"Can you promise that?" Tears hung on her lashes. "Can anyone, even him? In one morning, our parents, relatives, and friends died, leaving us to the beasts who changed our lives. We prayed to the goddess faithfully, but she never heard or saw, and offered no protection. Why should she do so now with him? I could never live through such sorrow again. I would rather be alone." She tore through the forest toward the courtyard walls.

* * * *

Royce fed his pigeons and cleaned their cage. A thankless task but he dreaded going to the library to tackle another lesson with Peter.

To Royce's surprise, Tristan was there, checking on Peter's schoolwork. "Well done. No errors."

"Can I take my ride now?"

"Only to the pastures and back. I want to tackle geography and history next."

"In the same day?"

"What say we add Greek too? And accounting. Royce may have other subjects he'd like you to undertake."

"I do. We can begin with mathematics, move on to literature, and end with science."

Peter hung his head. "I shall return shortly for history and geography."

Tristan closed the door and gestured to his charts on the table. "What are these doing out?"

"When Heath returns from his rock adventure, I want to show him the quickest and safest route to the other isle. Netta and Aimee are giving him a hard time about leaving."

"My, you have taken a liking to him to concern yourself with his love life."

"I was being unreasonable before. You know, as women often are. We men have to stick together."

"I'm with you on that. Did you get the bird off the other day? I forgot to ask."

"I did. It should return from Faucon before the week ends."

* * * *

"Ismay, Ismay, Ismay!" Fanette kicked Ismay's foot.

Ismay didn't move from the tree-shaded ground. Her hands pillowed her head. Legs hugged her chest.

Fanette ran to Yoland's house, waving her arms, screeching for help.

Canela had put too many herbs in the fish stew she'd given Ismay. A test to see how the sleeping herb worked and if Ismay would notice an unusual taste.

She hadn't. For the moment, she still breathed, though barely.

Canela sickened with fear. Not for Ismay's possible death. With her gone, control over the cooking would fall to Canela. A delightful prospect, unless Fanette accused her of poisoning the food and the others discovered the herbs she'd collected.

She'd never leave the isle then. They might cut her heels to make her a cripple or blind her so she'd be helpless.

Terror made her hot then cold. Shivering, she crawled to Ismay and shook her. "Wake up. Please. What is the matter with you? Are you sick? Tell me what to bring you to make you better."

Ismay's lids fluttered. She stared blankly at Canela as one would a stranger.

Canela shook harder and slapped Ismay's cheeks. "You have to wake up and breathe." She dumped stew from the bowl, filled it with water, and brought it to Ismay's lips. "Drink."

Yoland ran up.

Fanette followed and yanked Canela's hair.

She cried out.

"What are you doing to Ismay?" Fanette tugged harder. "Are you trying to drown her?"

"No!" Canela gripped Fanette's wrists to keep the hag from tearing her hair out. "Ismay opened her eyes. I gave her water to help wake her."

Yoland crouched near them, her form skinny and skin sagged with age. "Ismay, what troubles you?"

She swigged the water. "I fell asleep."

"Why?"

Canela yanked away from Fanette. "She works too hard. Put the burden on me. I can cook so she can rest. Heed my words or next time she may not wake up."

"Liar." Fanette spat. "You poisoned her."

"No. I love Ismay. She's kind and gentle. If the stew poisoned her it will do the same to me." Canela darted from Fanette, filled another bowl, and ate quickly despite the heat and foul taste. Finished, she ran her hand across her mouth. "Now all you have to do is wait for me to die or tell me I spoke the truth."

Yoland stroked Ismay's hair. She slumbered again. "You proved your words are true. Go back to the cooking. Fanette will leave and see to her tasks."

"I will not. She's lying. Why can no one see that?"

"You see only darkness where there is nothing except light." Yoland turned her back to Fanette. "Go."

"You will regret trusting her."

Canela made her face a mask and stirred the stew.

* * * *

Heath carried both sacks filled with rocks, many far from the description and color the book stated. He hadn't the heart to tell Ourson the pretty ones were unusable for their purpose. Childhood wonder only lasted a few years and should be encouraged not berated.

Ourson flapped his arms to mimic the birds flying overhead. "Are we finished?"

"For the time being." Heath could barely haul this load. His feet hurt from trying to keep up with Ourson and make certain he stayed far from trouble. "I promised your parents to get you back before the sun was too low." It skimmed the shortest treetops. "There's always tomorrow."

"I want more bacon and bread."

"Of course you do. You're a growing boy, but you ate the last we had a while ago."

"We have more at my house. Come with me. You can eat with us tonight."

Sleep beckoned, not food or polite conversation. Heath had fought desire and dejection during every quiet moment. There weren't a lot with a spirited child around, but enough to exhaust him. "Merci, but another time. I'm quite old, you know. I need my rest."

"Are you going to die?"

He halted. An animal rushed into the bushes next to him. Butterflies scattered. "What?"

"Kaarle said old people die when they're unable to work any longer."

"Who is Kaarle?"

"My friend. His papa told him our grandparents are gone because they were too old to work on the isle." He held Heath's hand. "Can you keep working? Please?"

"Of course. Many years will pass before I die. You may be an old man then." Ourson grinned. He'd lost another tooth.

They traveled with ease. Ourson chattered endlessly, Heath nodded and made occasional noises to prove he was listening.

He stopped at a path that veered to the left. "Here we are. Your home is just ahead. Be sure to tell your mother you behaved yourself and learned much today. Do you still have the pretty stone you chose for her?"

Ourson opened his hand. Bacon grease and crumbs coated the speckled pebble.

"What a fine lad you are. I'm sure she's going to love it. Now off with you."

"See you tomorrow." He ran, his feet kicking up red dust.

Esme and Michel waved.

Heath returned the greeting and shuffled home. An endless walk, the rocks and books a burden.

He dropped everything on his mattress, quaffed his remaining water, and cursed at having to go out for more. If he'd had any sense, he would have dug a well rather than making daily trips to the stream like the women did for their families. Perhaps he could install wells for everyone so they'd accept him and wouldn't mind that he wanted two women who kept their distance no matter how much that wounded.

A bullet wouldn't have hurt worse than Netta and Aimee turning from him. He couldn't suffer through more.

The urge to run hit him as it had when he'd been a child. Then, circumstances conspired to keep him in place, powerless to flee pain. As a man, he refused to accept the same restrictions.

He slapped the cowhide away and hurtled headlong into deepening gloom. Monstrous trees kept the remaining sun from bleeding through. On the shore, brightness lingered. Here, night began its approach.

Wind cooled, nocturnal animals stirred.

His feet pounded reddish earth, his chest pumped, and his side ached. Panting, he trampled wildflowers, stumbled past bushes and small trees, heedless of flaying branches or thorny growths.

Light pierced the darkness, dishes clinked, baking bread and frying bacon pleased as only civilized scents could. He didn't want to be alone. Not tonight. Not ever.

The fire illuminated Aimee and Netta.

Heath rushed into the light.

They stood.

He clutched his side and sank to his knees. "Please understand my reasons for going and try not to be cross that I must. I adore both of you. I've never missed anyone so much in all my days. We must fix this. Say you'll try."

Chapter 11

Netta cradled Heath's face. His longing and sorrow matched hers and Aimee's. They were all one soul, the refuge she'd needed for too long. Shamed by her doubt and selfishness, she kissed his forehead, eyelids, and both cheeks.

He drew her down to him. "Not enough. I want more."

Her tongue filled his mouth. Their combined heat, dampness, and taste renewed her. He smelled better than she recalled. Somehow each touch, breath, and caress seemed new tonight and miraculous.

He suckled her tongue and held her tightly.

Aimee joined them. Together they formed a family no country, man, or woman could deny or defeat. They'd belong together until time ended.

Netta wanted to linger in his embrace past dawn, but couldn't refuse Aimee the same pleasure she knew. "What are you waiting for, dear sister? Greet our man as you should."

Aimee smiled and settled into his arms.

Heath kissed her soundly.

Sounds flowed from Aimee that a woman in love must make. Ones expressing excitement, anticipation, yearning so deep nothing mattered except closeness and coupling.

Heath couldn't possibly deny them or himself any longer.

He pulled his mouth from Aimee, gathered Netta close, and lowered them to the ground. "I must have you both tonight and every day that follows. Loving you as a man should do with a woman. Tell me you agree."

Netta wanted nothing else but held back. "Not yet." She twisted from him.

Surprise and sadness crossed his handsome face. "I thought you'd forgiven me."

"I have. Can you do the same?"

"With what?"

"Me. I was wrong and willful when we spoke, thinking only of my hurt."

"We both behaved horribly. It's finished and forgotten."

She scooted back.

He reached for her. "Where are you going?"

"The fire. Our bacon and bread will burn. Once they do, the flames could destroy more than our meal."

"Of course. How stupid of me. Let me put it out then we can make love beneath the stars."

Aimee snuggled against him. "Our bed is better."

"Wherever you want. I shan't leave till dawn, if that's all right."

Netta laughed. "If you try to go, Aimee and I will hold on to your legs. She can be quite strong. So can I."

"I've no doubt. Here." He took the pan from Netta, put it aside where it could do no harm, and doused the fire.

Steam and smoke rose, mingling with the bacon aroma.

Heath removed the bread pot from the coals. He poured dirt over the glowing embers and extinguished fire. "Everything's done, including me interrupting your meal. I must make it up to you."

Netta kissed his strong fingers and weakened further. "Forget the food. I hunger for something more."

"I do too." Aimee held his other hand to her breast.

Together, they brought him into their house. An oil lamp lit the snug interior. Flowers delivered their sweet fragrances. His scent joined them to make this place his as much as theirs. Even without the priest's sacred words, they'd become one tonight, their love lasting until their last breaths.

Netta unbuttoned his breeches.

He tugged at the knot on her and Aimee's cloths.

Everyone's clothes fell at the same time, as they should.

Heath cupped Netta's buttocks and kept her close to him, away from escape.

She had no plan to leave. His calloused palm and sheer size aroused her as much as his good heart and tenderness. He used his strength with care, mindful of a woman's heart, her need to feel safe.

Within his embrace, Netta found freedom to be herself and a sanctuary against any cruelty the world offered.

She claimed his mouth with less restraint than she'd used at the fire.

He grunted and pulled her into him, his grip unbreakable yet protective.

His shielding her and Aimee bred loyalty more effectively than harsh words and a raised fist. Netta softened against him and cradled his thickened cock. It flexed within her touch. Her power was as great as his. She smiled.

Heath did too, the corners of their mouths lifting as one. He made a deep, satisfied noise, eased away from her, and kissed Aimee.

She gave her all, as she should.

Netta stroked his smooth, hot shaft, mesmerized by its beauty. She dipped to his crown and bumped Aimee's hand fondling his sac.

He freed his mouth and panted. "You're giving me too much to enjoy. I wager no man could withstand such temptation. No more delays. I must have you both now."

Netta pressed her furry mound against his thigh. "We have always been yours to take. Why are you still waiting?"

"I shan't." With them in his arms, he fell onto the mattress.

The wooden frame creaked loudly from their combined weight. The silk sheet fluttered. Delicate fragrances floated up and merged with their musk. The perfect place for love, the bed unusually large. Long ago, the islanders had built it for two young girls, women now. Its width and length accommodated a man's considerable size.

This had to be the goddess's work. Despite what Netta had said, her prayers hadn't gone unanswered. The goddess had brought Heath here.

Netta suckled his throat and worked his cock. Her hand and leg kept bumping into Aimee's who gave him her love.

He moaned and broke free. "Do I choose who to have first or would you ladies rather decide?"

Aimee smiled. "Love Netta."

She should have protested but couldn't. "Merci." She and Aimee shared a hug and kiss.

Heath settled between Netta's legs. "I'll take care. I won't hurt you."

As the pirates had. She pushed the past away and smiled gently. "I welcome your love."

His eyes glittered with adoration and male need, the mightiest forces on earth. "I must get closer." He settled her legs on his shoulders to expose her opening fully to him. "Is this all right? Are you comfortable?"

"Excited."

He laughed. Faint light softened his strong features. "I am too."

His breathing came hard, face flushed, muscles corded.

Netta gave him her most devoted smile, an invitation to have him inside her where he belonged.

Aimee watched with delight, no longer touching him. Instead, she squeezed Netta's hand in encouragement.

Tonight, she required none. Her dreams had never been as kind or wonderful as these moments. She needed to burn them into her memory, a reminder never to doubt him again. Too many days had passed. Hours lost when they could have been together.

She wouldn't repeat that mistake.

With skill and care, Heath entered her. His rod sank deeply within. Their curls touched.

His shaft stretched and filled. She could scarcely contain his full length and snatched a breath.

"Everything all right?" He searched her face. Worry pinched his.

His concern deepened her love. She cradled his cheek. "I never knew I could be so happy."

Heath's eyes filled, the same as hers. He kissed her deeply, affection and respect in his passion.

Their mouths enjoyed and explored. Tender delight turned to fierce lust. She craved his strength and animal need, no different from hers.

He pumped, slowly at first.

Testing her?

Netta squeezed her channel around his shaft.

Heath shuddered.

She cupped his sac.

He groaned, the sound muffled by her tongue in his mouth. He lifted his head and stared, eyes wild. "Continue to do that and you'll keep me from satisfying you. I can't last a moment more."

For the first time since childhood, Netta felt playful. "What am I doing? This?" She ran her nails teasingly over his lightly furred sac.

His moan filled the room. "Very well. Do what you must, same as I." He thumbed the hard kernel between her legs.

Delight struck from every direction. Her skin tingled and burned, limbs grew unsteady, the world careened out of control. Not wanting the pleasure to stop, she gripped the sheet rather than his sex and gave him peace.

A pleased sound rumbled from him. He stroked her nub quicker, pumped his sex into her faster. Their bodies met repeatedly and made faint smacking noises. His balls tapped her buttocks. The bed squeaked.

Her sheath dampened more than it ever had and hugged his impressive length and girth. The room smelled of sex. They wore each other's scents.

Longing, wonder, and joy battered her, stoking her passion. A carnal storm built between her legs and reached deep inside. Netta tried to resist the exquisite delight. She wanted this to continue without end.

Willful need defeated her and delivered intense release. Her channel quivered, the beats rhythmic, similar to an islander playing a drum. Though fevered, she trembled as she would when chilled. She couldn't lift her lids or hands. Helpless, she submitted to ecstasy.

Heath's breath warmed her cheek. He gasped nearly as much as she did. "You all right?"

She nodded, unable to do more.

He eased from her and fell to the side.

With her remaining energy, Netta touched his cock. Still hard. Ready for Aimee.

* * * *

The pleasant ache between Aimee's legs intensified and insisted on satisfaction.

Heath sprawled over the mattress, face crimson, neck and chest damp with sweat, breathing ragged.

He needed to rest.

She stroked his bottom lip. "Let me take care of you." Loath to have them separated another moment, she straddled him, positioned his stiffened cock on her opening, and sank over his flesh until they touched.

Her head fell back.

He choked out English words she didn't understand.

Aimee pretended he hadn't said anything and squeezed his shaft gently. Heath grabbed her hips. "Bloody hell. I don't think I can take it."

"This?" She tightened her channel.

His French came faster than his English, the words bumping into each other.

She brushed her lips over his. "Do you want me to stop?"

"No." The ridge in his throat bobbed with his hard swallow. "But do take things easy at first. I'm only a man, not an invincible god."

The greatest being couldn't compare to him. "I promise to take care."

She slid up his shaft and down, an easy rhythm meant to please, not drive him past restraint.

His breathing didn't quiet. His complexion matched James's when someone embarrassed him.

That wasn't supposed to happen. "Should I go slower?"

Heath blinked repeatedly and shook his head. "This is lovely. Do continue."

Recovered from her pleasure, Netta patted Aimee's leg in approval.

Bursting with confidence, Aimee not only pumped, she squeezed her breasts and thumbed her nipples.

Heath grinned. "Wicked girl. Do that again. I like it."

She laughed.

He stroked her nub.

Pleasure shot through her, impossible to resist. She lost her steady pace and clutched her hair.

"No. You're doing it wrong." He brought her hands to her breasts. "Rub and play with your nipples. Show me what I'll do with you and Netta's."

Giggling, Netta slapped Aimee's calf. "Do as he says. I want to see it too."

They asked too much.

Relentlessly, Heath teased Aimee's nub and drove her closer to release. She struggled to resist him and coordinate her movements. A hopeless task. Unnerved, she lowered her face. Her hair swept forward.

He brushed it back. "Look at me. I want to see what I do to you."

"You drive me wild. I can barely breathe. The room spins. My skin burns."

"I know. But I want to see that in your eyes. Come on. Give me what I want or I may stop this longer than a few moments." He ceased rubbing between her legs and rested his damp fingers on her thigh.

Surrendering, she met his gaze, squeezed her breasts, and pumped up and down his rigid shaft.

His pleased smile held a trace of arrogance at her bowing to his will. Aimee had and didn't mind. He'd do the same for her. She squeezed his cock with her sheath and increased her pace.

His smile fell away. Teeth gritted, he growled.

Aimee affected an innocent look. "Do you want me to stop?"

Netta laughed.

"Naughty girls." He swatted their buttocks playfully and spoke to Aimee. "I thought you were the shyer one."

Until meeting him, she had been. Heath opened her heart and world to wonders she hadn't imagined. Like Netta, he gave Aimee confidence and strength to do what she must.

Nothing mattered more to her than his pleasure and joy. "Threaten me if you will. Deny me your touch. You will never win. I can resist you too."

"Is that what you think?" He rubbed her kernel harder and faster.

She pumped more quickly.

The bed jounced. Her hair wiggled.

Heath roared.

His relief accompanied hers. Aimee's legs went rubbery. Her channel pulsed around his weary cock. Their breaths collided and filled the room with love sounds.

Spent, she released his sex from hers and sagged over his leg.

He stretched, puffed out breaths, and dragged them back in.

She patted his flat belly. "Everything all right?"

The question he always posed.

Netta giggled.

His breathing quieted. The only sound he made.

Aimee mustered her remaining strength and leaned over him. His dark lashes rested on his cheeks. His mouth hung open.

Netta crawled closer and spoke softly. "Is he asleep?"

"Oui." His helpless state tempted Aimee's mischievous side. She might have been the quieter twin but she could play as well as Netta. "What if I stuck my finger in his mouth?"

"Why would you do that?"

"To see what he would do."

"I prefer his sex." Netta rested her hand on his thigh. His rod hung over his ruddy sac, both slick from his seed and Netta's and Aimee's moisture. "What do you think would happen if I licked it?"

"Heath would grow hard as all men do and open his eyes. You tend his shaft. I can see to his sac. Together we can wake him and end our wait for more."

"What about his need to rest?"

"Once you crawl on top and take him inside you, ask him then. See what he says."

Netta sniffed. "With me pleasuring him, I doubt he could say anything, even the English."

"Perhaps. The only way to know is to..."

Heath regarded Aimee then Netta, his manner alert not drowsy. "Don't let me stop you two. You were saying?"

Aimee's face and chest heated. "What did you hear?"

"Everything. I was resting, not asleep or dead. So you want to stick your finger in my mouth." He spoke to Netta. "But you'd like my sex better. I must say, I do fancy your sweet lips and tongue on my cock. As to whether I'd be able to converse in English or French while you pleasured me, I would. How else would I be able to beg for more?"

Netta's cheeks turned bright pink. She covered her face.

"You have no answer? How about you, Aimee?"

She pretended offense. "You should be ashamed for listening to us."

"I had no choice. Both of you were leaning over me."

"We thought you were asleep. You should apologize."

"For not sleeping? I thought that's what you wanted. Me to be alert. I am. Can you forgive me?"

"I may." She kissed him.

So did Netta.

Aimee rested her chin on his arm. "Are you ready for more?"

"Not quite." He placed their hands on his limp cock. "But I will still see to your every need, beginning now."

* * * *

Heath left the bed and pulled on his breeches.

Netta grabbed his arm rather than his leg as she'd promised. "What are you doing?"

"Where are you going?" Aimee held his other arm.

"To finish the meal. You need to keep up your strength for me. I'll bring the bacon and bread to you. Relax and stay in here."

Past the entrance, he yawned and stretched.

They followed, knotting their cloths.

"If you want to watch to make certain I do nothing wrong, please do. But I'll tend to the food alone."

A small price to pay for all they'd given him. Even before Heath realized what he wanted, they knew what he should have. Them in his life. Him in theirs. Taking care of each other. Living out their destiny.

He wasn't a romantic, nor did he believe in fate. For some unknown and incredibly fortunate reason, he'd ended up here with them.

He set to work and located embers that still smoldered beneath the dirt. Half he used to start a new fire. The remaining ones he placed beneath the container they used to bake bread. "There." He slapped soot from his hands. "Your meal cooks. You can now await it in your house as I stated earlier."

They padded to it, whispering furiously to each other.

"I heard that."

Netta stilled. Aimee ducked past the cowhide.

Heath would have traded a month's sleep to know what they'd said. He loved teasing them. Given his bleak early years and endless labor as a man, he'd never had much chance to joke. When females were available and he could pay for their charms, he hadn't wanted to waste time with idle chatter.

How different to be with women who cared about more than a shiny coin or their next meal. Love made all the difference.

Aimee's and Netta's response to his touch told Heath what words never could.

They peeked from behind the cowhide.

He pointed the fork. "Inside, I said. I have a surprise." The idea had popped into his mind unbidden.

"What?" Netta sounded saucy rather than nervous.

"Wait on the bed and see or you might not get it."

Their feet slapped the packed-dirt floor. The bed frame creaked beneath their weight.

He had to put on a good show now. Thankfully, they'd nearly finished cooking the food when he'd interrupted, and no bugs had settled on the fare in his absence. After seeing to the fire and embers, he piled the bacon on one plate, the bread on the other.

At his return, Netta and Aimee stopped rocking on the mattress.

Heath washed his hands, removed his breeches, and blew on the food to cool it. "Take off your cloths and lie on the bed facing me. Not too close to each other though."

Netta made a face. "Why?"

Aimee regarded the food. "How can we eat lying down?"

"You shan't. Your meal comes after I eat. Do you mind that I'll go first?"

Aimee stared at his mouth. "I can see you talking, but what you say makes no sense."

"In time it will. Go on. Do as I asked...unless you don't want to play."

She removed her cloth as Netta did hers. They reclined side by side and held hands as frightened women would. Their bouncing feet betrayed their delight and anticipation.

He tested the bread and bacon. Both tepid. Perfect. "Promise you won't squeal or leave the bed no matter what I do."

Netta pushed to her elbow. "What have you planned?"

"It's a surprise." He ate a bacon slice. "Give me your word."

She exchanged a glance with Aimee. They shrugged to each other and nodded at him.

Heath sat between them and dragged bacon over their nipples. The dark circles tightened instantly. Nature had yet to produce a lovelier sight.

Netta grabbed his wrist. "This is how we eat?"

"It's how I do." He drew her hard tip and areola into his mouth. The meat flavored her velvety skin. He preferred her natural taste.

She released him and fell back. "Rub it between my legs."

"Mine too." Aimee spread her thighs and arched her back, her breasts presented to him.

She and Netta wore wide smiles.

He'd pleased them. A man couldn't receive a finer payment. Heath placed bacon pieces around their breasts, down their torsos, in their navels, and their springy curls. He followed his work with a breadcrumb trail. "How I hunger for you two. Should I eat?"

"Oui."

They'd answered as one, as they did most everything else, and had invited him into their lives. A privilege he wouldn't abuse. The affection they all shared with each other was an uncommon quality in a hard, ruthless world.

For them, he'd make everything pleasant, completely secure.

He sucked Aimee's nipples and licked Netta's breasts.

Each fought to get closer to him.

He gobbled the crumbs on their torsos.

They laughed.

The bacon in their navels didn't last long. He lingered to swirl his tongue around the small depressions before he shifted lower. Ravenous for their heat and scent, he found each crumb in their delectable curls.

Nothing on earth smelled better than they did.

Netta grabbed his hair, Aimee his hand. Neither let go.

They needn't have feared him leaving. At least not until death took him away. His place was at their side as protector, husband, and father to the children he hoped they'd both bless him with. He couldn't bear to see Aimee disappointed. Netta either, if they couldn't find anyone to say the vows over them.

A matter he refused to dwell on now. Tonight existed solely for pleasure.

He lapped their folds drenched with their womanly moisture. Further confirmation they wanted him as he did them.

They smelled of a fresh morning breeze, rich earth, sunshine, passion, love. Whether their goddess, or the spirit his people believed in, had created them, that being couldn't have done a finer job. Heath thanked both for a future he'd never believed possible. "Are you ready for me?"

Pure seduction widened Netta's smile.

Aimee licked her lips, her subdued manner in the past.

He wouldn't argue with that and selected her. A fair choice since he'd mounted Netta first the last go around.

Plunging into Aimee's tight, hot cunt made living worthwhile. The world stilled, silence closed in, and nothing existed except their joined bodies, her heat pouring into him, his into her. He sought greater closeness and wiggled his groin against her fragrant mound.

She pushed toward him too.

Exactly what Heath wanted. Still, he took care not to become too excited. He had Netta to satisfy.

He kissed Aimee deeply, stroked her nub, and pumped.

With each thrust, she grew wetter and more aroused. She clutched his shoulders and hair. Her channel narrowed around his cock.

Time for her to soar.

Fighting his base needs, he loved her hard and well.

She pulled her mouth from his. Her jubilant moan became a gasp and another delighted cry. Flushed and drenched with perspiration, she shuddered. Netta's turn.

Heath kissed Aimee gently and settled between Netta's legs.

She stroked his cheek with her maimed hand. "Do you need to rest first?"

Her trust in him gave Heath the energy he needed, coupled with boundless hope. "No. I'm ready for you."

"And I for you."

He kissed her scar, mounted, and sank deep.

Again, he knew heaven.

Chapter 12

Come dawn, Heath burst with plans for a well, irrigated vegetable and fruit gardens, a horse stable, pen for cattle, additional rooms, and lastly flowerbeds to surround his, Aimee, and Netta's house.

"Saves you ladies time gathering blossoms. Our home can smell as wonderful out here as it does within."

Netta sat on his left side, Aimee on his right. Sun colored the horizon light blue and gold, no clouds around to mar the sky. Another lovely day in store.

His stomach growled loudly.

Breakfast cooked over coals and a new fire. Using light from the bobbing flames, he'd drawn his plans in the dirt. A new thought struck. They'd have to have a stove in the house. Preparing meals out here was pleasant until the rains came. He added an X on his drawing to indicate the device.

Aimee covered her mouth to quiet a yawn. Netta blinked slowly, scarcely able to stay awake.

He'd given them scant time to sleep last night, his passion not easily satisfied. Despite the few hours he'd rested, he'd never been more eager to begin a day. "I hope you don't mind if we live here rather than my house." He'd failed to ask and wouldn't be that foolish again. They were a family now, everyone having an equal voice. "Or would you prefer a new place altogether? We can select a location we agree upon. Things will take longer that way. I'll have to develop new plans." He pointed at his drawings.

Aimee gestured to the one nearest her foot. "What is that?"

"Vegetable gardens. Over here is a spot for bananas and pineapples. We can even add a vineyard later."

"Tristan grows those things on the land beyond the stone house."

Heath cupped her chin. Her mussed hair, sleepy eyes, and lust-bruised lips made him fall more deeply in love. Same with Netta. Even after rest, they appeared identical. "If we have our own, you needn't haul the food from the courtyard."

Netta's delicate nostrils flared with her stifled yawn. "You could carry it for us."

"I shall until we have what we need here. We can trade our bounty with the other islanders for their help in building onto our house. We'll need a larger one surely. I suppose I could do the construction alone, but with several men at my side we can accomplish the goal far faster."

Netta shot a worried look at Aimee.

Confusion furrowed Aimee's brow. "You want to build a house as large as Tristan's? That could offend him. He is Capitaine. His word the final one."

"And things will remain as he wants. I have no desire to take over the island, people, or anything else. Our home won't be nearly as large as the mansion, but we do need extra room."

"Why?"

Netta frowned at him.

He wasn't sure how he'd offended Netta or what to say to Aimee. He'd merely discussed increasing their space for the children they'd have.

Ones Aimee might not be able to conceive.

What a bloody fool he was, excited about a matter painful to her. "Ah… Given how big I am, one room might not be enough for me…you…us to move about in freely. We don't want to be running into each other."

Aimee played with his fingers. "As we did last night? I like that."

"I do too. Enormously so." He tucked a stray tress behind her ear. The soft breeze tugged one out on the other side. "However, if you and Netta wanted to sleep while I prepared breakfast, it would be best if our kitchen was separated from our bedchamber so I wouldn't disturb you. See this?" He pointed to the X. "That will be our new stove to make meals indoors."

Netta scratched her shoulder. "Where do we get the stove?"

"I'll have to make one of stone, after the men and I build a smelting furnace to extract metal for utensils, pots, pans and such."

Aimee sagged to the ground, arm over her eyes. "Your words confuse me."

"Sorry. This evening, I'll show you drawings in the books I have. They'll explain everything."

"Why not now? We have light from the fire. Is it because I closed my eyes?"

"No. I need to get to the courtyard. I want to build a chair. I could use the one at my house, but it's not that sturdy. With the new one we can all sit at the table and eat a proper meal."

Netta laughed. "I like how you ate last night."

He draped his arm around her shoulders and gave her a hearty kiss. She was no less enthusiastic with him. Her hand roamed his chest and between his legs. The only place it should be. He finished their kiss and touched his nose to hers. "You, Aimee, and I shall do that again."

"At the midday meal?" Aimee lifted her arm.

"Fraid not. After the chair, I should start on the smelting furnace. Ourson will surely pester me until we start building the thing. I also have to speak with Royce. I was supposed to yesterday after I returned from collecting rocks, but forgot. If you're wondering, the rocks are for the furnace. I'll explain that tonight too."

The bacon popped. He turned it over.

Netta checked the bread. "Why does Royce want to talk? Did you two become enemies again?"

"We're getting along brilliantly. He's using Tristan's chart to map the quickest route for me to Faucon Island."

Aimee sat up. Netta leaned into her. They held hands.

Not as they had on the bed, their feet bobbing. Fear tightened their features.

If Heath had a choice, he would have avoided mentioning his departure until he sailed. He couldn't. They had to discuss him leaving and returning. Especially his homecoming. "Royce promised to find the safest way. One where ships rarely go. Please don't worry." He stroked their cheeks. "There's no need. The weather's fine. Mariners seek deeper water to reach the African coast for trade. That's not anywhere near here. Pirates follow them to board their ships. Those vessels are the ones with treasure, not what we use. The real danger I'll face is missing the only women I'll ever love."

He hoped his pretty words would produce a smile and put them back in his arms.

Aimee didn't look up.

Netta smoothed her cloth. "Will you bring the priest back?"

"He's another reason I'm going. Several islanders and Diana want their babes christened."

Aimee wound a tress around her finger. "Will you speak to him about us?"

Heath would rather face a pistol to his head. He'd had a bellyful of sermons at the workhouse, each filled with fiery threats for boys to seek a righteous way or else. Even as a child, he'd preferred the fury in Hell to the grim existence preachers inflicted on their flocks. At least before damnation, he'd have fun. "I won't tell him about us, if that's what you mean. It would be best if he and I got to know each other first. Become friends. That might ease the way for him to consider the vows."

"When he speaks of anything except his rules, the language he uses is different than ours." Netta brushed dirt off her foot. "Tristan calls it

Portuguese. Do you know it?"

He didn't. Could be a blessing. He wouldn't have to lie to the priest and remember what he'd said. "No. We'll have to wait until he's here and Tristan can have a word." Heath kissed their foreheads. "Breakfast is ready. I'm famished."

He ate heartily.

They nibbled their food. Their silence lengthened and held.

* * * *

In the courtyard, Ourson had laid out carpentry tools but no wood. The other boys flanked him. They regarded Heath as they would a god descending from on high.

"I told them about our rocks." Ourson circled Heath. "Put the sacks down so I can show them what we found."

"Take care and don't throw them at each other or anyone else."

"Only an infant would be so foolish. Not a quartermaster." He hit his fist against his skinny chest, indignation on his face.

Precisely the way Heath would have reacted. At that age, he'd longed to be a man too. Unfortunately, adulthood had proved nearly as challenging as his youth. "Of course, you wouldn't. I spoke in haste. Here you are." He lowered the sacks to the ground.

Ourson gestured his friends back. "No one touches these. Only me."

A younger child with light brown hair stuck his finger in his nostril. "Why?"

"They have fire inside." He pulled two out. "See how red they are. When you break them open, flames pour out."

The boys' eyes widened. The tallest leaned in. "Break them now."

"No." Ourson cradled the stones to him. "Heath and I have to build a…" He looked up. "What did you call it?"

"Smelting furnace." He opened the book and tapped the drawing. "Like this."

Ourson looked down his nose at the boys. "No one touches the book either. It belongs to Tristan."

Heath had to return it and the other volume, plus speak to Royce. "I must be going."

Ourson jumped to his feet. "Can I go too?"

"Not today. I'll come back shortly. When I do, we'll build a chair. Where is my wood?"

"I can bring it here." Ourson dashed across the courtyard.

Several boys followed, shouting they wanted to help.

No one was in the library this early. Heath returned the books to their proper locations but couldn't find Tristan's charts.

Tristan, Diana, Merry, James, Royce, and Peter were in the dining area. Diana wore diamonds and a blue silk gown. The men's chests were bare, but they had on new breeches. The surroundings were no less majestic. Sun streamed from an opening in the roof. Potted plants fluttered in the mild breeze. Fish, bacon, bread, and fruit filled silver trays on the table.

Though they lived a grand life in this place, Heath wasn't envious. He liked the home he'd share with Netta and Aimee. Hopefully, their pensive moods had passed and they'd get used to his departure. He dreaded them worrying even more.

Tristan peeled a boiled egg. "What brings you here?"

"I was looking for Royce." He spoke to him. "I returned late with Orson and continued home. Sorry. Are you still mapping the route?" A chart lay to his side.

Peter had another at his.

Heath prayed Diana hadn't changed her mind and Peter would now be accompanying him. Keeping Peter in line during the voyage wasn't a task Heath welcomed. His worry about Aimee, Netta, and the priest was enough.

Royce finished his tea. "Working on it now. We can discuss the details after breakfast."

Diana stroked Merry's back. She slept peacefully. "Would you care for something, Heath? We have plenty."

"Thank you, but no. I've already eaten. I would like to ask Tristan about the priest."

He finished his egg and gestured Heath to a chair. "What do you need to know?"

"What sort of man he is." Heath sat next to Royce. "His personality and beliefs. Is he strict or does he understand men can't always be proper when it comes to…" He couldn't go on with Peter here. "Perhaps we should speak in private."

"About Netta and Aimee?" Peter rested his arms on his head and grinned. "I already know about you and them. They came to me and I took them to Diana. Who do you think translated for everyone?"

Warmth shot to Heath's face and throat. "Thank you for being helpful."

James snickered.

"Enough." Tristan scowled at the men. "In a moment, you'll have Heath in tears."

Diana slapped Tristan's arm. "You're not making matters any better.

Answer the poor man's question."

"He didn't finish asking it."

Heath sagged in his chair. "How does he feel about women being with men? Intimately so."

"Oh that." Tristan swiped a linen napkin across his mouth and dropped it on the table. "He loves the ladies. Can't get enough for himself."

Diana regarded Heath sympathetically. "Forgive my husband. He loves to tease."

James laughed. "Not this time. He's telling the truth."

Peter nodded.

"What?" Diana sat up so quickly, Merry mewled. She soothed her. "Are you saying he indulges himself with women? Unheard of for a priest. I thought their church insisted on celibacy."

"As far as I know, they do." Tristan shrugged. "He doesn't hold firmly to that tenet."

"Clearly. What does that mean for the vows we exchanged before him? Were they true? Why didn't you tell me, and don't you dare say it's because I'm a woman and a mother. I had a right to know."

"Sorry, love." Tristan patted her hand. "He was the only religious man on the isle. I had no choice except to use him for our nuptials. Since the Church doesn't know what he does here, he hasn't been excommunicated. If they even do that for wayward priests. Perhaps they look the other way. In any event, he's still a holy man and the vows should stick."

"They had better. We have a child."

"And many more to come, I trust."

They exchanged an intimate smile.

Heath rubbed his neck. He admired Diana and Tristan's devotion to each other but their bloody passion kept getting in the way when he had real problems to solve. "Does this mean he'd be tolerant of my situation? Aimee and Netta have their hearts set on a proper wedding. I'll do whatever I can to make that happen."

"The most I can do is speak to him when he arrives."

Peter tented his hands and rested his chin on them. "You should threaten to withhold his food and drink until he agrees to see things as Netta and Aimee do. Given how he loves to imbibe and eat, he'd yield in a moment."

Diana stroked Merry faster. "Does he lack any vice?"

"Not that I know of. He sailed with me, Tristan, and James many times. When we boarded ships, he cut down several mariners before we had to."

"He murdered innocent men?"

Peter crinkled his nose. "They were hardly innocent. If he hadn't done them in, one of us would have been dead."

Hope sprang anew for Heath. Perhaps he could persuade the man to see matters his way. "This has been most enlightening."

Diana shook her head.

Royce pushed the chart toward Heath. "This is your best route." He ran his finger northeast from this isle to Faucon.

"Or he might try this." Peter brought his map over and showed another way. "James and I took this passage when we brought the prisoners there."

Heath's unfamiliarity with the area made him cautious. "I'm an excellent mariner, but I don't know these islands. Tristan, which do you think is best?"

Though Bishop had called Tristan a worthless fool, no man could have evaded capture as long as he had unless he knew the sea better than himself. Heath trusted his opinion.

Tristan pored over the maps and selected Royce's choice.

Peter crossed his arms. "I still say my way is best."

Heath committed the route to memory. "Perhaps the next time."

"Next time?" Diana bounced Merry, who'd awakened and whimpered loudly. A cry or shriek could be next. "If you're able to marry Netta and Aimee will you'll be doing this again?"

"Even if I can't wed them, this will probably be my last voyage. They worry greatly. For no good reason. Perhaps you could talk to them."

"My French isn't fluent enough yet. If I upset them and they start speaking quickly, I wouldn't be able to follow."

Peter leaned against the table. "I could translate. What would you like me to tell them?"

"To keep their man here." Diana transferred Merry to her other shoulder. "Where he belongs."

Peter pinched his nose. "I should have asked Heath."

"Very well." Heath rapped the table. "I'd have Diana say what I've told them repeatedly. The journey is short and simple. Absolutely no danger. Nothing bad will befall me."

* * * *

Vincent lay face down in the pen he shared with the other prisoners. He hadn't budged in three days except to sip water and take in scant food. An islander had whipped him for not hauling enough wood and not digging a hole fast enough. Bloody savage. Stupid fool. Matching wits with everyone on this isle proved easy for Vincent. He'd deliberately caused trouble to encourage punishment, pretended the welts on his back burned worse than they did, and feigned grievous injury by taking in little water and almost nothing to eat. At least while anyone watched.

When no one could get him to move, the healer had examined him. He supposed she said he was unfit for labor. Once she left, he didn't have to work any longer and everyone else stayed clear.

Not Canela.

Since he'd claimed this spot, she'd taken to strolling by at night. Close enough for him to smell her dark skin and the cloyingly sweet flowers she rubbed on herself. They didn't remove her island stench. She'd never be more than an animal to him. Her kind had no purpose except to serve his people. He'd bloody well make certain she did so.

He waited for her approach.

The waning moon barely lit the sky much less the earth. Even with his eyes adjusted to the inky blackness, Vincent couldn't see any better than a blind man. However, his hearing was excellent.

Across the pen, a man coughed. Surf swelled and broke. Bushes rustled when they shouldn't have. There wasn't significant wind to disturb them. Someone was out there.

Feet padded close. Canela's sickening fragrance wafted toward him.

He breathed through his mouth but didn't expect her to acknowledge his presence. Ample time had passed for the bird to deliver its message and return. She could have told him days ago.

Tonight, she laughed softly, derisively. The sound pinpointed her location.

Vincent jumped to his shackled feet, clamped his hand around her throat, and pressed his mouth to her ear. "You best not be treating me lightly unless you care to die."

She writhed and clawed him.

He tightened his grip. Not enough to strangle her but to prove she'd never best him. Not even in his current state, fettered and half-starved.

Her hands fell away.

A good first step. He loosened his hold slightly. "Tell me about the bird. Don't lie. I'll know if you do and you won't live to tell another one."

She stiffened.

He squeezed.

"It returned. Tristan's men sail here next month to deliver seeds and to bring the priest back with them."

The seeds made sense. The crops here were failing miserably. Damn islanders weren't intelligent enough to grow food unless an Englishman showed them how. The priest though… "Seems you do want to die. Tristan isn't a pious man. He wouldn't risk a ship or his crew for a bloody priest."

He pressed his thumb into her throat.

She clenched his wrist. "He would for Diana. They had a child and want the priest to christen her."

The last time Vincent had seen Diana, she'd been in her tub naked save for the diamonds about her throat. When he'd attacked, wanting them and her, she clutched her belly as a woman would when carrying something more precious than jewels or gold. "What do you know, Tristan's a father now. How interesting."

"Oui. We can use the child to bring him to his knees."

"Quite right. I'd wager him losing his little girl would drive him quite mad."

"And destroy Diana."

Canela's venom impressed Vincent. Once harnessed, her rage could prove most useful. "You claim they sail to this isle next month. The beginning? The end? When?"

"No one said."

"Of course not, but you'll tell me when they do, eh? Not good enough." He yanked her to him. "I want dates and details now. Everything you overheard. If you don't tell me, I'll share your secret with these savages. If they don't kill you outright, they may hack off your arms and legs. Other pirates told me they do that here to those they don't like. Without your limbs, how will you escape? How will you eat or even survive? They'll leave you to starve to death slowly. Perhaps on display for everyone to point at and laugh. If you cry out, they'll cut out your blasted tongue. That's another torture these animals love."

She whimpered.

Sounded fearful but could be an act. With her, anything was possible. He maintained his caution. "Talk."

Canela turned her face into his, her mouth on his ear.

"Bite me and you're dead. To hell with escape. I'll gladly kill you right here and now."

"If you tell them about my secret—our secret to leave here, the men would come after you next. Do you think anyone here would spare you?"

"I have no doubt they'd murder me in a second. I'm not talking about our plan. It's not the only thing you're keeping from them, is it?"

"What do you mean? There is nothing else."

"No? What about the cook nearly dying because you fooled with her food? Used too many sleeping herbs, did you? That was an unfortunate mistake. A damn foolish one too. You might have ruined everything. Luckily, she's as sturdy as a bull and survived. What do you think she and the others would do if they knew what you were up to?"

Canela stilled.

Vincent wagered she no longer breathed. "Betray me in the least, keep even the smallest information from me and I'll tell them everything I know."

"How?" She sniffed. "You only speak English, not French."

"I can point. First to you, then to where you hid the herbs in your pen, then to the pot you cook food in. Even a dolt would be able to figure out what I was trying to say. The cook might not believe me. I can see she likes you, fool that she is. But the large woman wants you dead. She's waiting for a chance to bring you down. Want me to help her?"

"No. We need to do this together, as you said, so we best Tristan. I had to test the sleeping herbs to know how much to use for our escape."

How sweet. She spoke of them as partners again, rather than him as an inconvenience. Vincent didn't trust her for a second. "Use all of it when it's time to leave. Who cares if these savages ever wake up? If they're dead they can't stop us, now can they?"

"No. What about Diana's child?"

"What about her?"

"She's mine, not yours."

"Take the brat if you like. Do whatever you choose with her. I want the jewels, gold, and Diana. At least until she bores me and I put a bullet in her head."

"Have you said anything to your men about this?"

"I bloody well can't if I don't know details." Even with the information, Vincent would keep everything to himself until the last moment. The safest way so no one could cross him. Except Canela. Protecting himself from her would prove difficult enough. "When do they set sail?" He squeezed her throat. A warning that her answer had better not evade the issue as it had before or disappoint him.

"The second week."

That would put them here during the third. Considering wind conditions, it should take approximately a fortnight to leave Tristan's island, arrive here, and return. Unless some island custom required a ceremony in addition to trade. Thus far, the natives here had traveled to Tristan's isle, not the other way around. "Do your people have a celebration after they trade with these savages?"

"No, but Tristan always gave them shelter and food so they could rest before they returned."

He'd expect the ones here to do the same for his crew. Tristan was hell bent on everyone behaving honorably. Vincent had no use for niceties. Every second here made his skin crawl. "What's the longest they stayed?"

"No more than two days."

Wasted time. Unless he used it to interrogate those who sailed here as he had the islanders who'd led him to Tristan.

Many had died in that quest.

He didn't doubt several would perish during this one.

Chapter 13

Netta climbed the hill, Aimee beside her. Wind lashed their hair, cloths, and the tall grass. Sun warmed cool ocean air.

The Lady Lark bobbed on gentle swells, waiting for her crew. Tomorrow morning, Heath would leave for Faucon.

Netta shivered as she would when lightning flashed or thunder roared. Loss and heartache had filled her dreams. Upon awakening, she tried to capture the pictures in her mind to ward off whatever trouble approached. The images remained elusive. Her dread mounted. She hid her alarm from Heath.

He promised to return, wanting to be at her and Aimee's side for a lifetime. Netta believed him. She'd felt the same about her parents, relatives, and friends. Then fate arrived and took them away on a day like this. One meant for love not ruin.

Nothing had been the same for her and Aimee until Heath landed on this isle.

At the hilltop, she gripped Aimee's hands. They lifted their faces to the seamless blue sky, the goddess's home where she looked down on them. Aimee had argued against praying for Heath's safety. Even mentioning a problem could rouse evil spirits. Best to be quiet so they couldn't find him.

Netta didn't know what to believe. She feared the destructive ones who brought storms, sickness, and death. Yet she couldn't allow Heath to leave without the goddess's protection and guidance. That could result in disaster he wouldn't survive.

Trembling, she prayed more fervently than she had when the pirates had taken her. Then, she begged for death to be with her parents again. Instead, the goddess had spared her. Netta had railed against the cruel decision not realizing how wise it was. Someone had to protect Aimee.

She hugged her twin.

Aimee clung to her. "Everything will be all right. He will return. He loves us. Tell me. Say the words."

They caught in Netta's throat. Darkness tormented her. Snatches from her dream came back and faded like smoke, too quick to grasp.

Aimee clutched her harder. "Say something. Stop frightening me."

"Heath will return. The goddess must listen to us this time. She will. We can speak to the priest's god too. He may help. We have nothing to fear."

Aimee wilted against her, accepting words Netta wanted to believe but feared might prove empty.

A bird squawked. Leaves rustled. An animal squealed.

"Netta? Aimee?" Heath asked. "What are you doing up here?"

He padded through rippling grass that reached his knees. A stiff breeze tugged his hair in every direction. His bronze skin glistened beneath the sun.

Netta ran to him. She wound her arms around his torso and rested her cheek near his heart. Its powerful thunder calmed and aroused her.

Aimee settled behind Heath, hugged him, and squeezed Netta's arms, desperate for reassurance.

He patted her hands and kissed Netta's forehead. "Are you worried whether the Lady Lark is fit for sea? Is that why you're up here? To look at it?"

"Oui." Netta couldn't tell him the truth. If he worried about her dreams, that might cause him more trouble. "We wanted to see how it looks."

"You'll have a better chance tomorrow before I set sail. I'll take you two on board if you want. Show you around."

"No." Aimee held him harder and dug her fingers into Netta. "Pirates said a woman on a ship brings bad luck."

"Not Tristan, I hope." Heath chuckled. "He's too wise for that superstitious nonsense. To find him, Diana sailed from England to Madagascar on the Lady Lark. She and Tristan are quite alive. Say you'll let me show you the ship. That will ease your worry greatly."

Until he left here. Netta wasn't certain she could watch him go. His absence would become too real. "Must we speak of this?"

"Not if you don't want to."

"Hold me."

Aimee made a pained sound. "Me too."

He gathered them in his arms.

Netta kissed his chest and dipped her hand to his sex. Nothing warmed her more than his hard shaft and firm sac. Both came alive within her embrace.

Aimee pushed Netta's hand aside, her usual deference lost beneath brutal need. They required him equally.

"You tempt me too much." He sank to the grass, bringing them with him. Within the fragrant blades, they undressed.

Hidden dew cooled Netta's skin. Heath's lips on her breast, his hand between her legs made her burn. She couldn't kiss him deeply enough, nor could he do so with her.

He freed his mouth to claim Aimee's.

Empty without him, Netta took his cock fully into her mouth.

He squirmed and grunted, the sound faint from his tongue between Aimee's lips or hers between his.

Salty fluid seeped from the tiny opening in his crown. Soon, Heath would release his seed, though not in her mouth. She wanted him inside her. She ached for his child and hoped Aimee would have an infant too.

Before Netta could release him, he broke free of Aimee. "Enough of that." He clasped Netta's shoulders. "I want your cunt."

His rigid shaft slipped from her lips and grazed her chin. "Fill me."

"Me too." Aimee kissed his biceps. Tears rolled down her cheeks.

Aimee's sorrow tore at Netta's heart. "Heath can love you first after I make a soft bed for you."

She spread her purple cloth and Aimee's yellow one over matted grass and rolled Heath's breeches to form a pillow.

Aimee kissed her cheek. She settled on the sweet-smelling growth and opened her arms to him.

He smiled at Netta then entered Aimee swiftly, his strong body tense with passion, muscles gleaming in the light.

Netta drank him in, enthralled by his potent masculinity, surprising grace, and wondrous scent. Yet nothing bewitched as his tenderness did. It made him more powerful.

He laced his fingers with Aimee's. They gazed at each other and smiled, their complexions ruddy, breaths rough, skin moist. With each hard thrust, his hair swung. Their tapping bodies made alluring music that stirred Netta's soul.

Aimee lifted her chin and closed her eyes. She squeezed Heath's fingers so tightly hers blanched.

As she sped toward release, he fought the same, jaw clenched, shoulders bunched.

Aimee cried out.

Lemurs raced through the branches. An animal darted about in the grass.

Heath stilled. Breathing hard, he brushed his lips over Aimee's. "Merci. *Je t'adore.*" I adore you.

"And I you. Love Netta now."

"I fully intend to."

Arms wide, she encouraged desire and kissed him leisurely, a slow exploration of his mouth and tongue. A lovely way to savor the man he was and give him a chance to rest.

Heath didn't allow her gentleness for long. His impassioned kiss stole Netta's breath and thoughts, leaving naught except indecent need.

They mated like animals and strove to get deeper, closer, to become part of each other's being. No matter how well, long, or much he loved her, Netta would never be sated or free from wanting more. He'd captured and claimed her readily. His smile, laughter, respect, and love toppled the walls she'd built around herself faster than any threat could.

He was too wonderful for this merciless world.

He had to return to her and Aimee.

Netta's release pounded into her. Heath's pleased shout announced his. Together, they floated down. Sated but not finished with each other.

* * * *

Excellent weather held the following morning, a few puffy clouds on the horizon. Island men gathered at the hidden cove to help Heath prepare the Lady Lark for departure.

Netta and Aimee stood on the bank, arms around each other, faces down.

He eased their hair off their shoulders and froze at his stupid action. If anyone saw him being too friendly, Aimee and Netta would endure their people's unkind words, or worse, while he set sail. He stepped back and crossed his arms. "Sure you don't want to board and have a look?"

With any luck, it would calm them. Neither had slept much last night. When he woke at dawn, they were outside, breakfast already cooked and cooled. While he ate and they didn't, he drew a map in the dirt to show the route he'd take. He'd explained tides, wind patterns, ocean currents, everything he could think of to give them a better understanding of why men did this without concern or regret. Traversing London streets was far more dangerous given the multitudes there, including equally depraved nobles and commoners. Out here, people were rare.

Nothing he'd said had any effect. They listened without comment.

Same as now. "Come and take a look with me, please. It's quite safe."

Netta pressed closer to Aimee. "We can stay here."

Tristan approached and tipped his head. "Ladies." He took a brace of pistols from his shoulder and handed them to Heath. "These are yours. The islanders will bring their own arms. There are additional weapons aboard the ship should you need them."

Aimee and Netta dashed away.

Heath wished Tristan had used an earlier moment to give him these and to make such a dire pronouncement. "Thank you. Excuse me."

He caught up with Netta and Aimee. "The weapons are simply a precaution, nothing more. The same as how you avoid snakes by staying on a known path rather than traveling through deep brush. Danger is all around but that doesn't mean it will come close."

"Heath."

Adamo. Given what he'd been through with Canela, he couldn't have agreed to take this journey.

Heath held up his hand. "I'll be with you in a moment." He bent down to Aimee and Netta. "Stay here, please. I'll return shortly." Heath joined Adamo and shook his good hand. "Are you accompanying us?"

"No. I wanted to give you this." He untied a cord from his waistband button. A medallion dangled from the leather, intricate symbols carved into the wood.

"This is excellent work. You're quite skilled. What do the carvings mean?"

"They offer good luck. When you wear this, it keeps demons away. Male and female."

He had to mean Canela. Given what everyone here said, Heath suspected he'd soon meet Medusa in the flesh. "Thank you, my friend." He embraced Adamo and lowered his voice. "Please see that Netta and Aimee are well during my absence. In helping them, we've all become close."

"You love them."

Heat crept up Heath's neck. "We're friends."

"Your eyes say more. So do theirs. Both are good women and need a brave man. My heart smiles for your good fortune."

"Merci. Others might not feel the same."

"The women you mean." He made a dismissive noise. "Who you love is up to you, but I promise to keep my tongue. So will Zola. We can visit Aimee and Netta every day and feed them so much both will be fat by the time you return."

Heath laughed. "You're a good man. I look forward to working with you in the coming days."

"We can help each other."

Anyone who called these people uncivilized was a damn fool.

Islanders carried food onboard. Enough for the crew and the other natives to tide them over until their yields improved. Tristan also provided horses, pigs, chickens, and cows. Diana had thrown in silk cloths for the women, new breeches and linen shirts for the men, and several cribs for the babes that Heath had built.

He suspected she was behind Tristan's extreme generosity, not wanting the Lady Lark or anyone here to depart these shores again for a long while.

Heath itched to leave so he could return. He'd once considered commanding a ship to be a man's greatest goal. He knew better now. Serving his family as a good husband and father mattered far more.

He stepped out of an islander's way and bumped into Michel. "Sorry." He shook Michel's hand. "Didn't expect to see you here. How is Ourson?"

"Proud of his papa."

Heath wasn't certain what Michel meant and simply nodded. Yards away, Orson danced in place next to mama Esme. He waved at Heath.

He returned the greeting. "Would you and Esme mind if I showed Ourson the ship?" Heath should have thought of that earlier. "I'm sure he'd be delighted."

"I showed him before you came here." Michel colored slightly. "I should have asked first, no?"

"Absolutely not. It's not my ship, and I'm sure Tristan wouldn't mind. Did Ourson enjoy himself?"

"Oui. He wanted to see where I would sleep during the voyage."

"You're coming with us?"

"To tend the horses, but also for another reason." He leaned in. "I want Ourson to boast about me as he does you."

Heath regretted befriending Ourson, coming between him and Michel. "You're his papa. There's no greater man on earth to a son. I'm a poor substitute. You don't have to take this journey to prove anything."

"I want to come if you can allow it."

"Of course." He clamped Michel's shoulder. "Another friend on board is precisely what I need. May I have a word with Ourson?"

"If he gives you time to speak."

Heath chuckled and motioned Ourson over.

He couldn't keep still. "The ship is so big. All the islanders' houses would fit inside with enough room for the stone house and courtyard."

"Aye. But size is no match for brains and good sense." Heath tapped his head. "Like your papa has. Only a skilled man could get horses onto a ship. The animals frighten easily. Without Michel, I don't think I could make this journey. I'm not as brave as he is."

Ourson took his papa's hand. "He protects me and mama all the time. He can carry more rocks than you ever will. He can lift a horse in his hands."

Michel laughed. "A foal, not one fully grown."

"You can. I know it. Show Heath your muscle."

"My what?"

"Like this." Heath held up his arm but barely flexed.

Michel did the same.

"Squeeze your fist, Papa. As hard as you can."

He did and produced an imposing bulge.

Ourson clapped. "My papa is the strongest man in the world."

Heath pointed. "And always will be." He put out his hand. "Shall we shake like men and say our goodbyes?"

Ourson squeezed quite hard.

"You're nearly as strong as your father. Well done."

Tristan joined them. "Are you close to leaving?"

"Only a few more things to do."

"Then I'll say my goodbye now so I can return to Diana and Merry." He shook Heath's hand and surprised him with a firm embrace. "You've earned my respect and trust. I'm proud to call you friend." He stepped back and waited until Michel and Ourson had left. "Promise not to do anything foolish. I wouldn't want to deal with Aimee and Netta if you're unduly delayed."

"I've memorized the route but I've also copied it and the one Peter suggested. Both await me in the cabin. The ship is sound, my crew excellent, the weather fair. The only trouble I can predict is boredom."

"That's a mariner's worst risk and greatest downfall. Trust the sea and she'll do you in every time. Always remain vigilant, especially when your surroundings are calm. That's when many men forget to do something and end up beneath the water rather than on top. Mind you, Diana will never forgive me if you don't return."

Heath lowered his voice as Tristan had. "Neither will Netta or Aimee. Can you and Diana see to their welfare during my absence? Make certain they don't worry too much? Adamo and Zola are going to, but they're islanders. You're capitaine. Aimee and Netta may listen to you."

"I'll do my best, but I won't promise anything. Before I forget, take this." He removed a pouch from his waistband and gave it to Heath. "Diana wanted Aimee and Netta to have these should they be unable to wear your marriage collar."

Two gold bracelets glinted in his palm, each carved with flowers and vines. Identical to the last detail and most likely priceless. "I can't accept these."

"You can and will. Your women can wear them to prove they belong to you. I know you're hoping the priest will relent, and he should, considering his proclivities. Should he hold firm to his teachings, you have those to fall back on."

"I can never repay you or Diana."

"Bring the ship, our people, and yourself back in one piece and we'll call things even. Best you say goodbye to your ladies now. The men are ready to leave."

Heath ran to Aimee and Netta. He directed them into a stand so the others wouldn't see and kissed them breathless. Still holding on, he spoke softly. "I'm leaving now. Before I go, I have something for you. Consider it proof of my devotion."

He gave them the bracelets.

Most women would have squealed and hugged him soundly.

Their tears fell faster.

"I will return, I promise. You'll wear these bracelets until I can replace them with marriage collars. Somehow, I'll do that too. I give you my word."

He kissed them a final time and bolted toward the vessel.

* * * *

Ismay gestured to the two fires and cooking pots. "Why is there more than one?"

"I woke early and did this to surprise you." Canela offered her sweetest smile. "Do you like it?"

"Is the smaller one for the children?"

"No, the bigger pot is for those born on this isle, young, old, male, female. The other holds the slaves' food. Why should they share with free men and women? They never earned the right." She lowered her face. "Nor have I. Whatever the prisoners eat, I will too."

"You can share mine. I want no argument. How did you think of this?"

Vincent had insisted Canela separate the food. He didn't trust her to keep the sleeping herbs from his bowl and promised to expose her if she didn't follow his plan. He wasn't as stupid as she'd hoped. Nor as pliant as Adamo had been. Destroying Vincent would be a challenge and her greatest joy, as soon as she didn't need him any longer. "If not for your people, the slaves would starve or boars would eat them when they sought food outside the community. None deserves your kindness, especially me, a foolish, stupid girl. I keep trying to learn and promise to be better. Tell me what I did makes you happy." She pressed Ismay's hand to her face. "I beg you."

"With your help, I sleep more than I ever did and have little to do when I wake. I like everything you do." She stroked Canela's cheek and crouched. "I can stir the larger pot now."

"You should rest. I put water and a soft pillow in the stand." Canela pointed. On such a warm day, the drink and shade would seduce the strongest man, even Tristan.

Ismay squinted. "Where did the red sacks come from? What did you put in them?"

"While you slept, I picked herbs and spices. You can choose the best for you and the islanders' meals and leave what remains for the prisoners. They hardly deserve anything except water and the smallest vegetables, but if you want I can make their fare tasty."

"They need to eat or they may grow too weak to work."

"They should accept whatever you give them. When my hunger's at its worst, I eat berries and sometimes leaves to keep my belly from hurting for more."

"We have enough food for the islanders and you." She scooped the vegetable stew into a bowl and handed it to Canela.

"No." She poured it back into the pot and barely filled her bowl from the smaller cauldron. "What I eat must be fit for a slave."

"Do you truly want that?"

Canela nodded. She had to accustom them to her not eating what they did so they wouldn't ask questions later. If Tristan's crew intended to reach these shores when they claimed, they'd leave his isle this morning. In days, they'd be here and she'd have to implement her plan.

This would surely be her only chance.

A scheme she and Vincent had decided together, though not the part she had yet to tell him.

* * * *

Islanders unfurled the Lady Lark sails. Wind filled them and pushed the ship toward the open sea. Its tang overwhelmed other scents Aimee preferred. Heath's musk, heated flesh, sweet breath, the flowers, forest, and earth surrounding them that made up their home. With him gone, the isle smelled different.

Her heart cramped. Terror pressed close. She wanted to scream that something was amiss, danger waited, and beg him to return. He wouldn't listen. Men never did. They challenged the devil or the demons her people feared and believed they would win.

Perhaps Englishmen could.

Hoping for that, she lifted her hand in farewell.

Heath smiled and mouthed, 'Je t'adore.'

The same as he had on the hill and in her dream last night. Once the words left his mouth then, the ship sank.

She ran.

Netta called, "Where are you going?"

Aimee bolted past others who watched the men depart. She tore through forest into a glade and up the gentle slope where Heath had made love to her and Netta. Birds fought the wind and changed direction so they wouldn't run into her. As she passed, thick insect swarms darted left and right.

Panting, she faced the water.

The Lady Lark leaned left. What Heath called east when he showed her and Netta his drawing by the fire.

Aimee climbed higher and pushed to her toes. Near the shore, the ship had loomed larger than she'd expected. It towered over the men and gave her hope they could seek shelter and protection inside. They'd be safe and would return. From up here, the Lady Lark became a mere speck again, surrounded by endless sea. Tiny. Helpless. Vulnerable.

She covered her mouth.

Netta raced through the grass and shook Aimee. "Nothing will happen to him. You must believe that. Say it."

Aimee couldn't. "Did you dream last night?" Their parents and the elders had thought Netta might have a gift for foresight. As a child, she'd predicted when a certain crop would fail or an animal would take ill. She's wasn't always right. She hadn't cautioned about the pirates. But her forewarnings on other matters were frequent enough for the men to take action to stop trouble before it arrived. "Tell me."

"I never slept or closed my eyes. I watched over Heath."

"Why? What frightened you? What did you see? Will he be all right?"

"I told you he will."

"I dreamed his ship sank."

"No." Netta backed away. "Never say that again."

"We have to beg the goddess for help. Ask her to ward off any evil that follows him." Aimee ran to bushes covered with fat, scented petals. The bracelet fell from her hand. She'd forgotten it and gestured Netta over. "We should offer the gold to the goddess, along with sweet flowers and herbs. Our gifts will please her enough to protect him."

"We also have our silk cloths. The goddess would like those."

"And our fruit, the grain, and bacon."

"She can have it all. The priest's god too. We can save some for Him and light candles as the priest told us. Come." Netta took Aimee's hand and pulled her down the slope. "We have much to do and many prayers to say."

"Wait." Aimee held back. "Did you dream last night? Tell me the truth."

Netta regarded the sea. The ship was on a straighter course now, what Heath called north. "No, I did not."

"Look at me and say that."

She wouldn't.

Chapter 14

Fresh bread, platters with meat, and fruit in bowls overflowed Netta and Aimee's table.

Even though they'd always provided for themselves, ever since Heath sailed everyone wanted to feed them. First, Adamo and Zola had come to offer food. At Diana and Tristan's request, Peter, James, and Royce brought more. Each day was the same. All smiled and asked if matters were well. If they could do anything else to make things better.

Netta resisted screaming at them to bring Heath back. He shouldn't have gone. Her dreams turned darker each night. She wanted him, not this feast.

Aimee scarcely ate. She stared at something only she could see.

This morning, Netta had reached her limit. Despite everyone's smiles, the gifts were a bad omen. Even the goddess didn't want them. Instead, she sent warnings during Netta's sleep that awakened her with a gasp and left her covered in sweat. "We need to go to the stone house and speak to Tristan."

Aimee pushed off the mattress. The dark circles beneath her eyes were worse. "About Heath?"

Netta gestured to the bacon, pineapples, boiled eggs, and more. "This. Why is everyone giving us so much? They tell us to eat but the amount they bring and keep offering makes no sense. The table is already full. Next, the chairs, mattress, and floor. You and I could never finish this."

Aimee brightened. "Perhaps Heath will return sooner than he claimed. This is their way to tell us."

"Why not speak the truth to ease our heartache?"

"They want to surprise us when he comes home."

"And worry us to death before he does? None of them is that cruel, especially Adamo. Even if they were, Tristan would never allow such a thing."

Aimee's mouth turned down. "Then they want us to offer these things to the goddess for Heath's safe return. The priest's god too. Neither has listened to us or accepted our gifts and brought him back sooner."

Netta tied a red cloth around her hips. "Tristan and the others are keeping something from us. The food soothes their guilt and stops us from asking too many questions." She put out her hand. "Come. We need to go to the stone house to find out what's going on."

Sun grazed the courtyard walls and streamed inside. Children played quietly, hair mussed from sleep. Mothers prepared areas where they worked. Something smacked loudly in the kitchen.

Gavra looked up from a bacon slab, her knife in hand. "Good. I could use your help. Laure's still asleep. Peter keeps her up too late." She muttered a French oath. "Put on the water for tea and—"

"Not now." Netta pulled Aimee past the table. "We have to speak to Tristan."

"Before he eats? Why?"

Netta had no patience for anyone's questions. She had her own that demanded answers. "Tell James not to bring food to me and Aimee. We have more than we need or want. Give it to the other islanders so they can rest rather than cook." She led Aimee into the cool, darkened hall.

Feet slapped behind them. Gavra watching.

Netta didn't care. She reached Tristan's bedchamber and knocked forcefully.

Merry shrieked.

Tristan hollered English words.

Netta could shout too. "*Je ne comprends pas ce que vous dites!*" I do not understand what you say!

"Netta?" He spoke French. "What do you want?"

"Aimee and I must speak to you. Now. Not later. Now."

"Why?"

She hit the door so hard her fist hurt.

Aimee covered her face. "Anger him and he may not tell us anything."

"Then you and I will stay here until he—"

Tristan yanked the door open. He wore breeches and a hard scowl, his face whiskered, hair uncombed, eyes mere slits from too little sleep. "What's wrong?"

Merry wailed. Diana crossed the room, her violet gown wrinkled, hair in disarray, face weary. She bounced Merry and paced. Merry wouldn't calm.

"Keep holding her as you are and her crying will never end." Netta brushed past Tristan to Diana.

She stepped back, eyes wide, but spoke French. "What are you doing?"

"I mean no harm." Netta calmed as much as she could and spoke slowly so Diana would understand. "I only want to show you how to quiet Merry's cries."

Tristan touched Diana's arm. "Did you understand that?"

She nodded.

Tristan gestured to Netta. "*Allez.*" Go on. "Say what you must. If Diana has trouble understanding, I'll translate. Show her what you mean."

"I would, but my hand…" She held up what the pirate had left her with, no longer ashamed for anyone else to see. Heath's love had made her strong. She wanted him back here today, now. Tears threatened. She pushed her emotions back. "Aimee can show her." Netta gestured her inside. "No harm will come to Merry."

Diana smiled. "I know. I trust you. Are you certain you don't want to do this?"

"Aimee would be better."

Diana handed Merry over.

Merry squirmed and screamed, her face darker than Netta's cloth and Aimee's cheeks.

"You fold her arms in front." Aimee showed them.

Diana watched carefully and nodded.

Aimee went on. "And put your hand lightly on her neck like this." She circled Merry's throat with her thumb and forefinger while also keeping the babe's arms down. "Hold her here, as I do." Her other hand cupped Merry's bottom. "Then you bounce her, but not too much." Gently, she moved the infant up and down.

Merry calmed.

Diana's eyes widened. "What you did was a, ah…" She breathed hard then brightened. "A miracle. I must say, a much needed one."

Tristan leaned against the door. "Why didn't we know about this sooner? The island women could have told us. Better still, Gavra."

Netta tapped her foot. "Did you ask them?"

"No." He scratched his neck. "My fault entirely. But it still doesn't explain about Gavra. Willy keeps James up many nights. Why didn't she do this too?"

"Perhaps she did but Willy is like his papa and wants her attention constantly and cries for it."

Tristan roared. "That could be."

Diana looked at them. "*Ce qui?*" What?

They'd talked too quickly.

He told Diana what they said and spoke to Netta and Aimee. "I can't thank you ladies enough. I must repay you both for this kindness."

Netta waved her hands. "We want no more of your food. Most will spoil before we can eat it. Why are you giving us so much?"

"Heath asked us to watch over you in his absence. We said we would. We thought you'd like to take a rest from gathering food and cooking. It goes no further than that. He's an excellent mariner. He's fine."

Diana touched Tristan's arm and spoke English. They conversed quietly. He nodded. "Diana wanted to tell you this herself, but she thought I could convey the thought with less trouble. She said my assurances about Heath don't ease your concern and if I wasn't by her side, she wouldn't be calm either. We do understand how you feel. She suggested while Heath is gone, you both might want to stay in this house. With people around, you'll have someone to talk to. I'll be here. You can stop me whenever you want and ask whatever you wish. Would that ease your burden?"

Aimee nodded.

So did Netta. "We promise not to bother you too much and we could help Gavra in the kitchen as we do when she needs us."

"I have a better idea. Let me confer with Diana first." He spoke to her in English.

She beamed. "Oui, oui, oui."

He laughed. "Seems she agrees with me. But you two must do so also. If you don't mind, you can care for Merry while Diana rests. She's gotten little sleep these last days. We can give you the chamber next to this one. Would that be all right?"

Netta couldn't imagine a more perfect solution. With Tristan close by, she and Aimee could question him about Heath whenever their worries arose. "Caring for Merry would be our pleasure. With us, her crying will be at an end."

Tristan closed his eyes. "I won't be able to thank you enough for that."

* * * *

Heath checked the stars against the map in his mind. His course proved steady. Despite the deep water and meager wind, he ordered some sails furled to slow the ship further. No need to race headlong into trouble, even if the nightly delays annoyed him.

At times, it seemed they crawled across the water rather than glided. He hadn't realized how much he'd miss Aimee and Netta. Everywhere he went, whatever he did, they loomed close, yet were too far away. He fingered the medallion and wished Adamo's carvings could bring him enough luck to reach home far sooner.

Michel joined Heath. "Capitaine."

Although Heath liked the title the crew used, he wasn't convinced he deserved it and certainly wouldn't have demanded the address. Their willing respect touched him and provided hope they, like Adamo, would see nothing wrong with him loving two women. "Oui?"

"The men you asked for are in the great cabin."

"Merci." Heath pulled his hair off his neck. The moist wind brought it back. "I'd like you to join us." Michel would have another tale to tell Ourson.

Before going below, Heath called to Phillipe in the crow's nest. "Everything all right?"

"Oui. Nothing is in our way."

Except too much blasted time. At the wheel, Heath spoke to Gérard. "Don't push yourself too hard. If you need relief or sleep, ask another man to take your place. I'll be in the great cabin."

Upon his arrival, Etienne, Rollan, and Julien stood. All young and strong with islander coloring and their people's handsome features.

Heath gestured them and Michel to their seats and took his. "I asked you here because you've been to Faucon before. You know their customs. We have only another full day before we reach land. What can we expect?" He should have asked before he left, but his concern over Netta and Aimee distracted him from practical matters.

Twenty-year-old Rollan sat shoulders above the others. "The community lies close to shore, not like our people's. They have few fine things to match what we have. Far less islanders. Half, I would say."

"No, even less than that." Julien spoke to Heath. "They barely survive with their poor crops and the sickness they had in the past."

Heath didn't like that. "What sickness?"

"The fever. Their chief said the priest brought it to them because their god was greater than his, who was jealous. The islanders killed the chief for those shameful words and a new leader arose." Julien rested his hands on his muscular stomach. "They have yet to recover from losing so many, especially the children. Without Tristan's help with the seeds and food, they may perish."

"So they're eager to see us. They'll be friendly."

"Oui. They need the wonderful things Tristan always gives them."

"What weapons do they have?"

Etienne spoke up. "Spears and knives. Also pistols Tristan gave them for protection from pirates should they come. They never have, but they might."

If they were smart, they had an armed lookout on their shores as Tristan did on his. "When we're in the longboat and have their beach in sight, do we need to do anything special so they know who we are? Some sort of signal for the lookout to keep him from firing on us?"

"We have a cloth of flowers and many colors, though mostly red. Tristan calls it cal-i-co. That tells them we mean no harm. Rollan waves it for them to see."

Heath clamped Rollan's shoulder. "And you'll do so again this time. Do the islanders have a glass as we do?"

The men nodded.

"When our longboat reaches shore, what happens then?"

Rollan spoke. "The chief, his men, and people hide until their strongest warriors tell them to come out. The chief wears a feathered robe and headdress, and has falcon talons around his neck. His men also have the claws but no feathers."

The protocol sounded simple enough, except few things in life were. "Will our weapons alarm them?" Heath wasn't about to chance arriving without protection.

"We take only one pistol and put it here." Julien gestured to his back waistband. "We can also take a cutlass, but no more than that."

Meaning a brace of pistols. He couldn't blame the islanders. If heavily armed strangers approached Tristan's isle, Heath would shoot their bloody heads off before their feet touched sand or they could explain themselves. "Anything else?"

Rollan folded his arms over the table. "Their community is far less advanced than ours, but everyone there is kind. None will give us any trouble."

* * * *

Canela finished her special stew. The fish stench and strong taste kept the sleeping herbs from being too obvious. Luckily, the afternoon heat made everyone drowsy. When they'd napped earlier, she worked without observation. Except for Vincent.

He stared at her from the pen.

She inclined her head slightly to let him know the plan was finally in motion, and to give him a false sense of his own importance.

He grinned.

Ugly fool. Vile swine. She would see him dead soon.

Nursing the violent images in her mind, she filled the chief's bowl and those for his men. She'd serve them first as she had these past days, familiarizing them with her slavish devotion. Like most males, they adored the attention.

Fanette had instantly objected to Canela's actions and the men's response to her. Until now, Fanette had made certain to keep Canela from their sight and lust.

No longer.

The chief and his men warned Fanette to keep her tongue or they'd cut it out.

Canela delivered the bowls to the chief's house where the men met each day. She sat on her heels, face down to await their request for more. They always wanted a second or third serving.

Today was no different. She took the chief's empty bowl.

He cupped her breast and rubbed her nipple. "Merci."

Pushing back outrage, she nodded submissively and gathered the other bowls. At the pot, she doled out generous portions for the islanders, except for the few children and infants. She barely filled Fanette's bowl.

Fanette kicked dirt on Canela's leg. "More, you stupid thing."

She gave it. Gladly.

Conversation ceased during the meal. The islanders rested against shaded trunks and devoured their food. None complained about an odd odor or taste. Not even Ismay. She grinned at Canela from across the yard.

Canela smiled in return. She poured the prisoners' stew from the smaller pot and brought it to them. They reached for it greedily, eyes crazed with hunger.

Vincent turned his bowl over. Steaming liquid and soggy vegetables splashed on the ground. "The key."

His men and those from Bishop's ship concentrated on their food, not his quiet words.

Vincent growled. "Answer me."

She kept her voice as low as his. "I have to wait for it until the right time."

"When will that be?"

"Not long."

She returned to the fire and refilled bowls for the chief and his men.

They proved too alert and ate their second helping as greedily as the prisoners did their first.

Canela's skin prickled. If she hadn't used enough sleeping magic or the wrong herb, she'd be here forever, serving Ismay, lying beneath these disgusting pigs. Panicked, she backed to the entrance. "There is far more. I can bring it to you."

She swiped the prisoners' empty bowls and filled them with fish stew.

Someone yawned loudly. The priest. His sluggishness meant nothing. If he wasn't eating, he slept and complained if anyone needed him for a blessing.

The others paid no attention to him. Nor did they show any effects from the herbs. Not even Ismay. She slurped and chewed happily, gaze on the water, face serene.

Something was wrong.

Canela backed toward the forest. Death from wild boars was preferable to living out endless days here.

Vincent pushed to his feet and motioned her back.

She shook her head.

He pointed.

A woman had closed her eyes. Two men slouched against trees.

That proved nothing. It was hot, the work hard, the...

Yoland stumbled out of her house, hand to her head. She sank to her knees and dropped to the ground.

Ismay pushed up and fell over.

Others didn't look, move, or open their eyes.

Canela ran to the chief's house. He sagged in his feather-covered throne, chin to his chest, lids down. Two men lay on the floor. One slumped in his chair. Another lay across the table.

She kicked his foot.

He didn't move.

She tested the others.

They slept.

Canela feared trusting it. She grabbed the chief's blade and pointed the tip at his chest. Prepared to kill him, she untied the cord from his breeches that held the shackle key. Next, she took his brace of pistols. The leather and weapons lay heavy on her shoulders and against her chest. Far from being a burden, they gave her strength and power.

She dragged the other braces and pistols outside.

Fanette's bowl slipped from her hand. She planted her stout feet widely apart but still swayed. Drool ran down her chin. "You."

Canela smiled. "Oui. Me." She rammed her elbow into Fanette's belly.

Fanette staggered and hit the ground. Dust puffed up.

Canela straddled her. "Now who is stupid and foolish?" She drove the chief's blade deep into Fanette's throat.

Her lips moved but only gurgling sounded. Blood filled her mouth. Her limbs quivered.

One man lifted his head and dropped it.

Canela stilled and waited.

He didn't move again, nor did anyone else, except the prisoners. Vincent gripped the top rail, his men and Bishop's slightly behind him.

Canela dragged the weapons to them.

"The bloody key." He put out his hand.

She trained a pistol on a man to the right. His hair was red, like James's, but he had no spots on his skin. "You. Come closer. To the fence."

"What in the bloody hell are you doing? This ain't no time to play games." Vincent strained and grasped wildly for her weapon.

Canela stepped back and spoke to the other man. "Do as I say or die." She cocked the gun as Tristan and James did before they killed a lame horse or a sick animal. The pistol was more unwieldy than she'd expected but fear made her strong. Revenge did too.

The man shuffled forward.

Canela tossed the key.

He and Vincent jumped for it. Vincent lost his balance, fell back, and hit the ground hard. The redhead held the key in his palm.

"Unlock your shackles."

Vincent bared his teeth and pushed up. "Me first."

"Do as I say. No one else." Canela held the pistol in both hands. "Defy me and you die."

"Free me first, Raymont." Vincent glared. "If you don't, you'll bloody well wish you were dead when I get my hands on you."

Raymont looked at Vincent.

Canela fired. The boom was louder than thunder. The gun jumped in her hands as something alive would.

Blood sprayed from Raymont's chest. He dropped.

The men recoiled. Vincent kept his tongue.

Canela avoided the hot barrel and returned the pistol to the brace as Tristan had done with his. She pulled out another weapon and directed it to a man with pitted cheeks. "Get the key. Unshackle yourself and the others I point out." She chose sheep amongst wolves. Those she could cow easily. Those who'd hungered for her.

A man from Bishop's crew held out his hands as one would when wanting to discuss not demand. "What about the rest of us?"

"You starve." She shrugged. "Or you can die now if you speak again." Canela pointed the pistol at him.

He said no more.

The men she chose gathered away from the others.

She spoke to the prisoner with holes in his face. "Toss the key to me." He did.

"Come out slowly. Bring Vincent with you."

He bellowed. "Shackled?"

She smiled.

* * * *

"*Terrain à venir.*" Land ahead. Phillipe pointed from the crow's nest. Faucon Island. Half the journey finished. Relief washed through Heath so quickly, he nearly sagged to the deck. Luckily, he hadn't or the men would've thought him daft.

He trained his glass on the deserted beach surprised not to see anyone. Though early, some should have been about. Perhaps idleness was another reason these people hadn't fared as well as Netta and Aimee's.

He inched his glass to the right and stopped on a large black pot. A native woman stirred whatever cooked, her back to him. Wind pulled her long hair.

Something moved to the left. Brightly colored feathers. The chief's cape and headdress were far more ornate than Rollan had let on. The chief's back was to them. He gestured to the forest as one would when giving directions then he ducked into a mud house.

Rollan rushed up. "Do we drop anchor here, Capitaine?"

"Oui. You, Etienne, and Julian will accompany me to the isle."

"Me too." Michel joined them. "I would like to go."

"Of course." Ourson would want to hear every detail, no matter how dull. "Once we give the chief and the others our good wishes, we'll make arrangements to transfer our cargo to them and tell the priest to gather whatever he wants to take for the journey home. Then we can be on our way."

Rollan shook his head. "We should stay here a day to listen to the chief and share his food."

Heath had hoped that wouldn't be necessary. "Given how little he has, it would make more sense if we simply left."

"To refuse would insult him."

"Can't have that." Heath quelled his frustration, ordered the men to drop anchor, and prepare the longboat.

He gave Phillipe his glass. Better it stay here than accompany Heath to the isle where the chief might want it, despite having his own. "Rollan. Do you have the calico?"

He showed it to Heath. Many an English maid had worn the pattern.

"Everyone have their pistols?"

They nodded.

"Not me." Michel's face fell. Exactly as Ourson's did whenever Heath disappointed him.

"There are several in the great cabin. Take one, but hurry back."

"Oui, Capitaine." He returned within minutes.

With four strong islanders rowing, the longboat approached the beach quickly. The chief didn't appear again. The native woman who'd stirred the food had left too.

Oddly enough, the priest lay on his back in a shaded area, asleep or unconscious from too much drink or women. Rich food couldn't have put him in that state since they had no fancy fare here.

Heath shaded his eyes. A naked child, possibly two or three years old, toddled through the community. His thin cries reached the longboat.

Where in damnation was his mother, or at least the woman who cooked?

Rollan had said everyone hid when a boat approached. They should have taken the poor child with them.

Expecting the warriors to come out, Heath twisted and craned his neck. Michel gasped.

Englishmen in filthy and torn breeches raced toward the longboat.

Its bottom hit sand.

A man with pockmarked skin wore the feathered headdress and cape. He held a pistol in each hand, raised one and shot. The crack pierced the quiet air. Julian fell over the longboat and splashed into the water.

The man shouted, "Anyone tries anything and you'll join your friend." The men flanking him raised their pistols. "Toss your weapons on the sand. Guns and blades."

Heath translated for the islanders.

He and the others obeyed readily.

Heath prayed those on the Lady Lark wouldn't come to investigate the noise. These men would cut them down in a moment. They had to be the prisoners Tristan had mentioned.

A young native woman padded toward the boat, her face an angel's, eyes belonging to a devil. Medusa in the flesh.

Canela pointed her pistol. "Welcome."

Chapter 15

Aimee settled Merry in her crib and kissed her chubby fist. With surprising strength, she grasped Aimee's thumb.

"No need to fear, little one. I promise not to leave until your mama comes for you." She wiggled her hand.

Merry gripped more tightly.

"How strong you are. The same as your papa. And as beautiful as your mama." Like Tristan, Aimee hoped Merry's eyes wouldn't change. Years from now, every boy on the isle would desire her, though only the bravest would win her heart.

Perhaps Netta and Heath's son. Or one Aimee might have with him.

She slumped. It was foolish to hope for an infant no matter how much she yearned. The goddess decided who would have a son, daughter, or remain barren.

Pirates too. They'd taken so much. First, Netta's fingers, then both her and Aimee's virginity, trust, and hope. Now, the future, leaving Aimee no chance to conceive.

She stroked Merry's tiny hand, reluctant to pull away. The infant's pale skin, long, dark lashes, and pink cheeks enchanted. She stopped squirming. Her eyelids grew heavy.

Diana must have rested too. No sounds came from her bedchamber.

"Netta, come look." Aimee spoke softly. "She sleeps but still holds on to me."

Merry's rosy lips moved as they would when she suckled. Perhaps she dreamed of being at her mama's breast. Nourished. Protected. Loved.

"Netta."

She faced the tall window and the sea beyond, arms wrapped around herself as she did when chilled. Even at this early hour, the day grew too warm and sticky.

Carefully, Aimee eased her thumb from Merry's hold and padded to Netta. Her color was poor, face worried. Aimee hugged her. "What is it?"

"Nothing."

"Tell me. Did you feel something bad? Did the goddess talk to you about Heath? Is he all right?"

Anguish filled Netta's eyes. "He has to be." She pulled away from Aimee. "I simply miss him. I have to stop being so foolish. You heard Tristan. Heath's a good mariner and capitaine. Nothing could be wrong."

* * * *

Canela ordered her men to haul the bodies from the chief's home and leave them in the forest. Vultures, boars, and other animals would welcome the corpses. The house would serve her until she left. Never again would she squat by a fire or sleep on the ground.

The tall Englishman stood outside the chief's mud dwelling. Even with a glass, no one could see it or him from the Lady Lark. He stared at the carnage Canela had left. She'd used too many herbs. Everyone dead. Even the priest. His prayers and god wouldn't help anyone now.

Before the visitors arrived, her men had hidden those bodies easily detected from the longboat or ship. The dead rotted in the shade beneath leaves and branches.

Each time the wind died down, the ripe odor returned.

The Englishman showed no emotion or fear. His handsome face might have been carved from the marble in Tristan's stone house.

Canela liked this man's courage but hated it too. He wouldn't frighten easily. Assuring his obedience would take more than force, though that would do for now. She pointed her pistol at him and spoke English. "Tell me your name."

"Heath Garrison."

"You serve as capitaine?"

He nodded.

Rollan, Etienne, and Michel stood mute behind him, unskilled in hiding their horror even though they were supposed to be men now, not boys. When the pirates came and killed their families, they squealed and wept like the girls.

Canela had propositioned the pirate capitaine, offering to delight him in his bed. She would have gladly killed anyone he chose in order to share his power and rule.

He'd enjoyed her as he had the other girls then gave her to his men. Like Vincent and Tristan, he preferred an Englishwoman, the whore he'd brought with him. He made her mistress of the isle, and later the stone house.

Canela would have those things now. She gestured to the pirate with ruined cheeks, wanting him at her side. Goodwin he called himself. A disgusting man who looked foolish in the chief's finery, but his meekness and loyalty to her rule made him valuable. "Who is the pirate with the scar on his forehead?"

"Zimmerman."

Zimmerman's scrawny frame and timid ways would fool anyone, especially a naïve islander. "When he returns from the forest, he and Michel will row out to the Lady Lark."

At his name, Michel drew back.

Canela pointed her pistol at him and spoke French. "How is Ourson? Is he strong or is he like his papa who is weaker than a woman?"

Michel's dark eyes sparkled with tears. No different from a helpless female. "Please, Canela, you cannot do this."

"I already have. If you want Ourson to live when I reach Tristan's shores, I expect you to row to the Lady Lark and convince the islanders to join you here. To feast and celebrate with the chief. Once everyone arrives, your friends will die then—"

"*Tuer mon équipage serait stupide.*" Killing my crew would be foolish.

Heath's French was flawless. He stared her down, the same as Tristan had always done. Canela liked a strong man, but not too strong. "What I do is no concern of yours."

"Perhaps not, but you strike me as an exceedingly bright woman." He used her language, not his. "Smarter than most men, given what you've accomplished here. Then again, I could be wrong if you kill me and my men."

Her cheeks heated from desire not embarrassment. He would be a worthy lover. His raw lust a perfect match for hers. "As I have my own crew, I hardly need yours."

"If you intend to get past Tristan's shores, you will. Have you forgotten his men on watch? The moment they see you in the glass, they'll cut you down, along with the prisoners you've recruited to help you. Tristan has a force of eighty or more men. All armed. You have what? Fifteen? Twenty? Think your bullets will last forever? What do you plan to do when you run out? That's not your only problem. Given the looks of the men here, they haven't had a proper meal in months. They're no match against strong and determined islanders. Your crew and you will be dead before one foot touches sand."

She clenched her jaw. "I will see Tristan and Diana destroyed. Their child too."

Something flickered in Heath's eyes. He hid it. "Not with your plan you won't."

"Speak again without my permission and you die first." She shoved her pistol in his face.

"Kill me and I'll be no use to you."

"Why would you want to be? You wear Adamo's good luck charm. That makes you an islander as much as the others. Speaking our language. Believing in our customs."

Heath laughed. "As though I had a choice when Tristan took me captive with Bishop's crew. Tristan said I could come here, which is hardly paradise, as you well know, or I could stay on his isle and serve him. I chose to feign loyalty to him so I could eat as a man should. As I deserve. The islanders there are nothing to me." He yanked the medallion from his neck and spit on it. "Superstitious nonsense. There's no goddess or god, only men who are brave enough to take what they want. What the world owes them." He threw the carving aside.

Michel gaped. Rollan and Etienne lowered their faces. All shocked at Heath's betrayal.

Facing death revealed a man's true nature. Canela wanted to trust Heath's, but didn't as yet and kept her weapon trained on him. "Why did Tristan allow you to be capitaine?"

"He has a child now. So does James. Simone is expecting one with Royce. An Englishman who was a castaway, or so he claimed. Each wanted to stay on the isle to protect his family. Peter's too young and useless to be in charge. Since the islanders don't have enough sense to command a ship as a white man would, Tristan sent me. I was the only Englishman left."

"With a ship you could take and then flee. Why would you come here instead? Why would you help these people or Tristan?"

"I want to enjoy his isle and its treasures. Takes less trouble to spend my days in his luxury than working myself to death on a ship or engaging in piracy. A shrewd woman like you should know that."

She understood far more than he would ever guess. "What does Tristan call his child?"

"Merry. A silly, stupid name."

Canela agreed. "Does she have Diana's eyes?" Tristan couldn't boast enough about their unusual color.

Heath frowned. "I wouldn't know. I've never been close to the brat."

"But you want Diana. An Englishwoman."

"Only for the price she'd fetch in Mozambique. A white woman as a slave would be quite enticing to most men there. She'd bring in nearly as much as Tristan took from merchant ships. Merry would set a fine price too. She won't always be little. Once she grows, her youthful, untried flesh will yield an enormous amount. A good investment for a wise businessman."

An island child toddled to Canela and grabbed her leg.

She shoved him aside. He fell to the ground and cried.

Heath watched indifferently. "Are there many more here like him?"

"Why?"

"They'd fetch a fair price on the block. Not as much as a white slave, but there would be adequate reward."

"We have fifteen." Goodwin had gathered the children in Fanette's house so their wailing wouldn't bother Canela. He'd missed this one. "Sixteen with him."

"There are many more on Tristan's isle, as you know. And young women. Imagine the gold or jewels for selling them."

Her pulse raced. "You know who to talk to in Mozambique?"

"Bishop had several agents there I can contact. All greedy for slaves. They tire of the dark ones. Your people's brown skin would fetch a much larger price."

None would match what a buyer would pay for a white woman and child. Even in slavery, they outdid her. Canela gripped her pistol harder. She preferred to watch Diana and Merry suffering and dying than have them survive. A secret she'd keep until the time came. "You can sail without worry, unlike Tristan? You have no price on your head?"

"Not yet." Heath smiled.

Canela did too. His long hair fluttered in the wind. Whiskers shaded his face. His bronze skin radiated animal heat. She'd enjoy their rule on Tristan's isle. Harsher than the pirate who once lived there. Longer too, at least for her. If Heath dared dispute anything she said or did, she'd bring him down in a moment and would choose another man to ensure her reign.

She spoke to Goodwin. "Collect the children. Stick bread in their mouths to keep them quiet and put them in the longboat." She pointed her pistol at Michel. "You and Goodwin will accompany them to the Lady Lark. Tell the islanders an illness has claimed most of this community, leaving only the little ones and a few prisoners who are so weakened they pose no threat. The men have no reason to unload their cargo here. As soon as you return with Heath, those with him, and the prisoners, the Lady Lark must sail. There is no choice if the children are to survive."

She pressed her pistol to his forehead.

He trembled.

His dread made her calmer. "If you fail me in the least, Ourson and Esme will die while you watch their pain and terror. After their deaths, I promise to cut out your tongue and blind you, making you completely helpless with no way to survive on your own. I may put you in a pen, like an animal, so my crew can watch you struggle for the food they throw. The men will point and laugh. By then, you may wish for death." She brought the gun back.

He turned to Heath. "Please, you must stop this. She is mad."

Heath backhanded him.

His head jerked.

Heath crowded Michel. "Take care what you say to the lady. Do as she expects and be quick about it. Your son's life depends upon you following orders rather than behaving like the fool I know you are. Convince the islanders or else."

Michel shrank from him and spoke to her. "To spare my son and wife, I promise to do whatever you ask."

* * * *

Heath stepped into the chief's house and stopped.

A man sat on the floor, ankles shackled, a filthy and tattered cloth on his head, the fabric faded to beige. Had to be Yellow Scarf. His skeletal frame, shabby breeches, and fetters contradicted the heinous stories Heath heard about him.

His eyes though…

Craven schemes seethed in them. Canela's male side. No wonder she'd kept him bound. He resembled a feral animal.

A smile spread across his homely face, revealing his long, gray teeth. "Chadwick Vincent, here. Who might you be?"

Canela hit Vincent with her pistol. Blood poured from a gash in his cheek.

He grasped for her weapon.

She skittered back, bumped into the table, and spoke English. "Move again and get worse than that."

Pure hatred poured from him. "You can damn well kill me for all I care."

"I would rather you suffer." She frowned at Heath. "Sit. You too." She gestured Rollan and Etienne to chairs.

They dragged theirs far from Heath's. Wouldn't look his way.

He didn't give a wit about their contempt for him. For the moment, they and the others, except for Julian, were alive. That's all that mattered, along with keeping them that way. Michel's death would destroy Ourson. Heath wouldn't consider what his demise would do to Netta and Aimee, along with another attack on the isle, new beasts hunting them. Canela leaned into him, her breast against his arm, the pistol tantalizingly close but useless. Even if he wrested the weapon from her, she could shoot first, the bullet hitting Etienne or Rollan. Should they escape that, Heath still had no defense. There weren't any extra pistols in here. All he had was brute strength to take Canela prisoner and threaten to break her neck unless her men lay down their arms then put their shackles back on. With the pirates' freedom at stake and Tristan's riches in sight, Canela's life was inconsequential to them. They didn't need her to get safe entry onto Tristan's beach.

Only he and his crew could do that.

Playing for time, Heath forced himself not to pull away or show anything except interest in her. Within reason. If he grew too friendly too fast, she'd sense deception and he'd lose whatever ground he'd gained. To keep Etienne and Rollan from further alarm, Heath spoke English. "When should we leave?"

She eased his hair behind his ear and stroked his lobe. "When do you think?"

"If the decision was mine, not until tomorrow morning. The chief expected us to feast with him. Tristan would surely wonder why we returned too soon and would certainly grow suspicious."

"So would the islanders who stand guard. Will it be Adamo?"

Vincent laughed. "Not likely with how I left him."

"You're right." Heath inclined his head in deference to Vincent's depravity. "Adamo's nearly blind in one eye. His arm doesn't work properly. He's as ugly as you now."

Canela ran her thumb over Heath's bottom lip. "Does Adamo suffer?"

"Every day. His pain never ends. The islanders shun him. His life is over."

"Is it?" She snapped her fingers at Rollan. "Adamo *souffre-t-elle? Il est toujours dans la douleur? Les insulaires lui détestez?*" Does Adamo suffer? Is he always in pain? Do the islanders hate him?

Sweat broke out on Heath's neck and back. If Rollan or Etienne didn't verify what he'd said, she'd kill him for lying.

He knew better than to toy with a poisonous snake but had flattered her thirst for destruction, her desire to humiliate. If he died, the islanders wouldn't fare as well as he had. They lacked her guile.

Rollan glanced away. "*Ils détestent le plus.*" They hate you more.

She laughed. Delight in her eyes. "As they should, along with fearing

me. No one will get in my way." She spoke English. "Will they, Vincent?"
He spat.

She trailed her fingers over Heath's chest. "Where does Diana keep Merry?"

A foul taste rose to his throat. He swallowed it down. "In her and
Tristan's bedchamber, I suppose. Isn't that what mothers do? I have no
idea." Thankfully, Etienne and Rollan didn't either. Nor did they understand
her question, asked in English.

Canela stroked Heath's nipple. "When Tristan goes to the pastures and
stables, he has no islander guarding her or Diana?"

There was no safe answer. Heath opted for the truth. "I don't know.
I don't spend time in the mansion. I work in the courtyard building
cribs and chairs."

She pressed her mouth to his ear, her pistol to his neck. "Does Tristan love
his child very much or is he indifferent because Diana failed to birth a son?"

Tristan's adoration and concern for his family would have stunned
Canela. And fueled her rage. "If you're asking if hurting Merry would
destroy Tristan, I don't know the answer to that either. He doesn't discuss
her with me. I'm not even a full citizen on the isle like the others."

"Do you have a woman there?"

Heath faced her. Their lips nearly touched. He fought revulsion.
"None like you."

"You mean beautiful?"

"No woman can compare." An easy truth. She was exquisite and
repugnant. Poison wrapped in a lovely package. Rather like preacher tales
about Eve's apple in Eden. "I trust you already know that."

"I do." She ran the pistol barrel over his jaw. One wrong move or word
and he'd be dead. "Now you do too."

Vincent snorted. "Don't be too certain. Ask him that when he has the
gun to your throat rather than his."

She swung the weapon to him. "I should kill you now but I want Diana
to suffer from your vile attention. Look at you. Nothing but bones with
dirty hair, breeches, and a stink worse than pigs. A perfect lover for Diana
in the bed she shares with Tristan. Your horrible face, not his, above her.
You using her while she screams and begs for mercy."

"She'll not get it from me."

"Nor me." Canela pushed away from Heath. "We go to the beach now
and wait for the longboat. Tonight we sleep on the ship. Tomorrow, we sail.
Etienne. Rollan." She spoke French. "Bring him outside." She inclined her
head to Vincent. "Drag him if you must."

Rollan eyed her warily. "What do we say about his shackles? Our people will want to know why only he wears them."

"Tell them I lost the key."

She'd tied its cord around her wrist.

Heath wagered it served as a constant reminder to Vincent how close his freedom was and how far away. "You best hide this if you want the crew to believe you." He tapped the key.

Canela spoke to Etienne. "Bring Heath his medallion." She trained her pistol on Rollan. "Delay and he dies."

Etienne returned promptly.

Holding the pistol in one hand, she used her other to untie the cord and tossed the key to Heath. "Fasten it behind the medallion and put it back on. My people will wonder why you no longer wear Adamo's good luck charm."

"Smart. Just as I said."

She didn't smile at his empty compliment. "Time for us to leave this loathsome place. Stay in front of me. If you signal to anyone in the longboat or on the Lady Lark, you die."

They piled outside, Etienne and Rollan in front, Vincent between them.

Heath squinted at the brilliant sun, brighter than he recalled, the air warmer, everything more colorful, his senses on high alert. He breathed through his mouth. The stench from death overwhelmed.

"Help!"

Men waved their arms and jumped within a fenced area. Some Heath didn't know. Many he did. His mates from Bishop's ship, as obstinate as Bishop had been. Tristan had offered them relative freedom and a fairly easy life on his isle. They chose Faucon. Perhaps they hoped to escape.

None could with shackles about their ankles.

"Move." Canela pushed her pistol into Heath's back.

"Aren't we taking them with us?"

"I have enough men."

Left here, the prisoners would eventually find a way past the fence. However, freeing themselves from the shackles...

While hobbled, they'd have to collect water, find food, and protect themselves from whatever roamed this isle. A death sentence that would prove slow and grueling.

No one deserved to die like that. Not even Canela. For her, a bullet in the head would do.

Several prisoners shouted at once.

"Wait!"

"Please!"

"Help us!"

Heath couldn't. Not if he intended to stay alive, keep his crew from harm, and find a way to keep Netta, Aimee, and the others safe on Tristan's isle.

* * * *

Canela wanted to taste Heath's mouth, revel in his cock pounding within her sheath, his large body on hers.

She didn't dare indulge her lust. He could turn on her in an instant as males always did and would take command, give orders, and choose an Englishwoman to rule beside him. She wouldn't chance it this time. Once they returned to the stone house, she'd keep Heath her prisoner, seducing him so he'd never consider another female in his bed. Wouldn't want anyone else except her. Only then would she allow him the slightest freedom.

Her men easily captured the unsuspecting crew. Michel had lied well. To reward him, she wouldn't kill Ourson. He'd go on the block with the other children and the younger, virginal women who would fetch the greatest price. His parents would die as hers had.

Canela hadn't missed them or her other relatives for a moment. With them gone, she no longer had to follow foolish customs and rules or pretend to. The pirates who'd invaded had their decrees to follow, but as long as she gave herself willingly to them, she could soar like a hawk, strike like a falcon, live like a man with no restrictions.

Her life with Tristan had offered that until he'd found Diana.

Canela looked forward to their anguish when she tore Merry from Diana's arms, and gave Diana to Vincent.

On Canela's orders, Goodwin and her crew tied up Heath and his men in the great cabin, the ropes sturdy, knots complicated so they couldn't help each other escape. Vincent and the children were also in there. Everyone packed tight like pigs in a pen, helpless to stop her. An armed pirate guarded the door. The remaining men took over the Lady Lark. Some slept. Others prepared for the coming journey.

No one spoke.

The soft night embraced, the air cleaner than she'd known in nearly a year, the sky vaster than it had ever been.

She should have been fatigued and hungry. Excitement pulsed through her. In days, she'd return triumphant and would crush everyone in her path.

* * * *

Netta sat on the windowsill, afraid to sleep or even close her eyes. When she did, Heath came to her, his face troubled, heart pained.

Diana said the unwelcomed thoughts were because Netta missed him so much.

Tristan showed her and Aimee his charts. He traced Heath's path and explained everything the ship would pass along the way. An easy journey. No rain fell, the clouds puffy and white, always allowing the sun to shine through here and on Faucon.

Peter and James said Heath had reached the isle by now and would set sail for home by tomorrow.

Netta begged the goddess and the priest's deity for answers and solutions. She offered them new gifts.

Her dread remained, more ominous than the darkness ahead.

Chapter 16

On the third day at sea, Heath worked his way next to Michel.

He leaned away from Heath. Not an easy task with so many crammed inside the great cabin.

The stink from too much humanity was sickening. Heat, hunger, and thirst put most in a stupor. Children slept draped over the men's legs. Vincent's chin rested on his bony chest. Heath worried most about him. Vincent would likely sell his own mother to the devil to get what he wanted. He and Canela loathed each other, but they'd band together to defeat anyone who stood in their way.

With no one watching, Heath pushed into Michel and pressed his mouth to the man's ear. "Forgive me for striking you on Faucon. I did so to save you and the others from harm, and to convince Canela that I lied to Tristan about my loyalty. Nothing could be further from the truth. The isle is my home too. Where I want to stay and help build our community. Ourson is the finest boy I've ever known. I love him as I would a son. I want you to return to him and Esme unharmed. If he lost his papa…"

Heath sagged back, unable to continue.

Michel stared, his eyes dull in the gloom.

Much more of Canela's treatment and none would survive. The few times she'd deigned to observe her prisoners, Heath had argued that without adequate water, she'd have bodies not pawns on her hand. She couldn't prop corpses in the longboats and expect to fool the islander who watched.

She'd increased their ration, but only enough to keep them alive not alert. She wanted them docile for her crew. The man who guarded the cabin door already showed improvement from ample food and drink. His step quicker, color less sallow.

Too much outrage burned inside Heath for him to be manageable to anyone. Hatred for Canela's injustice and his love for Netta and Aimee gave him strength he didn't realize he had. He pleaded with Michel. "Please try to believe me. It means your life. I have no reason to trick you or lie. If I were loyal to Canela and wanted you dead, I would simply ask her to shoot you."

Michel licked his cracked lips and leaned into Heath, his mouth on his ear. "How do we escape this with our hands bound behind our backs?"

They were lucky they didn't have their feet tied too. If Canela's crew could have spared the rope, no one would have been able to move. "She can't keep us bound when we near the isle. She needs us to row the longboats. Otherwise, the lookout will know something's wrong. The moment we reach shore, I'll distract Canela and her crew. That's your signal to run. Use the new path the islanders cleared after the last cyclone. She doesn't know about it. Go to Ourson and Esme. Take them to safety."

"What about everyone else?"

"I'll alert those in the courtyard and mansion. Once you take care of your family, run to those houses close to yours. Tell the men we need them to fight. There are more of us than our captors. Hunt them down. Before Vincent awakes, tell Rollan what I've told you. He should tell the next man until everyone knows what we've discussed. Caution them to speak quietly so Vincent doesn't see us whispering and the children don't overhear. They don't understand the grave situation we're in and may repeat something without thinking. Surprise is our only weapon. Canela and her crew can't suspect what we intend to do."

"How will you distract her?"

Heath didn't know. With her pistol and others likely pointed at him, he couldn't plan every detail and expect events to unfold flawlessly. He wanted to reassure Michel with a lie. He deserved truth. "I don't know yet, but I'll find a way. Trust me. Please. I won't let you or the others down even if it means my life."

"You need to keep safe too."

"Worry about your family. They're your first concern. The same with the others and their loved ones. Once on the isle, I'll get to Tristan, James, Royce, and Peter. Go."

Michel leaned into Rollan.

A child coughed.

Rollan flinched.

Michel bumped against Rollan and shook his head. They spoke so quietly, no whispers escaped.

The dialogue continued around the cabin. When the last islander heard the plan, he and the others looked at Heath and nodded. They were as prepared as they'd ever be.

Heath prayed to a god that he didn't believe in to keep the men safe for their wives and children. For himself, he hoped to return to Netta and Aimee but couldn't count on it. If he failed in his initial attack, many might die, including him.

* * * *

Aimee found Netta near the point where the islanders kept watch.

The sea stretched endlessly, farther than anyone could see, except the goddess. Water glinted deep blue. Flamingoes and other birds rode the wind.

Heath and the islanders would return there, the spot closer to their homes than the cove.

No longboats approached.

If they had, the islander at the cove would have already ridden to the stone house to tell everyone the Lady Lark had arrived.

She took Netta's maimed hand. Her forefinger and thumb were cold even with the heat. Aimee warmed her. "Tristan said Heath will arrive tomorrow. We can wait for him with Xavierre who has lookout duties. You can use the glass to see Heath in the lead boat and put your concerns to rest."

"When will the longboats arrive? Morning? Midday? Night?"

Tristan hadn't said. "I can ask."

"To learn what? Nothing?" Netta pulled her hand from Aimee's. "The wind may blow hard or slow down and keep the Lady Lark at sea. You expect us to stay here all day to see the longboats?" Her chin trembled. "What if he fails to come?"

"We wait another day."

"And another and another and…" She covered her face.

Aimee pulled down Netta's hands. "What have you dreamed?"

Netta shook her head.

Aimee felt ill. "Tell me, please. Did something happen to the boat?"

"No. I saw sickness that made the other islanders lay on the ground and not get up. Maybe the fever. It could strike Heath. He could be ill as we speak."

"No." Aimee refused to believe it. "He's strong. The fever has come here but the sturdiest men always survived."

"With Simone's healing. I fear for him."

"We mustn't speak of this. We mustn't even think it. If there was a fever on the other isle, the priest would have told Tristan when he sent the bird. Your dream is false. Your worry is needless. Everyone said Heath will return. You and I will be here for him."

"Not at the point."

"Then we can go to the cove and see the ship there and ride back here to meet the longboats."

Netta backed away. "Neither place is good. If he never arrives..."

"Stop it. He will. Please believe that. If you want, we can wait for him in the stone house. I can ask Xavierre to tell us as soon as the boats reach shore and are safe on the isle, not in the water where you fear something may happen. Come." She grabbed Netta's wrist and pulled her toward the wall. "Until Heath returns to us, Merry can keep you busy and brighten your spirits."

* * * *

Soon, the isle and its riches would belong to Canela. She'd already waited a lifetime.

Stars twinkled on the left, the rising sun shone on the right. The contrasting sky matched the darkness she'd known for too long and the light she would have for her remaining days.

They would be plentiful, filled with riches and wonder.

With the journey nearly at its end, she washed on deck, using precious drinking water to cleanse her hair, face, and body.

Goodwin and the other men watched. Their gazes were hungry, their moods restrained. Her pistols saw to that. She'd locked theirs away to make certain they behaved until she needed them to do her bidding. One pirate had actually asked why she'd demanded their weapons. She'd shot him dead for his impertinent question. She wanted meek followers, not those who challenged. On her command, the others hoisted him over the rail and gladly let her lead.

The wind dried her. She rifled through new silk cloths meant for the Faucon islanders and chose a violet one. Identical to Diana's eyes. Nearly a year ago, Tristan had the island women make gowns for Diana in the same shade. The morning they presented them to her, he'd told Canela that Adamo waited for her outside. Before she could respond or rail at Tristan, he turned away and joined his wife, leaving Canela forgotten, humiliated.

He'd chosen the wrong woman to rule beside him and would pay greatly for that.

She sat and slapped the wood. "My food. Now."

The men served her as she'd once done for the chief and his advisors.

As rulers, they'd worn silly feathers and talons like children at play. She'd clothe herself in silk and jewels, beginning with the diamond marriage collar around Diana's throat.

Canela ate fruit, bread, and salted meat ravenously. The first time she'd filled her belly since Tristan had banished her. She let Goodwin lick her fingers.

Vulgar animal sounds flowed from him.

She cradled his cratered cheek. "Throw bread and fruit to the prisoners, but no meat."

He kissed her palm. "What about water?"

"Only enough to keep them alive. Give Vincent what I left in the basin. Wait until he finishes then tell him where it came from."

Quiet laughter quivered Goodwin's throat. "He ain't going to be happy."

"If he opens his mouth, hit him. Make sure you draw blood." She stroked Goodwin's bristly upper lip. "You would like that, no?"

"I would. For the times he treated me poorly."

"Once we take over the isle, Vincent is yours. Do whatever you wish with him, except death. I want him alive. I expect him to suffer."

"I'll see he does, and anyone who gets in your way."

* * * *

Nothing the islanders could have said about Canela would have prepared Heath for her viciousness. This journey proved her people had good reason to loathe and fear her.

Goodwin tossed food into the great cabin as one would to penned animals.

With their hands bound, the men were helpless. Vincent shouldered a child out of his way, bent to the floor, and grabbed bread with his teeth.

The youngest boys and girls ate with no thought to anyone except themselves. Two older boys held bread and fruit to Heath and the islanders' mouths.

With a half-filled basin in hand, Goodwin sidestepped legs and held the thing to Vincent's lips. "Drink."

For the first time, Goodwin didn't ration.

Vincent drank quickly. Water streamed over his chin and flowed down his chest.

Children cried for a taste.

He ignored them and finished it all.

Heath expected him to fall over, dead from Canela poisoning him. A game she'd surely enjoy.

Goodwin shoved the empty basin beneath his arm and worked his way to the door. "Care to guess where that water came from?"

Vincent stopped licking the remnants off his mouth. "Where, you bloody bastard?"

Goodwin laughed. "You'll be my pet on the isle. Canela gave you to me. I'll fashion a collar to put around your throat and build a pen to keep you in. A small one fit for the swine you are."

"You won't live that long."

"Don't be so certain."

Goodwin delivered water to the rest. Barely enough to quell maddening thirst.

The scant food did little to quiet growling bellies.

The heat grew worse. Heath drifted and jerked awake. Light bled around the shutter that covered the sole window. Still morning? Midday? Early evening?

He strained to think, fuzzy from inadequate nourishment. His shoulders ached more than he could bear. He rolled them and stilled.

The ship had slowed considerably.

No one else had noticed. All slept, including Vincent.

Heath knocked his arm into Michel's.

He lifted his head and look at Heath dumbly. "*Quelle?*" What?

"We've arrived. Listen."

Something heavy splashed in the water followed by rattling chains. The anchor going down. Hurried footfalls sounded overhead.

The door swung open.

Canela.

Next to her prisoners, she might as well have been a monarch, her hair washed, skin clean, cloth new. She regarded everyone with disdain.

A little girl grabbed her fingers.

Canela slapped her.

The child wailed.

She pushed the girl away. "Never touch me unless you want to lose your filthy hand. Goodwin."

He joined her.

"Bring Heath out, then Rollan, Michel, and Etienne. Put them in the first longboat so the islander with the glass sees them before anyone else. Has Zimmerman found what I need?"

"It awaits you on deck."

"Bring them up now." She left.

After sitting so long, Heath swayed on his feet.

"Come on." Goodwin gestured him to the door. "I ain't got all day."

Vincent put out his foot to trip Heath.

He kicked Vincent's balls.

His howl followed Heath to the deck. The crew had anchored the Lady Lark in an area where a ship this size couldn't risk drawing closer to land. The water ahead wasn't deep enough. There were too many barriers to pass. Tristan's isle rose in the distance. On this side, his land had countless rocks and sheer cliffs. They'd keep even the most determined pirate from coming onshore.

No islanders watched from there. Wasn't necessary.

Canela had discarded her silk cloth in favor of breeches. She pulled a linen shirt over her naked breasts. Since the male islanders wore their hair as long as the women did, no one would suspect her sex. She simply had to keep her face down to avoid alarming the man on watch.

She padded to Heath and touched her lips to his.

He steeled himself against disgust.

"Do I smell sweet enough for you?"

"Far better than what I've become used to these last days."

Her laughter filled the balmy air. "You need to wash and change." She snapped her fingers. "Goodwin. New breeches. Water."

"Tell him I'd prefer to drink it than wash. If you don't mind."

"You can do both, but quickly."

Heath wanted to request water for the others but feared she'd wonder why he'd worry about them since she didn't. "My hands. I can't drink, wash, dress, or row until they're free."

Canela untied the rope and stroked his palms.

Heath squeezed her fingers playfully and endured her giggles. After drinking his fill, he washed and changed.

Michel, Etienne, and Rollan joined them on deck, along with Heath's remaining crew who would follow in the other longboats. The islanders finished their water hurriedly, her men's pistols trained on them.

Vincent arrived last, stumbling between two pirates he used to command. "I can't bloody well walk in these shackles. Take them off."

Canela snatched his scarf and threw it overboard. His thinning hair barely covered his scalp. "If he talks again, gag him. Find something to put over him in the longboat. No one can see him until we reach the beach."

Vincent swore. "How do you expect to get me in the blasted boat with my feet shackled?"

She slapped him, her full weight behind the blow.

He tottered back.

Canela snapped her fingers at Heath. "Unlock his shackles. Goodwin, if Vincent breathes too deeply, shoot him and throw his body over the side."

No one misbehaved. With everything in place, they piled in the longboats and rowed.

She pressed her pistol into Heath's back. Her crew did the same with the islanders.

* * * *

Diana hurried into Netta and Aimee's chamber, Merry in her arms, the infant's face red, cries shrill. *"Désolé."* Sorry.

One of the few French words Diana knew well. Netta nodded and waited for more.

"Ah, me montrer encore une fois, s'il vous plaît." Show me again, please. She wanted Merry quiet.

Unfortunately, Aimee had gone to gather bread, fruit, and beef from the kitchen. Netta hadn't wanted the midday meal. With that hour well past, Aimee insisted on getting Netta food to keep her nourished.

Given her maimed hand, Netta sat on the bed to avoid dropping Merry on anything except a soft mattress and showed how to soothe her tears.

As always, Merry calmed.

Diana sagged against the bedpost and rattled off more English than Netta ever heard and couldn't understand.

Aimee had been wrong. Caring for Merry didn't calm Netta's worries. They flared again. Harder and stronger than ever.

Diana smiled weakly and pointed at her room. She spoke hurriedly, her English and French words combined and laced with repeated *désolés.*

Before Netta could respond, Diana hurried out.

Left with no choice except to tend Merry, Netta rocked the gurgling child and ignored her building apprehension.

* * * *

Heath's pulse pumped wildly. They'd nearly reached the beach and he'd yet to formulate a coherent plan.

An islander stood on the point, a glass to his eye, hand on the pistol stuck in his waistband.

Canela jabbed her weapon into Heath's lower back. "Lift your arm in greeting. Smile."

He did both though his grin felt more like a grimace.

The islander waved in return. He pivoted and ran into the forest.

Heath's heart paused then raced.

If the islander told the others Heath had returned, Aimee and Netta might come down and risk a bullet striking them.

Canela dug her pistol into his back. "Where is he going?"

"I don't—"

He returned and hurried down the path to the beach, his glass gone.

The longboat hit sand, the others not far behind.

Heath piled out with everyone else.

Xavierre smiled widely. "Bonjour. *Avez-vous en un—*" He stared at Canela.

She lifted her pistol.

Heath rammed into her.

She staggered into Goodwin, both of them knocked to the beach. Heath grabbed their guns and shot the pirates guarding Rollan, Etienne, and Michel. "*Courir!*" Run!

Michel led them up the newest path. Xavierre followed.

The other longboats arrived.

Heath dove to the sand and grabbed the slain pirates' pistols. His aim was wild and missed his targets. He hurled rocks, the only weapon he had.

His crew fought the men.

Guns fired.

A pirate fell overboard. Several bolted across the beach to the brush and another path that would eventually take them to the courtyard. Women. Children.

Netta. Aimee.

Heath turned too fast and lost his balance.

Canela, Vincent, and Goodwin were gone.

Heath tore up the path. Canela and the others weren't in the woods or ahead at the wall. He ran past the opening. Women and children stared. Heath shouted in French. "Pirates, Yellow Scarf, and Canela are here. Get Tristan and the men."

Follie raced from the courtyard toward the stables.

Heath ran inside the mansion, Canela and Vincent's target with Goodwin possibly following.

It was too quiet. He crept quietly down the hall.

All the doors remained closed except the last that stood slightly ajar. Heath hurried to it.

Diana backed toward a bed, eyes narrowed, jaw clenched. "You vile pig."

Vincent chuckled. "Hello to you too. Looks like you're glad to see me. For once, you're going in the right direction." He lifted a pistol. "Strip then lie down and spread your lovely legs for me."

"Never." She edged back and bumped into the mattress.

"What say I threaten to kill your brat? Think that will change your—"

Heath kicked the door in. It crashed against the wall.

Diana fell on the bed.

Vincent whirled and lifted his pistol before Heath could attack. "Guess I'll have to shoot you first then take my pleasure with her."

"Only in your hellish dreams." Diana pulled a firearm from beneath the pillow and fired.

Blood blossomed on Vincent's chest. He clutched it and dropped to the floor.

A wail sounded in the next room.

"Oh my God. Merry." Diana pushed past Heath.

In the bedchamber, Aimee knelt next to Netta, food spilled on the floor. Netta clutched her head. Blood trickled down her cheek.

Heath crouched next to her. "Are you all right?"

Diana screamed. "Where is my daughter?" She knocked the empty crib over.

Netta sobbed. "Canela hit me with a pistol. I fell. Before I could get up, she took Merry and went out the window."

Heath left the same way and ran in one direction then another and another. She'd disappeared.

He returned to Netta and Aimee's room.

Tristan ran inside.

Diana grabbed him. "Merry's gone. Canela took her."

"I'll find her."

"Canela's not outside." Heath caught his breath. "I checked."

"Then she must have climbed in another window and is back in here."

They searched the mansion. Nothing. Islanders checked their homes. Not there. The longboats were still on the beach, Adamo and the men guarding them so the escaped pirates couldn't return to the ship.

Canela hadn't tried.

* * * *

Heath entered the forest, Tristan, James, and Royce on his left. Adamo and Peter on his right.

None spoke. They treaded carefully around twigs and branches, fearful of making any noise that would mask Merry's cries or alert Canela to their approach.

Heath longed to kill her for the ruin she'd caused.

That privilege belonged to Tristan. He'd aged years in the last minutes.

Nothing he said or promised consoled Diana.

Tristan tapped Heath's arm and pointed to a side path not often used. He gestured the others in the opposite direction and took this one.

Heath followed.

Sun winked through leaves. Animals and the breeze rustled them. Waves splashed.

Merry didn't cry.

Heath's belly clenched. She had to be alive. If anything had happened to her, he wouldn't forgive himself. He couldn't live knowing he'd brought her killer there.

Tristan slowed and pointed.

White flashed within the trees close to a cliff. The one Heath had nearly run off the day Tristan warned him against wanting any woman on the isle.

Heath would have given his remaining life to go back in time and begin anew. Fix things. Avoid this.

Canela stood at the edge, her back to them. Wind tugged her hair, shirt, and breeches.

Merry wasn't on the ground. There were no infant cries.

Heath pushed forward.

Tristan caught his arm and put his mouth to Heath's ear. "Go to the right. I'll take the left. We'll circle around her and hide within the trees. Once we're in position, I'll approach her carefully. With her distracted, make your move. Grab her around her waist. I'll get Merry."

"You see her?"

"In Canela's arms. They're close to her body, her shoulders strained." As they'd be when she held something in front. "I won't fail you."

Tristan nodded. They separated, circled quietly through dense foliage, and stopped.

Heath could scarcely breathe. Canela held Merry oddly, around her neck in back and on her bottom.

The child blinked.

Relief poured through him. She was alive. For now. Jagged rocks and the roiling sea waited below.

Tristan left the trees.

Canela stiffened. She stepped to the edge and turned to him. "Stay where you are or watch me throw your daughter over the side."

Tristan halted and held up his hands. "Tell me what you want. Whatever it is, it's yours. The stone house? The gold? Jewels? You can have it all. Just give me Merry."

"No." She edged back.

Heath inched forward.

"Please." Tristan's voice cracked. Tears filled his eyes. "I'll give you everything here."

"Everything?" She tossed her hair as a woman would when seducing a man, as if she hadn't just threatened to murder Merry. "I want more."

"What?"

Heath advanced another step.

Tristan pleaded. "Tell me."

"To rule here with you. To have Diana dead. Her body left for the birds to feast on."

Tristan's color rose. Rage and fear flared in his eyes.

A few feet separated Heath from her.

Canela laughed. "I expect you to kill her for me. Only you, no one else. I want you to bring her here and slice her open from her womb to her throat. Do so or Merry dies." She held her over the cliff.

"No. Don't." Tristan gestured imploringly.

"I warn you, stay where you are." Canela edged back. Pebbles fell beneath her foot to the crashing waves. Another step and she'd lose her balance.

Panicked, Heath rushed forward, swung his arm around Canela's waist, and pulled them to the ground.

Before they hit, Tristan snatched Merry. She wailed.

Canela punched, bit, and clawed Heath like one gone mad.

"Damn you." He struggled to control her. "Stop."

She wouldn't.

He let go.

She rolled over the side.

Heath scrambled forward and grabbed her ankle.

She waved her arms frantically. "Help me!"

"Stop thrashing." She kicked her free leg. Her ankle slipped farther from his grip. "Damnation, keep still."

"Help!"

Tristan put Merry to the side and grasped Canela's calf. "Don't move. If you fight us we can't pull you up."

"You want me dead. You always wanted me gone." She bared her teeth and kicked his hand.

"Have you lost your bloody mind? I'm trying to help."

"I hate you. I—"

She slipped from their hold and plummeted, arms and legs flung out, flailing wildly. Her scream pierced the air then stopped. She'd smacked the rocks below. Blood pooled beneath her and stained the surf.

James, Peter, and Royce rushed through the trees.

"We heard screams." James looked at Merry. "What happened?"

Royce peered over the side. "Canela's dead."

Tristan cradled Merry to his chest. "Vincent's old crew is still out there. We have to find every bloody one."

Peter stroked Merry's cheek. "When we do?"

"We kill them."

Chapter 17

Heath returned to the mansion for weapons.

Tristan grabbed his arm. "Stay here. You've done enough."

"Indeed, I have." He pulled away and put on a brace of pistols. "I brought the problem to this shore."

"You invited Canela and Vincent to ambush you and take over the sloop?"

"I failed in the one matter you trusted me with." Heath shoved two additional pistols in his waistband. "I won't rest until everyone's safe."

"You can see to that by staying in the mansion and helping me and the other men protect the women and children should the pirates find their way here."

"They won't, as I intend to cut them down before they get that far."

"You can't promise or predict that."

It was the only solution Heath had. If not for him, no one would have had to fight for their lives again. The pirates' fates belonged to him. "Promise to watch over Netta and Aimee."

Tristan stood in his way. "No. I'll not have their pain on my head. So you best take care out there and return unscathed. You've proven your worth repeatedly. If you can't see that, you're a bloody fool."

"I like you too."

They laughed softly to avoid disturbing Merry. She sucked Tristan's shoulder. "I must go to Diana then take my station here with the others. Don't do anything foolish. Your life matters as much as anyone else's."

That wouldn't be true until the last pirate died and the other men returned unharmed.

By Heath's count, nine fugitives remained.

James insisted Peter accompany him. "No arguments or heroics. If anything happens to you, Diana will shoot me."

Heath followed them outside. "She did a fine job with Vincent. Is it her habit to keep pistols beneath pillows?"

"Only since the last time Vincent attacked in the bedchamber." Peter walked backward as he talked. "Perhaps she and Tristan should move to another room."

Heath exchanged a glance with Royce. "Or we eliminate the problem for good."

Armed islanders joined them in the courtyard, empty now. Women and children sheltered inside the mansion. More mothers and their offspring arrived from the surrounding areas and joined the others.

With everyone's section agreed upon, the men fanned out.

It wasn't like Heath to hunt humans as he would animals. Some pirates might be unarmed. Most weakened by ill treatment. All would prove desperate to save their own lives. His would mean nothing to them.

If Canela had succeeded, they would have done unthinkable things to the women and children. Aimee and Netta. Given Netta's disfigurement, she wouldn't have brought in enough gold from a slaver. They would have simply raped and killed her.

He stalked his prey through the heavy forest. Every rustle and snap heightened his caution. He concentrated on beige and brown colors that matched the pirates' breeches and sun-darkened flesh. Rays broke through intermittently, showing how much time had passed.

Despite the long search, he felt no thirst, hunger, fatigue.

A shot rang out to the west, followed quickly by another.

With any luck, one pirate was down. Eight to go.

They had to eliminate the last before dusk. The slender moon would prove useless tonight. In the dark, a desperate man might work his way to the mansion, hoping for a chance to crawl through a window. Armed with a pistol, branch, or rock, the pirate could kill anyone in his path.

Michel, who stood guard. Or Aimee, Netta, and Ourson inside.

If a pirate dared harmed them or anyone else here, Heath would tear the bastard apart.

A shot cracked from the east. Another from the north.

Additional ones followed, though not enough. More vermin remained.

Sun dipped below the trees. Animals grew restless and noisy. The sounds competed with those a man might make. Heath sniffed the air, hoping to catch a scent that told him a human hid nearby.

Nothing.

He stepped around a fallen tree and worked his way toward the point, the darkest spot. Trees blocked the remaining rays. A good place to find countless shadows for shelter. Close enough to the longboats to chance escape.

Islanders guarded the boats. However, the prisoners wouldn't know that until they reached them.

A new shot rang in the distance. Heath couldn't detect the direction.

Twigs snapped.

He halted and held his breath. The noise came from the left. Couldn't be on the right. Nothing was there except the path leading to the beach.

Leaves scattered, with no wind to drive them.

Breathing sounded from behind.

He turned, crouched, and aimed.

Goodwin held a rock above his head, prepared to hurl.

Heath fired.

* * * *

Islanders poured from the mansion and streamed toward their homes.

Heath found Tristan and Diana at the dining table, arms around each other, Merry asleep between them.

Peter strolled inside. "James is off with Gavra. Royce with Simone. As Laure awaits me in our chamber, I must say good night."

Heath couldn't wait to see Netta and Aimee, but he had to know the truth first. "Any injuries?"

Peter grinned. "Only the pirates. We got every one. It's finished." He strode from the room.

"It's not entirely done." Heath spoke to Tristan. "In the turmoil, I forgot. Julian died on Falcon."

"Michel told us. He and Esme are consoling Julian's brother."

"There are also children on board the Lady Lark."

Diana kissed Merry's ear. "Adamo brought them inside earlier. Netta and Aimee agreed to care for them. They've been fed, washed, and are sleeping in the twins' room. Canela murdered every islander on Faucon?"

"The priest too. Poisoned them with a sleeping potion. Aimee and Netta weren't simply helping with Merry today? They live here now?"

"Only until you returned." Tristan pointed. "You asked us to see to their welfare. We did. How did you repay us for that kindness? You took off after the pirates here and were the last one to return. Netta and Aimee have been asking endlessly about you. Whether you're hurt. What you're doing. We told them you'd been helping the other men, assured them you'd come to no harm, and left it at that. You're bloody lucky you came back in one piece. I would have had your head if you hadn't. Shouldn't you be racing to their side?"

Heath laughed. "I will, but I must tell you this first." His good humor faded. "There are still Englishmen on Faucon. Pirates and those from Bishop's crew who refused to give you their loyalty. They're shackled and held in a pen. Canela left them like that. I feared arguing with her. They can't possibly survive."

Tristan frowned. "I hope you're not suggesting we go back and rescue them."

"Please, no." Diana looked from Tristan to Heath and back. "No one on this isle should do that." She lowered her face. "I realize this isn't the Christian thing to do but we can't expose anyone here to harm. The islanders have already been through too much. If we brought those men back, we'd never be able to trust them unless we imprisoned each for life. This isle would become no different from England. Soon, we'd be hanging people. Tristan, you promised we'd never do that here."

"We shan't. I gave Bishop's crew a chance to redeem themselves. They didn't take it. They chose their fate." He spoke to Heath. "Yours awaits you with Aimee and Netta. Why are you still here?"

"I won't be any longer." Heath rushed to the room.

The door was open. Children slept on the bed and mattresses spread across the floor. Many held hands or nestled against each other. All orphans now thanks to Canela's lunacy.

Aimee spotted him first and ran into his arms. Netta followed.

Heath closed the door gently and held them close. Their warmth and scents restored him as food and drink never could. He kept his voice low to avoid disturbing the little ones. "Are you all right?"

"Are you?" They'd asked as one.

"I am now that I'm back."

Netta hugged him hard enough to steal his breath. "Never leave again."

Aimee squeezed too. "Promise us."

"You have my word on that and far more." He'd already given his heart. Now, he offered his determination to make them his for all time. Not to hide their love in the shadows as they had.

During his darkest hours in the great cabin, he'd vowed to have Netta and Aimee as they and he deserved. Some might have deemed his determination a delusion. Heath preferred to call it hope.

* * * *

In the following days, Heath consulted Diana and Tristan first on an idea he had. "Would it bother you greatly if Netta, Aimee, and I had an islander wedding? The kind that used to take place here before white men invaded?"

Diana smiled. "I have no objection. Do you, Tristan?"

"Not at all, but you'll have to ask the islanders to see what they think. It's been quite a while since they indulged solely in their heritage. Do you have any idea what the ceremony consists of?"

"No, but I'll find out."

Heath next spoke to the islanders. His request surprised most. Many women were wary.

Michel defended him. "He's a true islander like us. He saved my life and the others so we could return to our families. Do we deny him the same for a belief that came here with the priest? From his people, not ours?"

The vote favored Heath.

Implementing his plan was another hurdle. Years of foreign invasion and rule had buried the islanders' culture. Thankfully, memories persisted. Stories told by grandparents about their ancestors' glory days. How the isle used to be. A place to love and laugh not hurt and restrict.

As Simone awaited her child's birth, she pieced together the oral history. She, Gavra, and Diana worked tirelessly to prepare for the isle's first wedding that would again follow sacred tradition.

On a sun-splashed morning, Heath and the entire community, islander and English, gathered on a hill overlooking the sea. Within a circle bordered by flowered branches, Netta and Aimee awaited him, their cloths red. The color represented the life force that flowed through everyone, white or brown. Blossoms decorated their hair.

He wore a garland around his neck and Adamo's good luck charm.

Women raised their voices in an ancient song their mothers sang when they'd been small. Children joined in. The sweet sounds drifted on the breeze.

Men stood shoulder to shoulder to create a wider circle around the group. A symbol of protection for their families, people, and homeland.

Heath entered the hallowed spot.

The song ended.

Ourson balanced a scarlet pillow on his palms, Netta and Aimee's marriage collars draped across it. He brought the items to Heath and grinned.

A bottom tooth peeked through his gums.

"I kept the collars from falling off."

"Indeed you did. Good man." Heath ruffled Ourson's hair and took the beaded leather. "You're the finest quartermaster a captain could have."

He giggled and dashed back to his parents.

Heath faced Netta and Aimee. They glowed from more than joy and peace. Both had experienced queasiness in the morning. A miracle from the goddess. She'd brought them other children too. They'd adopted two Faucon orphans. Remi, their new son. Laurel, their beloved daughter. Both toddlers in need of safety and love as Heath's women were.

He opened his heart and soul even further to them. "You are my life."

"You are our love." Aimee and Netta spoke as one and kissed his cheeks.

He slipped the collar around Netta's throat then Aimee's and took their hands. Joined finally and forever. "You are my hope. My happiness."

Together, they were each other's future.

The End

LOVING LIES

Read on for a taste of Tina's erotic historical series Dangerous Desires

Deception knows no limits. Passion knows no bounds.

When she is kidnapped, Senorita Isabella knows the men have been sent by her uncle in a murderous attempt to control her family's fortune. But when she is rescued by a dashing and mysterious warrior, Isabella can't imagine why a stranger would risk his life for her—until she discovers her rescuer believes she's someone else . . .

Fernando de Zayas loves nothing more than the cry of battle. Defying death is his way of life. But when he discovers his betrothed has been kidnapped, he rushes to her aid—never suspecting that spirited beauty would soothe his warrior heart . . .

With her uncle's minions close on their heels, Isabella finds herself drawing closer to Fernando. But as the desire between them builds, her secret could keep them apart forever . . .

A Lyrical Originals novel on sale now!

Learn more about Tina Donahue at
http://www.kensingtonbooks.com/author.aspx/24772

Chapter 1

The Moorish Kingdom of Granada, Spain—1488

Al-Caicería—The Great Bazaar

"Harem!" The slave trader's shout rose above other voices in the open-air market. He dug his fingers into the hooded robe hiding Isabella Lopéz de Lara's face and nudity. "Harem!"

The Arabic word seemed to linger in the still, warm air. Sweat trickled down Isabella's cheek. Her abduction in Andalucía, on orders from her murderous uncle, was far too real and horrifying now.

Someone brushed past, startling her. The individual's sandals or boots slapped hard against the ground, the sounds fading quickly. Isabella snatched a breath. The hem of her robe pulled away from her legs. She stilled, terrified to move. Work-roughened fingers slid over her ankle and up her calf.

Holding back a scream, she backed into the slaver. He released his hold on her robe and shouted in Arabic, his words incomprehensible to her. An object whistled close to her face, followed by a harsh crack and a man's agonized cry.

The hand jerked away from her leg. A series of brutal whacks and stumbling noises rose above the other sounds.

Swallowing hard, she listened for what she couldn't see.

Too many buyers shuffled close, stirring up dust to mingle with the scents of cooked meat, cloyingly sweet perfumes, the stench of animals and men. Crude male voices yelled the word *harem* repeatedly. Moments later, fabric snapped.

She pictured the slaver stripping one of the other captives, forcing the poor woman to display herself.

Murmurs floated through the crowd. The slaver shouted above them, making the men speak faster, louder.

As they offered bids?

She shuddered, expecting the slave to plead for mercy.

Whoever the girl was, she held her tongue, seemingly resigned to her fate the Moors deemed *qisma*, destiny.

Men pushed past with cruel indifference, some pressing so close Isabella could smell the grime on their robes. Sickened, she stepped back. The slaver said something and ran his fingers down her shoulder to her arm, touching the side of her breast. She jerked away from his filthy touch. Those surrounding them laughed. The slaver pulled her tightly against him, proving she was in his world, his property, even though she was the daughter of a grandee and duke.

Her late father's position hardly mattered now. Her only hope was in escape that seemed impossible.

Voices rose and fell during countless negotiations, sheep bleated, children played. Someone spoke above the din, the tone unusually high-pitched, sounding neither female nor male, marking its owner as a eunuch. A man who was no longer male.

His comments grew strident. The slaver shouted in return.

Her pulse pounded. If a way out existed, she had to see it. The eunuch and slaver argued on. She pulled at the hood of her robe and slowly lifted her head until she could see past the cloth.

The sun hung heavy in the sky, turning Granada's structures a blinding white. Squinting at the overwhelming brightness, she regarded the numerous towers to determine if guards watched from there and would see any attempt at escape. If not, where would she flee?

Granada was a city of countless dwellings and strangers who would never offer sanctuary to a Spanish noblewoman. The free women here were as shrouded as she was, with only their eyes uncovered. However, if she could secure one of the dark robes sold in the market and disguise herself as a Moorish woman, there might be a chance to flee. No man would dare break the sanctity of the veil, not even to search for an escaped slave. The Moors' religion forbade it.

The robes were tantalizingly close, though still out of reach.

The slaver's voice rose again. He spat on the dinars the eunuch had offered. The eunuch's palm looked as soft as a woman's, his dark face bearing no trace of a beard. Clearly impatient, he gestured to Isabella's robe. The slaver yanked the hood off her head. She gasped.

A flurry of excited murmurs rippled through the crowd. The eunuch stared openly at her elaborately braided hair, apparently stunned at its unusual auburn color. The slaver gestured to her robe, his words seeming to imply how the Moors had prepared her body for sale. The eunuch focused on her eyes, the same blue-green as Queen Isabella's, a color well known within Spain's Royal House of Trastámara.

The slaver's broad smile revealed most of his decayed teeth. When he spoke again, the eunuch grew thoughtful.

On a shuddering breath, Isabella searched the market for any means of escape and found none. Too many people pressed close with no clear route from the area. If only she could see what was behind her, she might find a way out.

A quick glance showed even more people and cramped stalls, proving how trapped she was. The eunuch's high-pitched shout suddenly rose above the slaver's angry growl. Wanting away from them, she inched back. The eunuch dashed to her right, blocking her. The slaver to her left and reached for her robe.

Piercing wails filled the heated air.

Isabella stiffened. The slaver's hand fell from her. He and the eunuch turned toward the sounds. Two dark-robed women pressed their hands to their veiled mouths. Children had stopped playing, their youthful eyes widened in wonder or fear at an aged man. His white beard trailed down his chest, and infirmity bent his tall frame, forcing him to keep his face lowered. He wore a turban and full robe, the voluminous fabric hiding the contours of his body.

Suddenly, he thrust his hand into a fire used to cook some manner of food.

Many in the crowd gasped. A young girl backed into a basket of olives, toppling it. The fruit rolled across the ground until it reached a pool of spilled honey where a black cat prowled.

The aged man kept his hand in the fire without bellowing in pain. He chose three smoking coals, tossing the hot embers from his right hand to his left much as jugglers did at fairs with brightly colored balls.

This was no fair nor was he a juggler, but a *fakir*, a holy man.

Isabella had heard tales of such beings who traveled the Arab territories. Fakirs had no homes or commerce, begging for food as they roamed from place to place, performing amazing feats to shock everyone, as he did now. Merchants, free women, and children waited to see what the strange man would do next.

With no one watching her, Isabella prepared to break into a run, to lose herself in the throng.

The fakir tilted his face and met her gaze.

Her heart caught. His eyes were arresting and strangely beautiful, his gaze so intent she stepped back. His expression changed. With a hard frown, he seemed to warn her to remain where she was. He turned to the eunuch and slaver, crying to them in Arabic, his voice reedy with age.

Her stomach churned. Was he warning them of her intent to flee?

When he looked back at her, raw power lit his expression, holding her to the spot.

Even if she'd wanted to move, she couldn't now. The eunuch and slaver stared at her.

The air grew heavier than before and far too still. The slaver adjusted his weight from foot to foot as he and the eunuch spoke to the fakir. The holy man answered in kind, juggling the hot coals. He drew closer to them, his movements inefficient and tottering, no different from a babe. The slaver stepped back. The eunuch did not. His shrill voice rose in what sounded like an oath. The fakir hobbled closer, the hot coals jumping more slowly between his hands. At last he responded, his voice low.

The eunuch scowled and shouted a string of foul-sounding words. The fakir grabbed the eunuch's throat, pressing the hot coals to it. Squealing in agony, the eunuch fell to the ground, rocking and mewling.

Frightened sounds rippled through the crowd. The holy man spoke to the spectators, who exchanged glances with each other and shuffled back.

The fakir grabbed more hot coals from another fire and staggered toward the slaver. Unlike the eunuch, the slaver offered no retort as he stepped back quickly. The fakir followed. It was a strange dance, the fakir plodding forward a step, the slaver retreating the same distance as he focused on the newest coals.

Again, Isabella realized no one noticed her. Before she could think to escape, the fakir was at her side, clutching her hair in his free hand, shouting at the others.

Again, they backed away.

He yanked Isabella toward him and whispered in Castilian, "When I release you, grasp your throat and cry out. Your freedom and life depend upon it. Do you understand?"

Her heart hammered so wildly she could barely breathe, much less think. With no time to consider why he would help her, she nodded.

The fakir shouted something to the others then brought the coals close enough for her to feel their heat. She clutched her throat and wailed.

The slaver spoke hurriedly, his words seeming to beg for mercy.

The fakir lifted the hot coals to his mouth and blew. Flames poured from his parted lips. Screams tore through the crowd with more than a few bolting.

The fakir gripped her wrist, his touch steel.

Again, he lifted the coals to his lips. Flames shot out of his mouth, which he directed to the black silk hanging on a stall. The cloth caught fire. He bolted, pulling her with him.

She struggled to keep up as they dashed through the narrow streets of the market, past stalls and startled people. Behind them, men shouted. She glanced over. Guards pursued them. The fakir ran faster, forcing her to follow. They darted down one cramped street after another. He knocked over goods deliberately. Both of them dodged buyers. Finally, he rushed into an unattended shop offering a variety of baskets.

Before she could question why this place was empty of a merchant or buyers, the fakir pushed her toward a shadowed corner near the entrance and shielded her with his body. She was so close to him her face and breasts pressed against his surprisingly muscular back. He shifted his weight. An object beneath his robe tapped her knee. She looked down at a long, thin outline hidden by the fabric. A sword?

Outside, the shouts grew closer. Moments later, guards ran past.

As their footfalls faded, the fakir turned to her. "No matter what happens in the coming moments keep quiet. Do only as I command."

He pulled Isabella to the back wall and a massive cabinet empty of shelves and merchandise. After shoving her inside the space, he joined her, bolting the doors so no one could open them from the other side.

"On your knees." He pointed down. "Now."

She fell to her knees.

"On the floor of the cabinet and to the left is a small door. Open it and take the steps to the bottom. There, drop to your hands and knees to enter the tunnel. Go. *Now.*"

As she opened the trapdoor, the sound of footfalls broke the silence. Too soon, numerous individuals poured inside the shop. She turned to the delicate latticework on the cabinet doors that gave her a view of the area. The guards lifted their swords as they searched for her and the fakir. One man's attention swept left and right before he ran to the cabinet and yanked on its doors. When they refused to open, he shouted what sounded like an Arabic oath and thrust the tip of his sword between the latticework.

She pressed her hand over her mouth to keep from making any noise.

The fakir kept pushing against her, forcing her toward the opening.

As she entered the narrow hole, liquid sprayed the side of her face and hand. She flinched and looked down. In the faint light, whatever was on her appeared to be red. Blood?

A scream caught in her throat. The man outside hollered and struggled to open the cabinet doors. On his knees, the fakir pressed his mouth to her ear. "The blood is a trick, nothing more. Stop only at the other end of the tunnel. No matter what happens, I will be behind you. *Go.*"

The moment she was past the steps, she forced back fear and entered the small tunnel. Earth pressed in on all sides, casting her into darkness so profound she might have been blind.

The men's shouts drifted down. The fakir pressed closer. *"Hurry."*

The robe wrapped around her legs, slowing her progress, the same as the blackness ahead. She had to feel what she couldn't see. The earth was hard and cool. It stunk of decay and death, the perimeters as confining as a grave. To die down here... She shuddered.

More shouts. The guards followed, intent on dragging her back to the market.

She pushed the robe over her hips, exposing her nudity, and crawled with greater determination though the journey soon seemed endless. After a time Isabella wasn't certain whether she was going in a straight line or if the tunnel was veering to the right, the left, perhaps deeper within the earth. Her elbows and knees stung from scraping against the packed dirt.

She could barely draw a breath. Quiet pressed in. She slowed.

"What is it?" the fakir asked.

"The shouting stopped."

"For the moment. The men will follow."

Faint cries drifted down the tunnel. She crawled as fast as she could despite her bruised elbows, aching fingers, and scraped knees. Repeatedly, the robe fell from her back and wrapped around her legs. There seemed no end to the time she'd been in here. She kept pushing back panic until she couldn't any longer. She wanted to shriek in terror and pain but didn't.

A faint gray light was ahead. The end of the tunnel?

She stopped and stared.

The fakir shoved her forward. "¡*Darse prisa*!"

After what seemed a lifetime, sweet air wafted in from the outside. Gulping it greedily, she was soon free of the tunnel's entrance, surrounded by a thick stand of mulberry trees. On her side catching her breath, she noted the angle of the sun. The journey through the tunnel had taken even longer than she'd thought.

She pushed to a sitting position. Countless leaves obscured the surrounding area, giving everything a strange green cast. Never had Isabella seen such a place. She'd hoped the tunnel would end beyond the walls of Granada or, better, within a Spanish village where she'd be on her way to safety. What if she wasn't? This might be outside the fabled Alhambra, a fortress and palace known for its gardens and the harem. The fakir could have led them to a tunnel going to the Sultan Boabdil in order to collect gold for selling her flesh.

Isabella pushed to her feet to flee. The fakir was immediately upon her, his arm around her waist, his other hand clamped over her mouth.

"Keep still." His lips were against her ear, his dirty beard trailing down her cheek. "Do you want our enemies to drag you back to their foul city?"

Then they were outside Granada's walls, though she had no idea where or why the fakir would speak of his people as their enemies.

"Do you?" he asked.

She shook her head.

"Then keep still. If you flee, I may not be the one who captures you, though you will be captured." He released her. At the mouth of the tunnel, he kicked away the planks supporting the roof. The tunnel collapsed upon itself, belching dust in a thunderous rumble. The fakir worked feverishly. Soft grunts poured from him as he forced stone after stone against the opening to cut it off completely.

Isabella hoped she was now safe from the Moors, yet what of the fakir? She kept witnessing his surprising strength. He appeared to have a sword hidden beneath his filthy robe. Now she saw the high boots he wore.

She backed up, ready to bolt. Before she could, he grabbed her wrist and looked over both shoulders. "Now we must run."

She stared. He expected her to stay with him? To go where? To what end? She had no chance to ask and couldn't match his mad pace. He tugged her roughly to follow. She winced at twigs, small rocks, and other debris digging into her bare feet. At last, she cried, "I cannot keep up."

"You must."

Despite his words, he slowed somewhat.

Mulberry trees swirled past. Greens smeared into browns, the sun darting between the heavy foliage. Isabella's breaths came hard and fast. At last, she was so dizzy the ground gave out beneath her. Before she could fall, the fakir wrapped his arm around her waist, holding her firmly against him as he slowed to a brisk walk, forcing her to do the same.

She panted. "Where are you taking me?"

"To safety. Ask no more, lest someone hears you."

No one was around. Even the guards had given up their chase. The only sounds were wind rustling foliage, their feet scattering fallen leaves, their breaths rushing out.

Good sense told her to fight him. She worried her struggle might make matters worse.

She tried to see the fakir's face. He held her so tightly she caught only brief glimpses of his beard and cheekbone as he scanned the area. They continued for what seemed an eternity. No village appeared through the countless trees. Did he expect them to walk forever? Fatigued and disheartened, she pleaded. "I must stop."

After a short distance, he helped her to a massive mulberry tree gnarled with age. Panting, she slumped against the rough trunk with him in front of her, his body huddled close.

Too close. His breathing slowed, his shaft stiffened, pressing against her thigh.

Her heart skipped several beats. She twisted to get away. He tightened his arm, trapping her.

She pushed against him. He didn't budge. She frowned. "Release me."

He looked at her.

Her mouth went dry. His face wasn't lined as it should have been for an ancient man. His eyes were even more striking than she'd realized, lushly lashed, the color of honey, an inner heat burning within them that imprisoned her...until he casually stroked her hip. Blood drained from her face. Her robe had parted, revealing her nudity. She yanked the fabric over herself and tried to pull away. He wouldn't allow her any freedom.

She spoke through her teeth. "I demand you release me."

His beautiful eyes seemed to smile, while his embrace remained strong with none of this making sense. Although his beard and brows were filthy from the tunnel, they were still white. Yet, he wasn't bent as he'd been in Granada. He stood at his full height, with it being considerable. Thinking back to their escape, Isabella realized when he'd spoken to her, he'd never sounded frail. His shoulders were broad beneath his robe, the look in his hooded eyes unmistakable. He was aroused.

She pressed against the trunk. "Who are you?"

His sensuous lips curled up in an unexpected and decidedly amused smile. "Your future husband." His voice was rich and deep with a young man's needs. "The man you will always yield to as a wife should."

Before she could comment on such madness or scream, the fakir lowered his mouth to hers. She froze. He brushed his lips over hers, tempting, coaxing, not yet demanding. She whimpered and ordered herself to flee but couldn't. He remained gentle and relentless as he teased the seam of her lips with his tongue.

She opened her mouth to protest, which allowed him to slip his tongue inside and kiss her longingly, patiently. Warmth rolled through her. He ran his fingers over her cheek. Her belly fluttered, her legs growing weaker.

He trailed his fingers down her throat, creating a burst of heat more surprising than the last, then slipped his hand inside her robe and cupped her breast. Her nipple tightened instantly against his calloused palm. His skin was dry and hot, his movements unhurried as he used the soft globe. Was he mad?

She tore her mouth away and shoved him back with all her strength. It wasn't a fraction of his, but she'd caught him unaware.

As he struggled to regain his balance, she hurried around the tree.

He followed and smiled.

His playfulness stirred Isabella beyond reason, the same as her memory of her peaked nipple rubbing against his palm. Her breasts ached for more. The breeze responded, hot and caressing, pushing the robe against her. The cloth was a poor substitute for this man who wasn't deeply lined and was quite strong even though he sported a white beard and brows, making him ancient enough to be her grandfather.

Not understanding any of this, she rushed around the trunk, retreated several steps and lifted her hand to stop his advance.

At last, he kept his distance, though unfulfilled need hooded his eyes. "Come now, is your manner befitting a woman who will soon be my wife?"

Again, he spoke of an absurd union. "Are you mad?"

He arched one eyebrow. "Mad? No. Dismayed? Certainly." He inhaled deeply before opening his arms. "Return to me. I have yet to satisfy myself with you, though I shall." He smiled.

It was quite beautiful, the same as his eyes. Never had Isabella seen such male beauty especially on one who was supposed to be old. "Satisfy you? Wed you?"

"You enjoyed our kiss, no?" He grinned. "You did. You cannot deny your response as easily as you pretend to be offended now. I felt your lips part to mine and your tongue caress my own."

She frowned. "What manner of holy man are you?"

He laughed as if she were mad and finally settled on an amused smile. "You must forgive me."

"Must I? Then you must wait an eternity for such grace."

His smile faded. "I am not a patient man." He shrugged. "In my haste to taste the sweetness of your lips I forgot my own appearance. For doing so, I request your forgiveness." He pulled off his turban.

Dark brown hair, shiny and thick, tumbled in waves over his forehead and around his ears. Before Isabella could recover from such a pleasant surprise, he used the turban to wipe the stain off his face, revealing bronzed, not brown, skin. He peeled away the white eyebrows. His own were the same dark shade as his hair. Next, he removed the white beard and mustache. Dark stubble dusted his firm jaw, cheeks, and upper lip. Beneath his robe, he wore a white linen shirt, dark woolen hose, a leather belt with a sheathed dagger, arming sword, pouch, and the high boots she'd already noticed. His legs were long and muscular, his chest broad, his form virile and youthful, his coloring and features those of a Spaniard, not a Moor.

She hardly trusted her eyes. Was this more magic as he'd performed in the market? It must be. She advanced until she was able to touch him. With her fingers against his cheek, she ran the pad of her thumb over his upper lip. His flesh was firm and warm, his coming beard bristly, his youth and masculinity quite evident.

Smiling, he turned his face into her hand. Isabella pulled away before he pressed his lips to her palm.

Despite his frown, his expression was playful. "Again, you deny me?"

"I shall always deny you."

He looked doubtful at her promise.

Perhaps if she hadn't sounded so uncertain and was able to understand this. How could he merely pose as a fakir, yet still breathe fire and handle hot coals without singeing his skin? She took his hands and turned them over. No blisters or marks of any kind marred his palms.

"Who are you?" She released his hands and danced back before he could pull her closer. "What manner of devil are you?"

"Devil?" He frowned, though it was still on the mischievous side. "I risked my hide to save you and for my efforts you call me a devil? Keep behaving in such a manner, keep denying me, and I may turn into a devil or worse."

"Do what you must. I shall always deny you and certainly do not belong to you."

"Oh, but you do."

He seemed so certain, Isabella could only stare until he advanced. She retreated several steps. "I was prepared to effect my escape when you came upon the scene."

"You were about to be sold and I rescued you."

"And you believe having done so gives you the right to take me as your bride?"

"Of course. However, you also belong to me as your papá wisely chose me to be your husband, Señorita Lopéz de Lara."

She stared. He knew who she was? How? She wasn't betrothed. Only her eldest sister Sancha was.

Isabella went hot then cold.

Sancha should have been in the slave market today, not her. As sole heir to their late parents' estate, Sancha was the one keeping their vile uncle Don Rodrigo from the wealth. He'd ordered her abduction to make certain she never wed and produced heirs with her betrothed, who she'd been promised to since childhood, hadn't seen since, and wanted not at all. She kept threatening to flee if he ever came to claim her.

This man couldn't be Sancha's betrothed. If he were, Isabella would have taken her sister's place to thwart their uncle's plans only to face this new trouble.

The world seemed to spin as the warrior in front of her bowed slightly and offered a dazzling smile. She was quickly lost in it.

Desire filled his eyes. "I am, you see, your betrothed, Fernando de Zayas."

* * * *

He expected her to be weak with relief and melt into his arms so he could enjoy another kiss. Instead, she looked unpleasantly stunned, leaving Fernando uncertain whether to be alarmed or offended by her response.

As her surprise dissolved into pensive reflection, and what appeared to be dread, Fernando was offended. From the moment he became a man, women had pursued him. Never had he lacked a female's comfort. When it came to this woman, his betrothed, he rather expected it. She was the girl his father demanded he wed despite Fernando's resistance to any union. He knew what marriage did to a man. How it subjected the poor fool to a wife's endless nagging or tears. It was better to die in battle.

Or so he'd thought before rescuing her today.

Despite her current behavior, her courage was refreshing, her beauty undeniable. Her milky skin, blue-green eyes, and those auburn tresses would bewitch any man, even a poor eunuch. Especially enticing was the promise of her ripe breasts hidden beneath the robe she clutched to her throat.

How demure and disturbing. Fernando recalled her reluctance to expose her flesh to an aged fakir who she'd kissed readily, opening her mouth to his. Now that she knew who he was, her kiss and continued modesty were beginning to worry him. Would wedding her prove to be a trial? Would she secretly crave other men? Would she actually refuse him in his bed? Was such a thing possible? How could it be? A woman refusing her husband would be against the laws of God, nature, and man. She simply needed some wooing. With little effort, he could teach her exactly what pleased him and only him, she could teach him the same about herself, and they would be drunk with happiness.

Until such time it would help if he could remember her Christian name. He'd heard it during their betrothal ceremony years before. The first and last time she was in his presence or thoughts. During the following years, he'd been busy with his own activities, going from page to squire to the battlefield and knighthood with no thought as to wedding.

Scouring his memory, he came up with Luscinda. Or was it Benita? Or perhaps Juanita? None of those names seemed to fit. What had those who'd requested today's rescue called her besides the señorita? Carmen? Maria? Hortensia?

As Fernando began to consider every name he knew, she edged closer. "Why were you in the marketplace? How did you juggle hot coals in your hands? How did you avoid burning yourself? How did you breathe fire from your mouth? Why were you in the marketplace when I—"

"You already asked the question."

"And you failed to answer."

"You never gave me the chance."

She lifted her chin. "You were upon the scene at the moment I was to be sold. Why? What was your purpose there?"

"I was informed of your dilemma and came to rescue you, what else?"

"Dressed as a fakir? Acting as a fakir?"

He sobered at her wary tone. "It was the only means I had of rescuing you and spying for Spain without being murdered in the bargain."

Her lips parted in apparent dismay.

Perhaps she did care. "I use my knowledge of the fakir's magical tricks and my ability to speak Arabic, Turkish, and Latin to learn of the Moors' military strategies. Others do the same. The merchant whose shop we escaped from is one of our own, as are the men who dug the tunnel we used. In time we shall rid ourselves of Granada's useless Sultan, the cursed *puto* you were to be delivered to if not for my daring and successful rescue."

"I had planned to escape."

He smiled. Until today's events, Fernando had always considered a woman to be no more than a means of physical release to a man. Whether as a shrewish wife who had to deliver her body and children, or as a willing mistress who would offer the most sensuous of pleasures.

He now knew better.

Here was a woman who'd shown remarkable courage in the marketplace, even though she'd been unaware of his plan to rescue her and was about to be sold as an odalisque. What other female was as resolute? To his way of thinking every other Spanish lady would have dissolved into tears and begged for mercy. Not this woman. She'd held her head high while searching for escape. She'd followed his orders with little pause, crawling through the stinking tunnel, running until her legs refused to carry her. As far as he was concerned, she was as fearless as any man. For the first time in his life, he'd met a woman who deserved his full respect. She was quite the prize, and she was his, whatever her Christian name was.

No matter. He would delicately approach the problem and soon learn how to address her. First, though, he needed to fix their sorry state, refusing to travel through the day's heat with them covered in grime.

He lifted his robe and approached. "Come." He took her hand and led her toward a stream in the distance. "You need a bath to wash the dirt and blood from you."

She held back and made a face at the brownish stains on her robe, then touched her cheek where blood had splashed her.

He nearly smiled at the face she made. "No need for alarm. The blood belonged to a lamb and will wash away easily. Come."

Again, she held back. "As I bathe, what will you do?"

"Assist you, of course."

She yanked her hand free.

Despite her rude move, he refused to be offended. She simply needed more wooing. He easily reclaimed her hand and kissed her fingers. "Come now, señorita. As my betrothed, I fully intend to have you stripped bare at some point, so it may as well be now. And a bath is what you need."

"No."

He paused. "You hardly realize how filthy you are. From the tip of your nose"—he kissed it—"to the soles of your feet."

Her lids fluttered. "The same as you."

He grinned and straightened. "How true. So you do see the wisdom of bathing together. After I wash you, you can wash me."

"No."

His smile faded. "Enough of your maidenly modesty. No one else is here. As your future husband I expect you to bathe."

Again, she tugged her hand from his. "I will never wed you. The truth is I—" She stopped.

When she failed to continue, Fernando crossed his arms over his chest and quelled his growing annoyance at how she insulted him. "You will never wed me? The truth of it is you, what? Go on, finish what you intended to say."

For once, she appeared at a loss for words. She lowered her gaze and whimpered. Her robe had parted, once more revealing her nudity. Covered again, she turned her back to him.

Was she going to weep now because he'd seen her flesh, or because he wanted to see even more of it? He held back a sigh and considered his next move. She needed to know all was well, only how to convince her, especially after her cruel words about never wedding him? As though she had a choice in the matter when their fathers had struck the deal long ago, or as if she was unable to endure such a transaction with a Spanish knight after she'd yielded to his kiss while he'd disguised himself as an aged fakir.

Fernando sensed she enjoyed the man he was. The way she'd stared when he'd taken off his disguise was quite clear. Yet, she refused to remain at his side for a lifetime.

What had happened in the days after her abduction and before her arrival at the slave market? He knew the Moors had prepared her for sale. Her parted robe had revealed evidence of their work. What else had they done to her?

Before he allowed himself to consider the matter further and added to her distress or his, he uncrossed his arms but kept his distance to put her at ease. "When did you last eat?"

She hesitated before facing him and looked even warier. "When I ate is of no consequence."

"Your growling belly says otherwise." He pulled an orange from one of the hidden pockets in his robe. "Here." He tossed the fruit.

She caught the orange easily, looked at it rather longingly, yet extended her hand. Wanting him to take it back?

He regarded her. "The orange is ripe, no?"

"I suppose." She still offered the fruit.

He didn't take it. "I expected my betrothed to be a lady, though not too pampered to peel an orange. You need me or a servant to do the work for you? Ah, señorita. You must learn the task quickly. After we wed I want you to peel all my oranges for me and feed them to—"

"I can never feed you as I can never—" She threw the orange.

It bounced off the trunk of a mulberry tree and rolled across the ground.

Again, he considered her abduction, what might have happened to make her behave this way. Although it wasn't likely anyone had taken her virginity, since no slaver would attempt such a thing with valuable merchandise, men found other ways to enjoy a woman's flesh. Ways in which her virginity remained intact while causing her to feel unworthy of the man who had a claim on her.

If such a thing had occurred, he'd hunt down the men who had dared defile her and bring them great pain before taking their filthy lives. For now though, she was safely back in Spain and on her way to being his bride no matter what she claimed. It was all he allowed himself to consider.

He turned to her. "Food is not to be wasted." With his hand clamped around her wrist, he brought her to where the orange had fallen, retrieved the fruit, and slapped it in her palm.

"Eat. Then we bathe. Afterward, we journey to your papá's castle for our nuptials. Say no more on the matter."

He gripped her wrist and led her toward the stream.

Meet the Author

Tina Donahue is an Amazon and international bestselling novelist in erotic, paranormal, contemporary, and historical romance for traditional publishers and indie. *Booklist, Publishers Weekly, Romantic Times* and numerous online sites have praised her work. Three of her erotic novels (*Freeing the Beast, Come and Get Your Love,* and *Wicked Takeover*) were Readers' Choice Award winners. Another three of her erotic novels (*Adored; Deep, Dark, Delicious; Lush Velvet Nights*) were named finalists in the 2011 EPIC competition. *Sensual Stranger,* her erotic romance, was chosen Book of the Year 2010 (erotic category) at the French review site, Blue Moon reviews. The Golden Nib Award at Miz Love Loves Books was created specifically for her erotic romance *Lush Velvet Nights. Deep, Dark, Delicious* received an Award of Merit in the RWA Holt Medallion competition. *Take Me Away* captured second place in the NEC-RWA contest. And *The Yearning* was honored with an Award of Merit in the RWA Holt Medallion competition. She's featured in the *2012 Novel and Writer's Market.* Before penning romances, she worked in Story Direction for a Hollywood production company. You can find her online at http://tinadonahuebooks.blogspot.com/, twitter.com/tinadonahue and https://www.facebook.com/DonahueTina1/.

www.ingramcontent.com/pod-product-compliance
Lightning Source LLC
Chambersburg PA
CBHW020609270626
47155CB00022BA/1593